PANNING

FOR

LOVE

Rachel!
I hope you love this!
MegCuenig
10-13-20

PROLOGUE

"Anna, are you sure about this?" I asked my best friend through the phone. "I could go pick up a bunch of ice cream pints, and it just might do the trick. Ice cream would be cheaper, and we wouldn't have to go for a week without electricity—win. We've come so far in modern advances that I feel trying to go back in time would just be a slap in the face to Benjamin Franklin. He worked so hard." I tried one last attempt to change her mind. She wanted to go live for a week in an old mining town like people did in 1866. The craziest part was that she wanted me to come with her. I knew I would end up giving in, and that my rebuttal was as good as a sinking ship, but I wouldn't go down without a good fight and not until the last flare had been fired.

"Maggie," Anna said as she sighed. *This was it.* This was the moment I had no choice but to give into Anna's very extreme method to get over her ex-boyfriend once and for all. "I need this. I need time to clear my head of Ryan completely. I know it's been a few months since the breakup, but I still feel like I'm not *free* of

1

him. Everywhere I turn, he's there—either physicatly or mentally: social media, my coworkers/his friends, every restaurant within a five-mile radius of my apartment, the bakery…"

"The bakery?"

"He loved pie."

"Oh, right."

"Maggie, I'm also ready for some uninterrupted bonding time with you. We haven't had more than two consecutive hours together since high school—between your job and mine."

A certain guy named Ryan was a big factor too, but I wasn't going to be the one to bring him up. "Okay, okay, we'll go," I surrendered.

"Yes! You won't regret it! This trip is a once in a lifetime experience!" She was right because it wasn't every day that I could fork over the same amount of money it would take to put a down payment on a car. "So, we'll be going the last week of September. Remember to put my name on the registration application so that we can share a room. You'll get a confirmation email once you have completed the registration. Text me when you get the email, no matter how late it is!"

"Will do." I forced a smile, hoping she could feel the smile through the phone and not the forced part. My goal this trip was to help get Anna's confidence back and to catch up without interruptions. I hung up the phone and stared blankly at the registration website. There was a picture of a cowboy riding on a black horse, and I couldn't seem to look away from his eyes. I rubbed my forehead. *What am I getting myself into?*

1

One month later, we boarded the plane at LAX and touched down at the Salt Lake City International Airport in Utah at 10:02 am. Instead of waiting for the shuttle, we got an Uber and were on our way to the old mining town of Summit Springs. We drove through the capital city until we reached a canyon. The mountains on both sides of the freeway rose hundreds of feet. Green trees covered the inclines and side canyons. It was beautiful. After about an hour of weaving our way through the canyon, we hopped on the freeway, veered left, and then drove until the car's tires met dirt road.

The driver slowed the car to a stop and met our eyes through the rearview mirror. "This is your stop," he said. We thanked the man, grabbed our bags, and made our way down the dirt road. The large leafy trees touched overhead, creating a green tunnel over the road. We passed an open metal gate, as powdery dirt and small rocks crunched under our shoes. A small clearing in the trees appeared in front of us. The squeaking of metal overhead caught my attention, and I noticed a sign swaying back and forth that read, "Welcome to Summit Springs."

"Anna, I've been trying to be positive about this whole Wild West thing, but let's be real, we are walking straight into a horror movie—not a western. Where are all the people? Creepy metal signs are always a foreshadowing of horrible things to come."

"Mag-gie."

"What do you say we get the Uber driver back and spend a nice week in the city instead. I overheard a lady on the plane say that there's an Italian restaurant in Salt Lake City that spins your hot linguine noodles in a wheel of cheese before serving it to you. If a melty wheel of cheese doesn't fill the cracks in both of our hearts, then I don't think we can be cured. Let's get out of here." I turned on my heel and started back towards the living.

"Maggie, wait! A man is waving at us."

I didn't want to turn around. I wanted to run, but I couldn't leave Anna on her own to play out the eerie scene we had just walked into. I turned to see Anna waving to an older man standing next to a wood cabin that was half-hidden by large pine trees.

"Anna, we can outrun him if we turn back now. We're twenty-three years old, which is like a third of his age. We'd have a head start too."

Anna laughed. *Why was she laughing at a time like this?*

"No more scary movies for you," Anna said. "Come on, let's go!"

"I haven't written up my will yet, and I only put two of those week-long fish feeders in Alan's tank. He'll die if I die, Anna. Please. Think of the cheese wheel. Think of Alan." She wasn't thinking of the cheese wheel or my pet fish because she looped her arm through mine and pulled me down towards the cabin.

"Howdy! Welcome to Summit Springs, where the west will always be wild! I'm Bill, and you are?"

"Leaving," I said as I tried to steer our two-woman chain around. Anna stayed put, and Bill only laughed at me.

"She's a spitfire, ain't she?" he said.

"You nailed it." Anna smiled.

"Hey! You're supposed to be on my side!" I glanced over at Anna with a look of surprise on my face. She gave my linked arm a squeeze as Bill chuckled to himself before turning and making his way up the rickety steps.

"Come on in, and we'll get you where you need to go," he said. I had no more words for Anna. I gave her a we-can't-go-in-there look, but it didn't have the effect on her that I had hoped. She didn't hesitate before following Bill into the cabin, so up the stairs we went. Our shoes clunked on the wooden floorboards as we made our way over to a small desk in the corner. "I'll be back shortly with the paperwork."

Once Bill had disappeared into a back room, Anna and I slowly made our way around the cabin. Flickering flames danced in the lanterns around the room. It was homey minus the wanted posters that hung all over the walls. I started to read the bold black words: "REWARD FOR THE ARREST OF EXPRESS AND TRAIN ROBBERS" and a few that began with "WANTED DEAD OR ALIVE…" I made my way over to the fireplace, and a specific outlaw on a wanted poster caught my eye. It was the cowboy from the registration website. I could pick out his eyes in a crowd any day. Whoever made the poster made this guy out to be the most dangerous of them all. His bounty was set higher than the rest at $500. I stared into his eyes. Even in this "old fashion" photo, I could tell that his eyes were light and his hair was dark. His jaw was squared, and the 5 o'clock shadow from the picture on the registration website had tripled in length—it was more of a midnight shadow now. He looked roguishly handsome all the same. I wondered what he would look like when he smiled or what his laugh might sound like, and that thought made the side of my mouth turn up slightly into a smile. A manly throat cleared, and I blushed as though I'd been caught eating someone else's takeout from the fridge. "What a fella…felon…this one looks like, right?" The words managed to tumble out of my mouth.

"The most dangerous of them all if you ask me," Bill said as he dropped the papers on top of the desk. "Read through the guidelines, and then sign and date the bottom." He put two dip pens and an ink well on the desktop for us. Anna and I took a seat at the small wooden table near the window and began to read. Anna and I both made eye contact without moving a muscle as if we just read the same line at the same time.

No technology of any kind beyond this point.

"This rule doesn't apply to us," I informed Anna.

"All the rules apply to us, Maggie."

That comment was rewarded with an eye roll. We read through the rest of the guidelines, and then each grabbed a pen. I acted like I knew what I was doing and submerged the whole tip of the dip pen into the ink. I tried to write, but only a small pool of black ink leaked out onto the paper.

"You need less ink, and to write on a 45-degree angle," Anna said. I watched as she signed her name in elegant cursive.

"Here. Sign mine too." I turned my papers around and slid them across the table in hopes that Anna would forge my signature. "M-A-G-G-I-E C-A…"

"I know how to spell your name, Maggie Carver. What kind of friend would I be if I didn't know by now?" She handed my papers back, and I smiled at my fancy new signature. The ink hadn't dried just yet, so I blew on the paper until it did.

"If you ever decide to quit your day job, then I think you'd do well in the calligraphy field."

"There's no such thing," Anna said.

"There really is. Addressing strangers' envelopes for events is a thing now. I saw it on Instagram."

"That is so strange. Well, thanks for the heads up. It's comforting knowing I have something to fall back on."

I knew she would never quit her job being a middle school Spanish teacher because she loved her students too much. "Well, it's official. My dreams of learning how to churn butter and pan for gold are finally coming true." I tapped my papers on the table until they were lined up and perfectly stacked.

"Really?"

"Nope. Let's go."

Anna smiled and rolled her eyes. We stood and walked over to Bill, who was waiting for us behind the small desk.

"Here you are," I said to Bill. We both handed our forms to him. He seemed surprised by my penmanship but didn't comment once he saw the pool of ink and drenched pen nib. *Smart man.*

"Changing rooms are through that door, and a trunk to lock up your belongings for the week is in there as well. You'll find a change of clothes hanging on the back of the door. A wagon will be up shortly to take you back to 1866," he said.

There were makeshift changing stalls in the back room. Bill was right; clothes were hanging on the back of the door. I never doubted him, minus when we first met and up until now.

"This is going to be fun! Look at my mine!" Anna hugged her long-sleeved, floor-length dark green cotton dress against her as she swayed. Her dress was going to compliment her long strawberry blonde hair and hazel eyes to the max.

"You have to put that on right now!" I told her as she squealed and disappeared behind the curtain. I unhooked my ensemble from the door and hugged it just as Anna had done to hers. It was perfect. My pretty top was off-white with a large intricate lace semi-circle around the neck. It was paired with a full, high waist, floor-length, deep sapphire blue colored skirt. I knew this outfit would complement my long dark brown hair and equally dark eyes. "We're going to get along just fine," I whispered to my new borrowed clothes before sliding into an empty stall. I heard Anna's curtain slide open as I was tucking the last of my blouse in. I walked out just as Anna was tying a bonnet on her head.

"Maggie! You look stunning!"

"Thank you. You do too!"

"I wish there were a mirror in here so you could see yourself, and so I could see if this bonnet makes me look ridiculous," she said.

"Not ridiculous at all. It even matches your dress! You know my vote." I smoothed my hair, then pulled my phone out of my bag.

"Are you really sneaking that in?" Anna looked at me with wide eyes as she tucked a few loose tendrils up under her bonnet.

I slid the phone into my leather boot and smiled up at her. "Yes, ma'am!"

"Wagon's here!" Bill's muffled voice sounded through the door.

"You are going to get us both in trouble!" Anna whispered.

We locked up our things (well, most of them) in a small trunk that would stay in the cabin for the week, then hurried out.

"Ready to go?" Bill asked.

"Yep," Anna said.

Bill started to pat his shirt pocket, then his pant pockets. "Shoot! I forgot my phone and need to let my wife, Carol, know you both on your way. You wouldn't happen to have a..."

"Oh, sure!" I said as I reached down and pulled at my hemline. I dropped my head in the realization of Bill's tactic—*he's quicker than I initially gave him credit for*. I slid my phone out from its hiding place and held it up before my audience. "I will be putting this away now."

Bill laughed as though he was pleased with himself, and it was obvious that this wasn't his first rodeo. He showed Anna out to the wagon as I went to lock up my phone in the trunk. Once the trunk had been locked, with my phone inside this time, I slid the key into my skirt pocket and closed the door behind me. Something willed me to turn back around towards that familiar wanted poster near the crackling fireplace. I walked across the floorboards slowly and stared into his eyes. I reached up and touched his jaw. The coarseness of the paper made his midnight shadow almost feel real. The man on this poster staring back at me was sure to be living at least two lives. My stomach started to get twisty just thinking about how if the paper version already had this effect on me, then what effect would the actual man have? I knew I'd need to double the guards around my heart this week because falling in love in a place like this could only end in tears. I let my fingers trace down his jawline before I thought twice about what I was doing. *What is going on?* I snapped my hand down to my side as I rubbed the other hand across my forehead. *I need to get out of here.*

Bill offered me a hand up into the buckboard wagon, and I slid in next to Anna on the wooden bench. I said hello to the driver, then noticed two new trunks near our feet.

"Do you know what those are?" I asked.

"Our clothes for the week."

I raised my eyebrows at Anna just as the wagon lurched forward into motion. We bumbled along the dirt road through a large cornfield. I could barely see the treetops in the distance over the bright green stalks. The tall mountains surrounded us from every angle. The sky was bright blue with wispy white clouds. The air felt like summer, but the wind felt like fall. I couldn't deny that the weather and my surroundings were nothing short of perfect. My eyes closed, and I let the sun warm my cheeks. I breathed in the crisp air long and slow, and let myself enjoy this reverie. Something about this moment felt like home, but I couldn't place it. I had never been to Utah before.

"Maggie! Look!" Anna said. My eyes opened and followed hers until they landed on the cutest little town I had ever seen. It looked like a rickety old wooden ghost town—straight out of a western movie. However, this town was very much alive. To the right of the town, people were picking red apples from an orchard. To the left of the town, horses grazed in a large fenced pasture, and chickens pecked at the ground under the trees nearby. Straight ahead, people bustled around the town and crossed the dirt road from one building to the other. The hum of their voices sounded, but they were still too far away to make out their words. The birds were chirping all around us in the trees. We stared in awe as our wagon rolled closer and closer to the old mining town of Summit Springs.

Once we came into town, I noticed a barn-like building off to our left. It had two swinging doors large enough to fit our entire wagon inside, and above it were the words "Hudson's Livery." On the right was a small wooden building with a sign on it that read "POST." At Sutter's General Store, three horses were tethered to a wooden post on the road. A few men loaded crates of potatoes, apples, and corn into a wagon. We also passed by a bathhouse, a bank, an assay office, a sheriff's office, and "The Broken Spoke Saloon." There were people all around, and they would stop what they were doing and wave at us as we passed by. I felt like we were in a parade. Anna and I both stared at each other with wide eyes but said nothing. *This feels like a dream.* As if reading my thoughts, Anna nodded slowly in agreement. The dirt road came to a "T," and at the end of it was a large wooden two-story building. A sign that read "Gold Mine Hotel" hung on the rungs of the second-story balcony. A little cafe sign hung near the front door, and its hinges squeaked in the breeze.

Our driver reined in the horses in front of the hotel, then hopped down to help us and our trunks down from the wagon. "Enjoy your stay!" our driver said. He smiled and tipped his hat. "Carol's apple pie is the best in the West, so be sure to get your fill!"

We stood on the dirt road with our trunks and looked out at the town. I was convinced a time machine had brought us to Summit Springs, instead of an airplane, car, and wagon. All of these people were playing a part, and as I looked down at my skirt and shoes, I realized that I was too.

"We don't have to eat any pie," I said.

"Deal. Shall we?" I could tell Anna was nervous and excited all in one.

"Let's do this."

Anna and I both tried to pick up our trunks, then we both tried *really* hard to pick up our trunks. We decided to move one trunk at a time instead because clearly, they were filled with bricks and not clothes.

"Let's try moving yours first," I said. "On three. 1... 2... 3..." We both held our breath and shuffled to the stairs stirring up the dirt as we went. We dropped the trunk with a "thud" near the bottom step and tried to come up with the best plan of attack.

"Should we try sliding it up the stairs?" she asked.

"Yeah, good idea." I wiped a bead of sweat, forming at the top of my forehead. We held our breath, pushed, and heave-hoed for a while. We finally made it to the top of the four-plank staircase with Anna's trunk. Hands on our hips and breathing heavy, we stared down at my trunk in the dirt.

"There's no way," Anna said between breaths.

"There really isn't."

"Where's one of those cowboys when we need him?"

My cheeks turned red at the thought of one specific cowboy/outlaw.

"Well, hello! I'm Carol." We turned to see an older woman, with light brown grey-streaked hair, standing just outside the front door while wiping her hands on her apron. "Maggie and Anna was it?" We both nodded. "Room twelve," Carol said to someone behind us. Anna and I slowly turned back around, and there he was in the flesh—the handsome cowboy turned outlaw. He hoisted my trunk onto his right shoulder with ease. As he stood up straight, the brim of his hat tipped upward and revealed his eyes that traveled up slowly until they locked on mine. In less than a minute, he had already managed to take out the first line of the guards around my heart. I couldn't look away, and I couldn't move until he looked away first. Finally, his blue eyes shifted from mine to Carol's, and air instantly filled my lungs again. I looked down at a rock in the dirt while I tried to pull myself together. *What just happened?* I dared to look at him once more while he was talking with Carol. He wore dark brown boots that were meant for hard labor, brown cotton pants, and a tucked-in, off white button-up shirt with the sleeves rolled up his forearms. Under his cowboy hat, he had dark brown hair—just like I thought he would have.

He also made wearing suspenders look natural, unlike the hipsters back home. The fabric around his biceps looked as though it might surrender, and I'd deny if ever questioned that I wished it would. I snapped back to attention at the sound of my name. My arms literally straightened at my sides.

"Yes?" I asked.

"Nothing dear, I was just introducing you to my nephew, John Hudson."

"Oh, hello," I said to his…shirt collar. No way was I looking into his eyes again until I had figured out a better defense. This guy had a quiet cool confidence about him, and it was causing the remaining guards around my heart to quake. A bump on my arm brought my mind back to reality…*again*. Anna looked at me expectantly, and I looked at her like a deer in headlights and mouthed "what?"

"We were just invited to go horseback riding after we get settled in. What do you say?"

"Oh. Um, no. Thank you…John."

Carol looked surprised, Anna didn't, and John didn't flinch. I made the mistake of making eye contact with John again, and I knew he was looking into my soul at that moment, trying to read me. His eyes did that connection thing again, but this time it's as if they were having a secret conversation instead of holding me captive. I could see in his eyes that he knew there was more to the story, but said nothing. Thank goodness nobody else pressed the horse riding invitation either.

"It will just be me today." Anna broke the silence. John's attention diverted, and the corner of his mouth turned upward into a slight smile. He nodded to Anna, then bounded up the stairs with the trunk still on his shoulder. He dipped his head slightly to me as he passed by on the porch, and all I could do was stand completely still staring at him until he was out of sight. When the hotel doors clicked closed behind me, I closed my eyes and took a deep breath. *He's acting. He's acting. I better get a grip on my wits and fast, or else my heart will be all but his before this week is over.*

"Well, come on into the café, you two!" Carol said. "I'll bet you both are hungry from your journey! I have hot cornbread inside and some cool milk to go with it."

After devouring the best cornbread smeared with sweet butter that I had ever tasted, Carol started going over the itinerary she'd just handed to us.

"Each day, there will be different trades to be learned and activities to participate in should you choose to do so. They are all listed on the second page with the time and place at which they will be held. Most everyone in town, who is not passing through on their way west like yourselves, carry pocket watches with them. They will let you know the time, should you need to be somewhere at a specific hour. There is always something going on, and while there is a structured itinerary, you are free to do as you please during your stay here in Summit Springs." Carol explained the layout of the town and what took place in each of the buildings. My ears perked up at the mention of John's name and how he was the one who ran the livery. "Any questions?" Carol asked. Anna and I both shook our heads. "If you need anything, feel free to come to me for any reason."

We both thanked her and stood to leave. Anna went to check out where the bathrooms were while I made my way up the staircase to get settled into our room. My footsteps made the floorboards squeak as I walked down the hall, counting the room numbers as I went. *Twelve.* I slid the old fashion metal key into the lock and slowly turned it. As I turned, I could feel all the gears turning inside the door until...*click.* The door creaked open wide. The room was clean and simple. The simplicity was foreign but refreshing. It was strange recalling how just this morning, we flew on a plane and were surrounded by a busy world, and now we were in a small mining town in what felt like the middle of nowhere. The walls were painted powder blue, and there were two twin beds on opposite sides of the far window. I walked across the wooden floor to get a closer look at the small desk underneath the window. I slid open the drawer, and as I did, the scraping sound of wood against wood filled the room. Inside, there were pieces of paper and one of those impossible dip pens and an ink well. I sighed and pushed the drawer closed. I knew that if I was in a hostage situation, I couldn't resort to writing a letter if needed or document any of my time here should I want to remember something. I looked up to get our bearings from the window. Our window faced the apple orchard and some of the dirt road through town. Looking out past the orchard, hills, and tall mountains that surrounded us, I looked up and wondered what the night sky would look like in Summit Springs. I'd heard that without city lights, a person could see so many stars it would be impossible to number them all. I turned back and walked towards a small table against the far wall. Before I made it to the table, I noticed our trunks at the foot of each of our beds. My trunk was to the right, and heat rose to my cheeks, remembering just how it got there.

"Maggie, there are no bathrooms in the hotel. Not one," Anna said. Her voice startled me because I hadn't heard her come in. "There are, however, four outhouses outside behind the hotel with the moon cutouts on the doors and all."

"Oh, man!"

"You can say that again."

"Oh, man!" We both laughed and talked about the worst possible scenarios that could happen if we had to go out to the outhouses during the night. The wheels in my mind started to turn. "Do you think there are any bears here?" I began to low-key panic.

"I don't know, but I'll find out. I think the riding group is meeting at the livery soon, so I'll need to go. Are you sure you don't want to come?"

"One hundred percent sure, but thank you. Have fun!"

She squealed and slid out the door. This place was exactly what Anna needed, I could already tell. I was a little deflated, remembering the reason I couldn't go with her. The horrible experience I had while riding when I was a little girl still affected me all these years later. A small piece of me wanted to go to see the mountains up close, but there really was no chance. My head raced for a couple minutes debating on whether I should go and at least watch, but I quickly talked myself out of it and tried to think of what I could do instead. I could walk around town or maybe go see if Carol needed any help with dinner. I locked up our room, made my way down the narrow hall, and went down the long wooden staircase. Only a few people were seated in the café. Some of them turned to look at me when I poked my head in while trying to find Carol. *Where could she be? Anywhere in this town, really. What was I thinking?* I spun around, intending to go back upstairs and sort through my trunk when I smacked into something hard. *Ouch!*

"Oh, I'm sorry," a man's voice said. I looked up, and a man with light brown hair stared down at me.

"I'm more sorry because I think I not only flung myself into your un-expecting arms, but I also stepped on your foot!"

He jumped a few feet back, bent his knees, and held out his arms as if he were ready to catch something. "I'm ready now, and my arms are expecting you. On three!" He smiled big, and I quickly found his smile was contagious. I laughed as he stood up straight and walked back to where I was. "The offer stands if you ever feel the need to fling yourself into my arms again, just warn me first, and I'll be ready."

"That is a very kind and odd offer. Thank you."

"I'm Devin." He extended his hand, and I shook it.

"Maggie."

"I'm glad to have run into…let me rephrase that. I'm glad you ran into me because I was just coming to find you. I'm supposed to come and do whatever it takes to get you outside."

"I'm a little confused…why—"

"Smart girl! Let's go!" Devin led me out the door. Our boots clunked down the wooden steps and onto the dirt road. He laced my hand through his arm, and we started walking down the street. It felt a little strange holding the arm of a man I'd just met, but when in 1866, I always say! *I've never said that.*

"And where might we be going?" I asked.

"We are taking a stroll through town."

"I don't know you at all, but I know enough to know that is not the full truth." All I got was a smile from him in return. He waved at people as they passed by and introduced me to a few of them. Soon enough, we had walked to the end of town and the only buildings left were the post and...*the livery*. My stomach dropped, and nausea kicked in. I stopped in the road, and Devin had no choice but to turn back and face me.

"Ah, you've figured out where we're going, haven't you?" he asked. "Most people don't know what a livery is until the second day, so I thought I'd be able to at least get you through the doors."

"Carol mentioned it to Anna and me during our orientation. I can't go in there." I dropped his arm and stood there unmoving.

"She must've just added that into the orientation then." He snapped his fingers in defeat. "I made a bet that I have to carry out, but how about I make a second deal with you, so we both win?"

"Who did you make a bet with?"

"Someone who wanted you to come to the livery, but he said nothing about getting you on a horse. Here's my deal, if you come inside the livery, then I'll tell you a secret," he said. All that got him was a raised eyebrow from me. "Come on! Don't you want to get to know me better," he teased.

"I'm not so sure." I smiled. He put a hand on his heart as if he had just taken a devastating blow. "Okay, okay. You've got yourself a deal." I didn't want to hurt his ego too much.

"A secret is coming your way as soon as you cross the livery threshold." He smiled. I made an exaggerated step over the stone threshold and turned to face him with folded arms. He leaned in and cupped his hand next to my ear and whispered. "I love tuna fish juice, and I drink it straight from the can."

My brain took a minute to process what he had said because we were supposed to be in the Wild West in 1866, where canned tuna fish wasn't a thing yet. *He's not acting.* Devin pulled back slowly as if he had just confessed his deepest secret. Trying not to laugh, I rose on my tiptoes and cupped my hand to whisper in his ear. "That…is…disgusting." I could sense him smiling next to me, and we both couldn't keep it up anymore—we laughed out loud. This friendship between Devin and me was a fun charade. *I just might survive this week and possibly enjoy it.*

"I'll be right back," Devin said. I watched him jog out the back doors and disappear. While he was gone, I took in all that was the livery. The building was dimly lit, and when my eyes adjusted, I could see a long worktable to my right. Tools, ropes, and other things were stacked on top of it. There was a loft full of hay overhead, and a small window that let in a ray of sunshine. The light made every floating particle of dust in the air visible. Watching the dust swirl and float through the air was oddly soothing until my nose started to tickle. A loud life-altering sneeze sounded throughout the livery, and it took me a moment to recover.

"Bless you," a deep voice said from behind me. A startled yelp escaped my mouth, and I spun around to face the man standing in the shadows. *John.* How long had he been standing there? Long enough to have witnessed mine and Devin's exchange, most likely.

"Whew! You scared me."

"Sorry." He slowly walked out of the shadows, cleaning something off in his hand with a rag. "I thought you wouldn't be riding today?"

"No riding for me. I only came because apparently somebody needed me here. Do you know who it was?"

He shook his head before looking back down to his task at hand. "I didn't know you already knew my younger brother…"

His brother?! "We just met, actually."

"Really?" He raised his eyebrows in genuine surprise. "I noticed you both carrying on like old friends just a moment ago. How was I not fortunate enough to receive such a greeting when we first met?"

"I…um…it really was nothing." It was my turn to look down and try to gather my thoughts. I could barely do that with his blue eyes watching me. I'm pretty sure his eyes got bluer the closer I got to him—but that wasn't important right now.

"Let's give it a go then," he said. I looked in his eyes and opened my mouth to say something, but no words came out. I wanted him closer, but it also terrified me that I wanted such a thing from a stranger. As if reading my mind through my eyes, he slowly stepped forward as if approaching a wild animal until we

27

were only inches apart. I could feel the heat from his body through his shirt as he neared and noticed he smelled like a pine tree in the best kind of way. I tried to slow my breathing, but my heart rate was in "full steam ahead" mode. If he felt my pulse, it would give me away. "So how does it go?" he whispered. The timbre of his voice was deep and smooth. I swallowed hard.

"Um…we exchange secrets. I'll go first," I whispered. It wasn't like me to be so bold, but maybe it was knowing I was playing a part for a week that allowed me to let my guard down a little bit more than normal. I wasn't supposed to be letting my guard down for this specific man, though. I softly put a hand on his chest and another on his shoulder to position my mouth close to his ear. He tossed whatever was in his hand into the dirt, and it landed with a *thud*. He put his newly freed hand on my waist. His confidence made my heart race. I leaned in and whispered softly into his ear. "I used to love to ride, but I was thrown from a horse when I was young and landed hard. I couldn't move and could barely breathe for a few minutes, and it scared me enough to never want to ride again." I took in a shaky breath. "I promised myself I would never put myself in a position to let that happen again. I guess the rubbing sound from my parka coat spooked the horse. No one told me until after I had been thrown that the horse had been known to spook easily with certain sounds." I slowly eased down from my tiptoes and looked into his eyes as he searched mine. "Trust doesn't come easy when it comes to…horses." I started to slide my hands off his shoulder and chest, but as soon as I did, he smoothly pulled me closer to him. His hold on my waist had tightened, and his other hand held one of mine just over his heart. Our eyes locked, and I could see his eyes searching mine for more, not necessarily more details about the spooked horse incident, but just more about *me*. I was holding my breath. I knew from an EMT training course I had taken a few years ago that I could survive without oxygen for four minutes. I would wait as long as it took for him to speak, or at least four minutes, whichever came first. He gently lifted my chin with his hand and gave me a look that said I could trust him. He slowly lowered his mouth to my ear and lifted my hair back.

"You being thrown had nothing to do with you. The horse would have thrown anyone, and no one should have been allowed to have been so close to him—especially you. There are good horses—more good than bad. You just have to try again to find out, but with a horse you can trust." John pulled back so he could look in my eyes. "It had nothing to do with you. There is nothing wrong with you."

My throat tightened, and my eyes started to sting. *What was happening?* I usually didn't let things strike such chords with me—especially from a stranger. His simple words started to untie internal knots, ones that I was so sure would never come undone.

I never told John the horse was a male, and he referred to it as such, which gave me the feeling we weren't talking about horses at all. I looked down just as a tear fell and no doubt landed on his shirt.

A voice cleared loudly behind me. I turned around slowly out of John's arms.

"I challenge you to a duel at high noon tomorrow in the town square!" Devin took a wide stance with a hand on his belt. "I know we may be family, but she's mine, and I will fight to the death!" Devin lowered his head slightly as though he would charge like an angry bull. *What on earth is going on?*

John slow-clapped while he walked around to put himself between Devin and I. He bent down to pick up what he was cleaning earlier and started at it again. "Now take a bow, Devin. That was some of your best work."

"Do you think so?" Devin asked eagerly. "I won by the way," he said to John and then turned to me. "I got what we need." He held up a bag full of something. "Let's go!" Devin snapped out of his dueling cowboy character and led me out through the back doors. I turned back to see John look down and slowly kick something imaginary in the dirt.

John. Bill was right; he was a dangerous one. I didn't know how much of what just took place was real and what was an act. Whichever side of him that was, though, was good—*too good.* He probably gets a sheriff's star or something if guests fall head over heels for him. If I was smart, I'd distance myself from him. The scary thing was that I could already feel myself starting to fall. A place like Summit Springs, where guests changed weekly, was one of the most dangerous places to let it happen. I felt like I was falling without a parachute, not knowing if I had a place to land in the end. I rubbed my forehead to try and clear my mind of what just happened in the livery and the thoughts that followed. Outside, I could breathe again, and it felt like I was able to take in my first deep breath since seeing John in the livery. I looked up and saw Devin smiling over at me.

"Whaaat?" I asked for the motive behind his smile.

"Oh, nothing at all," he lied. I let it slide because I had a feeling he knew exactly who had been on my mind, and I didn't want to blush in front of him about it. We walked along the wooden fence that surrounded the horse pasture. Chickens pecked the ground near our feet under the big shade trees. "So, where are you taking me now?"

"To the pond, of course," he said.

"Of course! What was I thinking?"

"With you? Only heaven knows." The look of surprise on my face was the reaction he wanted, and he beamed with satisfaction. "I'm kidding."

"What's at the pond?"

"Ducks. A plethora of ducks."

"What are we going to do with these ducks?"

"If I had my way, we'd roast them all."

"Devin!" My dropped jaw was all he was after again. He lived for a reaction, and he was saying all the right things to elicit many from me.

"But unfortunately, they are the ones who will be fed today." He opened the bag he had been carrying and revealed two loaves of bread. "I snuck theses out of the kitchen earlier. Don't tell my aunt." I smiled wide, and so did he.

"Is Carol really your aunt, or is she your pretend 1866 aunt?"

"Real one. My parents own Summit Springs, but Bill and Carol run it." We weaved our way through some bushes, and suddenly he pulled me behind one and crouched down low. "Are you ready?" he whispered with a touch of seriousness.

"I…I think so. I've been preparing myself for this as long as I can remember."

He almost smiled, but then I saw a glint in his eye. I think he was surprised I could hold my own in the sarcasm department.

"Good. Here take this." He handed me a loaf. "Whatever you do, watch out for Quacky."

"Which one is—"

Before I could finish my sentence, he was up waving his loaf of bread in the air for all the ducks to see and letting out loud "quack quacks!"

"Wait! Devin! Which one is Quacky?"

"All of them!" He threw his head back and laughed an exaggerated evil laugh that made me laugh in return. Within moments, the "quacking" was so loud we couldn't hear each other laugh. There had to be at least two hundred ducks, and they were all swimming towards us!

"We won't have enough bread," I called out to Devin. It took four attempts, increasing the volume each time before my words finally reached his ears.

"We'll just have to come back tomorrow too!" He smiled, and I knew this was the real Devin and not the actor. I smiled back. I broke the bread into as many tiny pieces as possible, and as fast as I could. I flung the bread into the masses by the handfuls so more ducks could eat at once. There were even ducks that took the subtle approach of letting me know they were hungry by nibbling at my skirt and boots. They had Devin and I surrounded, and I couldn't help but laugh until happy tears started to pool in the corners of my eyes. It had been too long since I'd laughed this hard. When all the bread was gone, and the ducks realized more wouldn't appear, they dispersed and waddled around looking for any other edible items along the pond shore.

"Devin, that was nuts," I said while brushing breadcrumbs and feathers off my skirt.

"I had fun."

"Me too."

"My aunt has no doubt concocted up something delicious for dinner. You ready to go find out if I'm right?" He smiled, and I nodded in response. We made it back to the livery just as the riding group started unsaddling their horses and brushing them down. I saw Anna up ahead, and she turned to wave as we approached.

"Hey Devin, I'll catch up with you later. Thanks again," I said. He looked up and saw Anna, and then tipped his hat to me before walking over to a group of guests to help carry their saddles into the livery.

"Maggie! Look at you!" Anna said as I neared.

I held out my skirts and knew that the rest of the feathers and muck wouldn't be coming out without a good wash. "I know I'm filthy, but…"

"I'm not talking about your skirt. Although, now that you bring it up, you're right. You look like you've just gotten into a tussle with a goose. The man next to you just moments ago was more of what I was referring to. Maggie, he's really cute!"

"Oh, that would be Devin. He's just a friend," I said, linking my arm through one of hers to head back to the hotel. "How was the ride?"

"It was so good! I knew this place would do wonders for my soul. You were right by the way—letting my hair down and galloping through the wind like a romance novel heroine proved to be very freeing. Being on a horse again was just what the doctor ordered, and no doubt, I will be completely cured by the end of all this. What's his name will only be a memory. I'm almost positive I could eat pie right now without even thinking of him!"

"Good!"

"Remember how he said that the lack of spark between us was my fault. He turned out to be such a jerk!"

"Times ten! Yeah, I remember, and I'm sorry again that you went through it. You deserve someone who knows what they have when they have you."

"Thanks. I want the same for you, you know."

"Thank you," I sighed. "I just don't know if I'm ready to jump in with both feet yet. I'm gun shy, even after two years. I'm scared to trust someone with my heart again, because what if I stumble upon a closet packed to the brim with skeletons like I did before?"

"We all have skeletons, but the problem is when they're not laid to rest."

"This conversation has taken a morbid turn."

"It normally does with you," Anna said as she smiled over at me.

"I think it has to do with the cadaver lab I had to do for anatomy class. I still have nightmares."

"Anyone would." Anna and I put overly peppy smiles on our faces and waved at some townsfolk as though we weren't just talking about stuff that could be used in horror movies. "Moral of the story, and your new mantra…innocent until proven guilty, and not, guilty until proven innocent. Let yourself trust again. Only you can make the call when you're ready, and remember not every guy is going to be like the last one."

I let out a big sigh before confessing what my mind and heart had been battling over for a few hours now. "Anna, I think I like John. It hasn't even been 24 hours, and that terrifies me.

"Is he the one who saved us from having to carry your trunk up the stairs?"

"Yep, that's the one. I saw him in the livery earlier too. I don't know him, and what I do know about him is most likely an act. I'm normally not so reckless with my heart." I looked over at Anna as she nodded. "John and I have this mind-reading thing, though. No matter where we are or who we're with, all we have to do is look into each other's eyes to know what the other one is thinking or feeling. I've never had that with anyone else besides you and my mom. It's like he and I are having secret conversations around the actual conversation going on around us. I want to know him—

like really know him—not the actor. That scares me because of the situation we're in."

"And what situation is that again?"

"1866. Thanks to you." We both smiled at each other.

"You're welcome," she said.

I did an exaggerated cry face before lifting my head to the sky. "What if he has somebody waiting on him?" *I really hope he doesn't.*

"Ask him."

"What? I can't do that."

"Yes, you can. Ask him."

"We're all playing a part here, and I'm starting to find it hard to discern fact from fiction anyway."

"If the two of you have an eye thing going on, then focus on what you see in his eyes when you ask him and not so much the words you hear."

"But I…"

"Maggie, just give it a shot. What have you got to lose?" she asked. I mulled it over in my mind.

"Did I hear something about shooting?" a man's voice called out from the hotel porch. Both mine and Anna's heads turned to find an elderly man dressed in a dark grey cotton shirt, a leather vest, and chaps towering over us on the porch. His worn hat had a feather and some white looking beads on it. "I'm the one you're looking for! Meet me by the orchard, and I'll take you both out shooting. As soon as you wake up tomorrow morning, make your way over along with the others."

"What if we don't wake up in time?" Anna asked, slightly panicked.

Half of the man's mouth curved upward into a small smile. "Don't go worryin' about that. You'll be awake."

We nodded slowly as he turned and walked away. He walked down the porch, then around the corner of the hotel and out of sight.

"We didn't even agree to go," I said. We both stood in the dirt road, stunned.

"I know. How did that happen?"

"I'm not entirely sure."

"Do you think somebody comes around and knocks on our doors each morning to make sure we wake up at a proper time?" Anna asked.

"Only the shadow knows, but I have a feeling we're going to find out." We walked up the stairs and into the cafe to find it empty and not a footstep to be heard upstairs either. "I need to go and change really quick because I don't want to look like a walking pillow fight on our first night here." We lifted our skirts and scaled the staircase up to our room.

I opened my trunk for the first time and saw a pretty blue floral dress. I gently laid it across my bed and lifted the next dress out—*blue*. Lifting each outfit from my trunk proved to be a very blue experience. Blue in the sense that every clothing item was blue or paired with something blue.

"It's like whoever put together my outfits for the week knew my hair was strawberry blonde!" Anna squealed. "This deep purple day dress is perfect! I wonder if they'll let me take it home if I begged?" She twirled around and around next to her bed. She looked perfect, but I couldn't help but feel deflated that my wardrobe had not been so carefully selected.

"I promise I'll do whatever I can so you can take that dress home—if you let me borrow a couple of your dresses this week. All of mine are blue!"

Anna looked over at the clothes on my bed, then bent down and sifted through the rest of my trunk. She flopped the remaining contents onto the bed one by one. I'm sure she was convinced she would find something that wasn't blue because she started to breathe a little heavy and toss things quicker than before. We both stared down at my bed with our hands on our hips.

"I don't get it. Why would all of your clothes be blue? Clearly, there are other colors of clothes available." She made a sweeping motion over her colorful outfits strewn across her bed. "And of course, we can trade whenever you want. Do you want one of mine to wear to dinner?"

"No, that's okay. This floral dress will be great, but tomorrow I might want a change of scenery."

"Mi ropa es su ropa!"

"Anna, you know I can't understand you without Google translate."

"My clothes are your clothes!"

"Thank you!" We both laughed and clicked the bedroom door behind us.

Later that evening, Anna and I found everyone out behind the hotel getting ready for dinner. There was easily over two hundred people back there. Long wooden tables were set up in rows with benches lining them all. The closer we got to the crowd, the louder the conversations and laughter were. I couldn't help but search for a specific pair of blue eyes. A loud whistle sounded, and the crowd hushed into silence. Everyone looked around for the source of the whistle, and all eyes eventually rested on Bill.

"Howdy, everyone!" Bill called out. "The town of Summit Springs is happy to welcome the new settlers and prospectors who have arrived from all over the world today! We hope your time here is enjoyable. We'd also like to thank the members of our community who have joined us for this meal tonight. Women and children will take their meals first, and the men are to follow.

There's enough food to go around at least twice." Bill took off his hat, and every other hat was removed as well, while Bill prayed before the meal.

"Amen!" the large crowd sounded in unison. I did hear one man say it much louder than the rest and knew immediately it was the mountain man we had met on the hotel porch. Anna must've realized it too because the sound brought a small smile to both our faces.

Everyone stood and started to make a line. Luckily, Anna and I were standing close to the front already. As I was nonchalantly scanning the crowd, I noticed Anna doing the same.

"Who are you looking for?" I asked.

"No one," Anna said a little too quickly to go undetected.

"That's a weird name."

"That's not his name."

"Caught! Who is he?"

"Okay, his name's Ricardo, but I call him Ricky."

"Very *I Love Lucy*," I said.

"Right?! I met him on the horse ride today. I like the way he rolls his "r's" and the way he says my name."

"How does he say your name?"

Anna's cheeks blushed in an instant. "You'll see."

I turned just in time to see a man with tan skin and jet-black hair under a hat hold out his hand for Anna's. He raised her hand to his lips and kissed it softly. "Señora Anna, you look beautiful this evening." He raised her hand higher as if to show her off to the world. Anna being on the shy side, tilted her head slightly to the right and blushed deeper. *Okay, they are cute.* I couldn't help but full grin smile.

"You must be Maggie," he said as he held out his hand for mine. He kissed it quickly like a gentleman. Over my shoulder, I mouthed "Señora Anna?!" to Anna before Ricky could see. She beamed.

"I am Ricardo Jose Gonzalez Moreno...Junior." I stared wide-eyed, only remembering the "junior" part. "But my friends call me Ricky."

"What a relief!"

We all laughed. Someone called Ricky's name from farther down the line. He held up his hand to whoever it was and then locked eyes with Anna. "Save me a seat?" he asked. Anna dipped her head and smiled, and Ricky returned the smile before excusing himself.

"An-na!" I whispered.

"I know, I know. I should've told you sooner, but I didn't know how to tell you. After seeing how Ricky treats me, there's no doubt I was in the wrong relationship before. I'm not ready for anything serious right now, though, so we're just friends."

"Her famous last words."

"Yes, they are," she said. I almost believed her. We scooted up in line and picked up our metal tin plates and utensils. "We spent the whole ride side by side, just talking. His family is from Mexico, but they moved to Arizona when he was young. When he was 19, he went on a two-year service mission to Guatemala, and that's where he met John. When they got home, Ricky moved here to Utah to go to college and has been working here in Summit Springs off and on each summer since."

"Molasses beans?" a nice woman asked.

"Yes, please!" I said a little too eagerly—knowing my stomach had been growling ferociously under the crowd's chatter.

"Me too," Anna said when it was her turn.

We thanked the woman and postponed our conversation for some corn on the cob, a roll, and some beef roast. We grabbed metal cups, like the people in front of us did, then dipped them in a barrel full of water. Anna and I walked in concentrated silence, so we didn't trip over any rocks and lose our precious food. We found a seat near a tall bushy tree in the back. Anna scooted in on the bench to save a spot for Ricky, and I did the same, so I was seated in front of her but on the opposite side. She and I didn't say anything while we devoured the most tender beef roast as quickly as a carnivore could.

"Twenty-four hours," Devin said as he sat down next to me with a plate full of food. "That's how long they roast the beef underground on oven spits."

"Really?" I tried to chew and swallow quickly, just in case I needed to talk again. Between bites, I introduced Devin to Anna. "...and Devin is John's brother," I said to Anna. She just about lost the mouthful of water she had just drank, but pulled it together at the last second and swallowed hard.

"That was my exact reaction to the news when I learned of our relation, too," Devin said and smiled in satisfaction at Anna's reaction.

Anna composed herself and apologized. "Oh no, I just thought there was a bug crawling on my leg." She bent down and shook her skirt. She was turning into quite the actress. "No bug!"

"Oh, good! You never know out here!" I added for effect.

"Hey, man!" Devin greeted Ricky as he slid into the space next to Anna.

Ricky sent a smile my way before turning all his smiles and focus toward Anna. I could tell Ricky and Anna wanted to talk for a moment, so I shifted Devin's attention to me.

"So, I'm thinking about going shooting tomorrow morning," I said.

"Oh yeah, who with?" He asked as he took a drink.

"I'm not sure, actually. Some man with a feathered hat outside the hotel asked us to go. We assumed he was one of your men, you know from the community, and that it was on the itinerary."

"Some man? Maggie, you know you shouldn't talk to strangers." I tipped my head down in a you've-got-to-be-kidding kind of way. He laughed. "We call him Old Tom. He's a bit more of a genuine mountain man than the rest of us. Do you want me to come with you?"

I just stared at him with a smirk.

"Oh, I get it. You're choosing right now not to talk to strangers. Good thing we're not strangers, though, because you already know my deepest, darkest secret."

"Is that so?" A deep familiar voice sounded directly behind me. *John.* He moved to the head of the table and leaned over it with a glint in his eyes. "So, she knows about that one time you—"

"John!" Devin warned before he shoveled more food into his mouth. John patted him on the shoulder, and the air lightened up a bit. Ricky held up a hand and shook John's, then turned to introduce John and Anna. John shook her hand and explained to Ricky how they had briefly met earlier.

"Then, I assume you already know Maggie as well?" Ricky asked. John and I made that connecting eye contact where we both knew there was more to the story, but neither one of us was going to share the details.

"Yes, I know Maggie," John said softly without looking away.

I smiled, and he did too before turning to Devin.

"Oh, hey Dev, I actually was coming to ask a favor. The Hansens wanted to get an early start on panning and need a guide upriver. I'm out with the cattle in the morning, or I'd do it myself. That all right?"

I saw Devin take a deep breath in. "That'll be fine."

"Thanks." I sensed John as he walked behind me and noticed him out of my peripheral vision sit down at the next table over. I lifted my head slowly to sneak a glance, and he was looking at me. *Shoot.* I smiled and quickly looked down at my plate, suddenly very interested in my corn on the cob. I didn't dare look in his direction for the remainder of the meal.

After we washed our plates, utensils, and cups in the wash buckets, Anna and I went and found the outhouses before going up to bed. We finished our first outhouse experience and opened the wooden doors at the same time. As we stepped off the step onto the dirt path, we heard a strange loud gargling sound coming from behind us. A huge black rooster strutted out from behind a rock and stared us down.

"Anna?" I asked cautiously.

"Yeah, Maggie?"

"Run!"

Just as we did, the massive rooster charged. Its feathers were puffed out and flying in the wind. I screamed, Anna screamed, and the rooster seemed to have screamed in its own war cry way as well. We both about tripped on our skirts, but somehow made it to the hotel's back door. Where the door led? I didn't know, but I hoped for all I was worth that it wasn't locked.

"Anna! The door!" I called out to her.

She made it to the door first, and I could hear the rooster closing in. The door opened. *Yes!* Anna opened it wide as I sprinted through. She shut the door quickly, and a loud smack sounded on the other side. *Crazy bird!* Anna and I breathed heavily with our hands on our knees, trying to catch our breath.

"I… am never…going… to the bathroom again," I said.

"Me neither!"

With that unrealistic pact settled, we started to breathe normally again and realized where we were. The room was dim, but we were in some kind of pantry from what we could see. There were two closed doors, both on opposite sides of the room.

"Which one do you think we should try first?" I asked. In that instant, loud crashing and banging sounds came from the door on the right, causing us both to jump and run to the door on the left. Just like that, the decision was made. Once we closed the door, we rested against it with eyes closed. My eyes shot open at the sound of a cupboard closing softly. At least five pairs of surprised eyes from the kitchen staff stared at us, not knowing how to handle our sudden arrival.

"Excuse us," I said before leading the way out of this maze of a kitchen and into the café. We hurried around the chairs and tables and out to the staircase. As soon as we made it to the safety of our room, we flopped down on our beds. I was exhausted.

"I asked Ricky about bears on the ride today," Anna said. "I guess there are bears around, but they don't come down into this valley very often. No one has seen a bear in the valley for a long time, so we should be safe."

"I hope so because the birds around here are already out for blood."

"Maggie?"

"Hmm?"

"Thanks for coming on this trip with me."

I rolled over onto my side to face Anna. "Of course."

"I still can't believe Devin and John are brothers!"

"I know! It's weird. Sorry I didn't mention it earlier on our walk."

"All is well. So, Devin is really okay with you and John?" she asked.

"Well, John and I aren't even together, but Devin would be fine with it if we were. He and I really are just friends. Anna?"

"Yeah?"

"It wasn't the electricity thing that worried me about coming on this trip." I took a deep breath. "I saw a picture of John on the registration website and got nervous about the possibility of falling for a guy who is living a double life—again. The people in this town are paid to do exactly that—live a double life. *John* is being paid to do that."

"In his defense, we don't know how much acting he's doing. I think only time will tell. Trust your instincts because yours are good ones. Except for that one time when you had a 'good feeling' about us taking that sewing class in middle school."

The memory of us opening our report cards made me laugh out loud. "We did get a cool pillow out of that class, though."

"That's true," she said. I could hear her smile as she said those words.

My eyelids started to close. "Oh, and Anna?"

"Hmm?"

"Ricky does roll his "r's" just right, doesn't he?"

"He really does!" Anna squealed.

"Goodnight, Anna."

"Night, Maggie."

• • •   — — —   • • —   • — • •

What on earth?! I woke up in a panic. "He's in the house!"

Anna sat up straight, "Whose here?!"

There was the sound again! The rooster crowing! "The rooster! It's here in California!"

"We're still in Summit Springs, Maggie. Come look." I rolled myself out of bed and joined Anna next to the window.

My eyes took a minute to focus because it was first light outside where everything seemed to blend together. After a few moments, Old Tom came into view and was holding that horrible black rooster up in his arm as if it were a puppy. He marched up and down the dirt road in front of the hotel at least five times while that noisy bird sounded off the whole time. I heard bumps on the walls to the left and right of us, which meant the rooster had done its job. People were waking up. This whole scene would be funny if that piece of poultry hadn't just tried to eat us the night before, and if I wasn't so tired.

"What time is it?" I asked.

"I'm not sure, but the sun isn't up yet."

"Ugh! If the sun isn't up, we shouldn't be either. Can I wear one of your dresses today?"

"Yeah! Come pick one!" We both knelt next to her trunk and sorted through her outfits for the week. "You can pick anyone you want…except this one." Anna held up a cream-colored dress with pretty lace. "I want to wear this one to the Pasture Party Friday night."

"It's all yours. I think I'll borrow this pink floral one."

We changed into our dresses for the day. Anna wore a deep gold skirt and cream top with her hair up in a twist. I wore the pink floral dress and left my naturally wavy hair down. The sleeves on my dress reached just passed my elbows, and the A-line silhouette made me want to spin around to see how far the skirt would fly.

"I think I'm going to be daring and wear the poofiest of the petticoats today," I said.

"You are feeling brave, aren't you?" We both laughed as Anna attempted to help me get the petticoat situated properly, then stood back as I spun around a few times. "Maggie, you look like a Wild West princess!"

"Were those a thing back then?" I asked.

"Probably! Remember how I wanted to figure out if there's a way to take a dress home with us? Well, I think you should fight for that one. It looks *that* good on you."

"Thank you. I will only agree to take this one if it comes with the petticoat, and if you agree to help me get it on when we get home." I laughed and continued to sway back and forth, clearly enjoying the extra volume the petticoat gave my dress.

"Done and done!"

We laced up our boots and made our way downstairs. We got to the bottom step when the scent of bacon stopped us in our tracks. Anna and I both looked at each other. "Bacon!" we said in unison. People had already started lining up to plate their breakfast in the café. Once we reached the front of the line, we filled our plates with bacon, fruit, and delicious looking things called lacy-edged corn pancakes. We doused the pancakes with honey and butter. By the time we finished breakfast, the cafe had filled up with more people until there was hardly any open seats left. Anna and I slid outside and walked down the dirt road over to the orchard. There was already a small group gathered near the apple trees for the shooting lesson.

"Well, *Anna* Oakley, are we ready for this?"

"As ready as I'll ever be."

5

I smiled at Old Tom as we approached and thanked him for his wake-up call this morning.

"Don't thank me…" He gave us a sly smile, knowing that loud bird was the one to thank. "We'll wait about ten more minutes before heading to the range." People talked among themselves as we waited for more people to join us.

"Hello there!" an elderly woman said, as she slowly walked over to us.

Anna and I greeted her in unison.

"I'm Marge, and who might you be?"

"My name's Maggie."

"I'm Anna."

"It's good to see some women in the ranks this morning!" Marge said. "Normally, it's just me showing all these boys how shooting is done, but it's nice to have allies today! What brings you girls to Summit Springs?"

"We wanted to take a break from the busy city," I answered, so Anna didn't feel the need to explain the real reason for us coming.

"Mmmhmm," she nodded while closing her eyes. "I understand completely. My first year in Summit Springs was ten years ago, and it was the best experience of my life. That was my reason for coming too. Times are simpler here, and the people are friendly, just like they used to be long ago. That's why I buy out a spot every week in the spring, summer, and fall. I'd live here in town year-round if they'd let me!" She laughed loudly as though she'd just told a really good joke. Anna and I smiled and laughed too—more so at her hearty laugh. Marge had grey hair and was shorter than Anna and me by at least a foot. She had wrinkles on her face that grew deeper when she laughed or smiled, and I loved that about her.

"All right, stay on the trail," Old Tom called out.

"See you girls up there! Good luck!" We watched Marge disappear into the crowd. The group took about a ten-minute walk over to a clearing where a mountain served as a backdrop for the shooting range. There were bottles and cans lined up on top of crates near the mountain. Old Tom gathered everyone around and talked about the parts of a gun and gun safety, then we were split into groups. Everyone lined up, and I volunteered to go first in my group on the end. A lifetime of shooting at those pretend Wild West arcade shooting ranges had prepared me for this moment. Each person shooting had a more experienced person assisting them, except me. Old Tom assisted a group, and Marge was with another. Two other men helped the other two groups.

"I'm here!" I heard a man's voice call out through the crowd.

"On the end." Old Tom nodded.

John and I smiled at each other as he jogged over to me. He did a once over at my dress before looking away. My pulse started to race, and I got self-conscious in an instant, wondering what had caused him to look away so quickly. I looked at my dress to see if I had dropped something down the front of it at breakfast. There wasn't anything on my dress…besides a lot of pink. *Does he hate pink?* I shouldn't care, but I found myself doing exactly that— *caring.*

"You ready?" John asked.

"MmmHmm."

I picked the gun up from the wooden table and pointed the barrel downrange just like Old Tom had just instructed. I loaded the shells and took a deep breath. A piece of me wanted to pretend I didn't know how to hold the gun, so John would come closer, but a bigger piece of me wanted to impress him. I held the gun up close, aimed just like I used to at the arcade shooting ranges, and pulled the trigger. *Crash!* I hit a bottle! The sound was satisfying, so I fired four more. *Crash! Crash! Crash! Crash!* I set the gun down on the table for the next person in line, then looked up to where John stood. His eyes were wide and locked on mine. He was standing tall with his muscled arms folded across his chest, unmoving. A small smile was on his lips, and I could tell by the look on his face that he was impressed. There was something else in his eyes though, and I just needed a couple more seconds to figure it out—

"Well, I'll be!" Old Tom walked over to where I stood. "Who would've thought the girl in the pink dress would turn out to be Little Miss Sure Shot! Atta girl!"

I said nothing, but I was sure my blushing cheeks filled everyone in. Everyone within earshot could overhear the praise exchange, and I wasn't a girl who felt comfortable with all eyes on me.

Every person got to take three turns before we headed back into town. Anna fell back in the group to praise some of the boys who had missed some bottles. She really was the best teacher and has always tried to build up her students, no matter their background or their academic performance. She always seemed to know what each student needed, and if she didn't, she would take different approaches until she found out. She was no different here, and I was proud of her.

"You did good back there." John fell in step beside me.

"Are you saying you'd pick me to be on your team for laser tag?"

"That's exactly what I'm saying, and I'd even pick you first."

I opened my mouth to say something back, but no words came. The corners of my lips turned upward, and I looked down at the dirt trail. "Did all the cows behave this morning?"

"We only have obedient cows here in Summit Springs," he said while trying to keep a straight face. I looked up into his eyes and smiled first, thinking about our conversation's bizarre turn. He gave in with a smile in the next moment. "So...I...um..." He took off his hat to run a hand through his dark wavy hair. Something was telling me that nervousness wasn't something this tall, strong, and confident man felt very often. "I was wondering if you wanted to come down to the livery with me?"

Panic took over. *Horses.* He probably was going to try talking me into riding one. "I can't."

He nodded, and I saw a flash of hurt surge through his eyes; then, it quickly left, just like he did. John tipped his hat to me before walking away in the direction of the orchard, instead of back into town with the rest of the group. I was saying 'no' to the possibility of riding, not to John. He didn't know that, though. I remembered our conversation in the livery; *I had a feeling we weren't talking about horses at all.* A sick feeling took over, and

I knew I had made a mistake. He was talking about horses, but he really wasn't. The thought of getting on a horse again terrified me to the point of nausea, but I couldn't let John walk away, thinking I was saying no to *him.*

I picked up my skirts, as much of them as I could, and ran. *Of all the days to wear the poofiest petticoat!* Looking like a flying pink cupcake, I ran as fast as I could. I didn't want another minute to pass by, letting John think I didn't want to be with him. I wasn't sure what I wanted out of this week when it came to John. All I knew right now, though, was that I wanted to spend time with him—as much as I possibly could.

"John!" I called out while running through the apple trees. He didn't turn around at first, so I called out his name again. He heard me the second time because he slowed and started to turn around towards me. I dropped my skirts and slowed my pace. When I was an arm's length away, I stopped and looked up into his eyes. "I don't want to get on a horse today, but I do want to spend time with you." I took a deep breath. "Is that liver option still on the table?"

The corners of his mouth started to curve upward slowly. "I don't know what's for lunch today, but I have a feeling it won't be liver." I was confused by his response. My forehead crinkled, trying to think back through the last of our exchanged words, and then it clicked. "Livery! Livery! Not liver! Gross. Why is it even called a livery?"

A big grin spread across his face, and suddenly I didn't have to wonder what the outlaw from the wanted poster looked like when he was full-fledged smiling. His smile was even better than I had imagined. I was already thinking of ways I could summon that smile from him again. Confidence started to fill his eyes before he turned and plucked two apples from the tree next to us. Some men pick flowers for their girl, but mine picks me fruit. *Mine.* He wasn't really mine. *Please don't have someone waiting on you.* I watched him as he rubbed both apples on his shirt and held one out for me to take. We walked and ate our apples while a light breeze blew through my hair and the trees around us.

"A servant's uniform used to be referred to as livery," he said. "During the Middle Ages, a high-ranking servant was entrusted with the care and keep of the horses. The name 'livery' kind of stuck, but throughout the years, it's often been referred to as a livery yard or livery stable as well."

"You've sure got the definition down pat, don't you? It's as if you've had this conversation once before." I smiled before taking another bite of apple.

"Once." He laughed a little. "Yeah, I've tried to convince Bill to let me repaint the sign to say Hudson's Livery Stable, but he thinks it's more authentic just as "Livery," and he doesn't think I could fit all three words onto the sign."

"Well, Bill has a point with the three-word thing. I'm not sure you could do it." I smiled over at John, who quickly turned his head in my direction before picking up on my sarcasm. He turned back to take the last bite of his apple, but right before the crunch sounded, I saw a smile spread across his face. We walked out of the orchard and over towards the post.

"So, what's his name?" John asked.

"Whose name?"

"The lucky guy waiting for you back home."

"Alan. I'm hoping he's alive when I get back." John looked at me, slightly alarmed. He didn't move a muscle, and I forced myself not to laugh. *Two could play at this acting game.* "He's never been on his own this long before. He's really good at holding his breath though, so I'm thinking he'll be all right. Alan is also a fish." I'm pretty sure I saw him let out a breath of air that he'd been holding.

"You are unlike anyone I've ever met," he said.

"I'll take that as a compliment."

"You should." John unlatched the lock on the large livery doors and swung them wide open. He grabbed a bridle as we walked through the livery, then some carrots from a small box near the back doors. "I think we're all set. Let's go find us a

61

horse." John and I walked out to the wooden post fence. He handed me the carrots. "I'll be right back."

I watched John walk away with the bridle in his hands as he clicked his tongue and let out three short whistles. I hated to see him go, but I loved watching him walk away. Today, he wore a steel blue button-up shirt with the sleeves folded up his forearms again, with black pants, and a brown brimmed hat. His broad shoulders and back muscles pulled against his shirt as he walked over a small hill and disappeared. I started to wonder what his other life was like, and what he did when he wasn't here. Just as I tried to place which occupation I could picture him in, he crested the hill and led a horse in my direction. As they approached, I could see the horse a bit better, and it was beautiful—tall and jet black. John stopped about twenty feet from where I stood and positioned the horse sideways. I was relieved to be on the opposite side of the fence from the horse.

"Come on in. I've got him," John said.

"That's okay. I like the view from right here." John and I realized what I had just said at the same time. My eyes widened quickly. He raised an eyebrow into a surprised arch, and a small smile followed. "…view of the horse!"

John lifted his head back at a diagonal in a "come on over here" kind of way. I shook my head side to side in a "not a chance" kind of way. I heard him laugh for the first time, and it was deep and hearty. As soon as that sound stopped, I instantly craved to hear it again. He dropped his head before I could see his full-on smile, but I did see a dimple on the right side of his cheek, and it made my heart skip a beat. He dropped the reins and closed the distance between us until he stood directly in front of me—only the fence separating us.

"Maggie," he said while staring me right in the eyes.

"John." I held my ground, and a smile started to form on my lips.

"What is it going to take to get you to come over to greener pastures?"

"Something you can't give."

"Try me." I saw a fire ignite in his eyes as he leaned in and rested his hands on the fence on either side of me.

"Guacamole," I said while I forced myself to keep a straight face.

"That's it? That's all it will take?" he asked in a surprised tone.

"Yeah." I attempted to fake the confidence I was trying to exude. Maybe I should have thought of something harder to get in Summit Springs. *Him?*

"Consider it done. Come on over."

I let out a nervous sigh. "Okay, fine. If I don't survive this, though, I need to know you'll go back for Alan. Deal?"

"The fish?"

"Of course, the fish! Until you commit to taking care of Alan, if anything should happen to me, then I'm staying put."

A small challenging smile spread across his lips—not that I was looking at his lips. *I was definitely looking at his lips.* "Brine shrimp or bloodworms?" he asked.

I smiled really big. He knows fish. "Brine shrimp."

He gave a quick nod and took a step back to make room for me to come through. I handed him the carrots and bent down to duck under the posts that were parallel with the ground. My left leg slid through to the other side, and John offered me his hand. I took it and realized our hands fit together perfectly. When he gripped my hand, I got the same feeling I did when pressing the very last puzzle piece into place. *Right where I belong.* His hand was coarse, strong, and gentle, all at once. I didn't want to let go of it, of him—kind of like how my petticoat didn't want to let go of the fence posts. I was stuck. My skirts were too big to squeeze through the space between the posts. "I can't move," I said. Embarrassment quickly sank in, and I closed my eyes. *This was so not happening right now.* My cheeks were reddening by the second.

"Oh, hold on," he said as he slid his arms under my arms. He gently tried to pull me through the fence, but my petticoat wouldn't budge.

"I promise to never wear another petticoat ever. Maybe I should sit this one out today. I'll just wiggle back and stay on the other side of the fence. I—"

John pushed my poufy dress down under the fence and pulled me close to him at the same time. My skirts made a whooshing sound, and then I was free! We both toppled over into the grass and dirt. John kept his hold on me the whole time and took the brunt of the fall.

My hands splayed across his solid chest, and I could feel his heartbeat start to quicken. My eyes widened. John's hat had fallen off, giving me a better view of his face. He was the most handsome man I'd ever seen. His five o'clock shadow was already starting to show itself. His lips looked soft. As they began to turn upward at the corners, I shifted my focus to his eyes. They were stumbling blue. Time stood still. I noticed a scar near his left eyebrow but was too nervous to ask for the war story. My eyes fell on his lips again, and they spread into another small smile. That's when I remembered exactly where I was and who I was with. This was not the position I should be in if I was cautiously getting to know him.

"I…um…thank you." I scrambled off of him with close to no grace while struggling to get control of my petticoat and not to trip on my skirts. We both brushed the dirt off our clothes. John bent over and picked up the scattered carrots. The horse surprisingly stayed in the same place grazing, even with all the...*commotion* that had just taken place.

"Are you ready?" he asked. His eyes softened. I was nervous, and he could see it. "I promise I'll keep you safe." It was time to try overcoming this fear of mine, and I was grateful I didn't have to do it alone.

John's hand stroked the horse's shoulder, then down over its back. "I'm letting him know where we are, so he doesn't get spooked by any sudden moves. He already sensed us coming over long before we got here, though. You can always tell by the movement of his ears." John moved around my back to the front of the horse, and as he did, he put a hand on the small of my back for a brief moment—*letting me know where he is*. The horse's head started to rise from grazing, and I backed up out of reflex. John moved behind me in the next second. He pulled me back into his arms and held me close. "It's okay. I'm right here." He reached around and gently took hold of my hand and raised it to the horse's mouth.

"What are you doing?" I resisted his hand a little.

"Letting him get used to your scent by smelling your hand."

"Are you sure? This feels a lot like a human offering."

I felt the deep rumble of laughter in his chest before I heard it. "I'm sure," he said. Easing up on my resistance, I let John guide my hand up to the horse's mouth. The horse's breath warmed my fingers. "All right, it's carrot time." He handed me a carrot, and I cautiously raised it to the horse's mouth. It snatched it up so fast that I barely had enough time to move my hand away. The horse's lips flapped around, trying to maneuver the carrot deeper into its mouth.

"He's beautiful, John," I said.

"He's fast, too. If you ever want to outrun something, this is the horse to do it on." John bent down and grabbed the reins.

"Sounds like you've had experience. What would a guy like you be running from?" His silence was enough for me to know there was a deeper story, but I sensed I should bring it up at a later time. "I know what you're running from."

"Yeah?"

"The law. I've seen the wanted poster. If I was smart, I'd turn you in and cash out on my $500."

I noticed him tense up slightly. "And what would you spend it on first?" he asked.

"Your bail."

He looked directly at me, and his lips parted slightly. My response had caught him off guard. I stared right back at him. He was trying to read me. I wasn't going to let any of my explanations budge, though.

"You'd set me free with the reward money?"

My eyes said yes, but my mouth stayed closed. He caught it. I decided to try and blur the line between 1866 and modern time with another tactic—distraction. I had to get to know the real him before the week was up. "Let's take a walk," I suggested.

"You take the reins." I was sure my wide eyes and obvious hard swallow gave me away, but the horse was not supposed to be part of the plan. "You got this. I'll be here the whole time, and I'm not going anywhere." He was being sincere; I could see it in his eyes. If I didn't know any better, I'd wager that statement held more weight than just words. I sighed in an attempt to calm my nerves.

"Okay, if I'm going to be taking this massive untrusting animal for a walk, I ought to know his name," I said.

"Shady."

"Fitting."

"I thought so, but for probably different reasons than you." John gave me a small side smile.

"Well then, *Shady*, let's be on our way." My movements were a little too stiff, but I pulled gently and was able to set the horse in motion. John let out a small laugh, and we were off. *All three of us.*

We walked across the large pasture kitty-corner to the livery. We didn't talk a whole lot until we reached the far fence. The silence allowed doubt to creep into my mind, and I realized I really knew nothing about the stranger walking beside me. A part of me wanted to keep it that way. Another bigger part of me wanted to know him well enough to not call him a stranger. This situation with John felt delicate—like the whole thing could all disappear by Saturday afternoon. There was a good chance that it would, and it scared me enough to not want to open up. I hadn't let myself trust anyone or be this forward in two years. It wasn't a normal way to get to know someone—trying to read between the lines and gauge whether they were acting or not. It was now or never, and I knew I had to try. He opened the gate, then closed it behind us. I held onto the reins and hoped the horse would stay put and not try to run away. I'm sure John would not be thrilled if I lost his horse. I was starting to panic. I forced myself to remember the original plan of distracting him while trying to get real-life information out of him. *It could work.* It might take my mind off of the horse too. I needed to get on with it before my doubts took command again.

"Speaking of names, we should play a game. It's called six questions. It's like twenty questions, but there's just…six." I smiled, and he did too.

"All right, but I'm making a clause," he said. "The questions can only be ones that require a yes or no answer. Deal?"

"Deal." *Start out small and nonchalant.* I needed to pace myself. "Is John your real name?"

"Yes."

"Is Hudson your real last name?"

"No."

"If I guessed it, would you tell me?"

"Yes, but it will cost you. You get three guesses before you sign away your firstborn."

"Okay, Rumpelstiltskin. I think I might need a prize if I guess it right, though." The forwardness of his comment was not lost on me.

"All right. Fair enough. What will it be?" he asked.

"If I guess your last name, will you let Anna and I take one of our dresses home when we leave?"

His eyes averted down toward the ground for a few moments. Bringing up leaving seemed to have dampened the mood. "I'll see what I can do," he said as he looked up at me and forced a smile. I didn't know much about John, but I already knew when his smiles were forced and when they weren't.

"Next question. Do you like pink?" I grabbed a handful of my skirts and swished them back and forth, making a show of it. If I didn't need to hold the reins connected to the giant animal next to me, I would've done a twirl too. I think John would've even laughed or at least smiled. *I am getting to know him—at least a little bit.*

"Are you asking if I like your dress?"

"I ask the questions around here, Mr. Christensen." John stilled next to me. "Not Christensen, huh?" I asked.

"Is that one of your three guesses?" He cleared his throat.

I stared in his eyes and tried to gauge his reaction, and I even squinted for effect. "No, not a guess."

"I like the color pink on you. A lot," he said as he looked forward. "You look beautiful today, you looked beautiful yesterday, and if I was a gambling man, I would bet you'll look beautiful tomorrow too."

My cheeks colored, and I looked down at the passing field grass. I didn't point out that he expounded on his answer more than just the agreed-upon yes or no, but I was not complaining in the least. The distraction of the game was working. *Here goes nothing.* "Are you ready for the last question?"

"Let's hear it."

"Do you have somebody waiting on you?" I asked, then held my breath. *Silence.* Anna told me to look him in the eye when I asked that question, but he was facing away because we were walking. I needed to see his eyes. I instantly wished I could retract the question and save it for a later time. Now that the words had escaped my lips, though, I desperately wanted to know the answer.

The horse started to sidestep, and it shook its head back and forth a few times. I looked up at the horse and mentally reminded myself to keep holding onto the reins. His ears kept turning towards the trees. John stepped in, and I was relieved to pass off the reins.

"Whoa, Shady. Come on, boy." John calmed the horse down until he was still. Well, everything except for the horse's ears. John stood and brushed his hand down the horse's nose and its neck. Things were quiet—too quiet. Maybe he's going to break it to me that he's taken, remind me that he's playing a part and that this is just a job for him. I took a deep breath and braced myself for his next words. "Maggie," he said. *Here it comes.* My chest started constricting, and my eyes started to sting a little bit. *Not again. Not the double life let down.* "I need you to hold completely still. There's something in the trees across the stream up ahead." I was not prepared for those words. I held my breath as I scanned the bushes and trees near the stream. *There it was!* It was large, black, and crouched over. The horse let out an anxious breath, pulled its head back, and tried to reverse out of John's grasp. John held the horse tight against its protest. Within the next second, a bear stood up tall on its hind legs and stared directly at us. *No, no, no.* "If the bear crosses that stream, I need you to get on Shady and ride as fast as you can back into town," he said quietly. "Don't look back, okay?" John slowly pulled the reins over the horse's head while never turning his back to the bear.

"No."

"What?"

"I'm not going to leave you here," I whispered. I meant it. I was petrified, but there was no way I would leave him here alone with a bear.

"I need to know you'll be safe. Promise me?"

"I can't. Why don't we ride together?"

"Shady won't be able to run at full speed with the two of us," he said.

"There's no way I'm leaving you here alone with a bear."

The horse started to spook, and the bear started to cross the stream. John held the reins and calmed the horse as much as possible, before bending down and lacing his fingers together to help me up. "Please, Maggie," he asked. He looked in my eyes, and what I saw there broke my heart. He seemed desperate for me to get on the horse. My lips parted slightly, and I started to shake my head. I looked up and saw the bear was almost completely across the stream on our side.

"Please. I'll be all right. I just need you on this horse, so I can think straight." His voice shook slightly. A quick nod of my head was all I could muster. I put my boot in his hands, a hand on top of the horse's back, and the other on John's shoulder. In one fluid motion, John lifted me up, and I swung my leg over the horse's back. I was so high up—way too high. My hands shook as he handed the reins to me. The horse's footing started to shift. "Shorten the slack a little bit. There you go. Hold onto the mane to help keep your balance, and lean down low. You can do this. He'll keep you safe. Are you ready?" John asked. He looked at me for the briefest moment to search my eyes, and he nodded at the answer he saw there. "Don't look back," he reminded me.

There were too many emotions in John's eyes to decipher them all, but I caught one. He'd already come to care for me in the short time we've been together. I wasn't sure what he cared for me as— a human in general, a Summit Springs guest, a friend, or maybe something more? The bear had crossed the stream now and was headed towards us.

"All right, hold on tight," John said. He clicked his tongue a few times and swatted the horse's rump. The horse dipped slightly before it took off into a run in the opposite direction from where John stood. I was terrified. All the layers of fabric from my dress weren't allowing me to hug the horse's sides as tightly as I wanted with my legs. My legs had to work double-time just to keep me upright. It was harder to ride a horse than I remembered, and I was too nervous to let my past knowledge of riding calm me at the moment. I was too afraid of falling. Two gunshots sounded, and the horse picked up its pace even more as if understanding the urgency to get far away and fast. I could feel myself slipping with each bound. *This is horrifying!* I could let myself fall off and probably get hurt in a big way, or try to face this head-on and hold on for my life.

I chose to hold on and to try to take back what little control I could. I slowly sat up and squeezed my knees together a little tighter. I held onto part of the mane with one hand and slowly started to pull back on the reins with the other. The horse slowed from a gallop to a trot, to a walk, and eventually stopped. I closed my eyes to the heavens and whispered in complete relief, "Thank You." I turned my head around to see if I could see John. He wasn't anywhere in sight. All I could think about was getting back to him to make sure he was okay. I pulled the reins to the left and tried to turn the horse back around—it didn't budge. I clicked my tongue once and tried to rock the horse into a forward motion, but it stayed put.

"Come on. Let's go!" A soft kick of my heels to the horse's sides did nothing either. I kicked a little harder in desperation. *This horse had to be part mule!* As I began to panic, I caught movement on top of the hill. *John!* When he saw me, he slowed his pace. I saw the relief on his face, and I'm sure the relief on my face mirrored his. The bear was nowhere in sight. *John's safe.* I sighed. He jogged towards me and let out three short whistles. The horse immediately turned and started to trundle towards him. "Really?"

I asked the horse. "You only respond to whistles?" The horse didn't reply, but I'm sure it found my failed attempts to get it moving entertaining. When we reached one another, I brought the horse to a stop. "John, this horse is faulty. It apparently only responds to whistles," I said. John smiled as he caught his breath.

"By faulty, you mean highly intelligent and expertly trained, I'm sure." Half of his lips curved upward into a small smile. "He'll get a move on with three short whistles or three tongue clicks."

"That's all it takes? Exactly three? Are you serious?"

"Yep. Like I said, expertly trained." The other half of his lips curved upward. "Are you all right?"

I nodded. "Are you?" I asked.

"Yeah." He let his head fall, and even though his hat blocked the view, I could tell he was rubbing his forehead. "I'm so sorry."

"For what?"

"The bear. The spooked horse from your past. Shady. I promised to keep you safe."

"You did, John. You can't control the animals; you're not Noah. Which I'm pretty relieved about because I'd rather be on this mountain with you." I smiled a reassuring smile when he looked up at me. I could tell the stress was dissipating a little.

"I was supposed to protect you, and the horse thing…"

"What horse thing?"

"I put you in a situation that I shouldn't have and all but forced you to ride a horse when you didn't want to. I wanted you safe, but I also wanted you to trust a horse again, then maybe you'd..." He looked off in the distance.

"Maybe I'd what?"

"John! Maggie!" Ricky's voice called out from an approaching horse. I could see two other riders coming in hot behind Ricky.

"We're fine," John called out, not looking away from the tree-covered mountains in the distance.

"John," I whispered before the others came close. He looked up at me, and I could see defeat in his eyes. I wasn't sure why he felt defeat. He dropped his head, and it made my heart ache to see him like this. I wished I could read his mind or at least look into his eyes long enough to reassure him somehow.

Ricky was the first to reach us. "We heard the gunshots," he said.

"There was a bear on the tree line. Luckily, it was more curious than hungry, I think. It was spooked by the shots and headed upstream," John said. The others caught up and were silent as they waited for instruction. "Hey guys, will you go find Bill, and let him know there was an adult black bear on the upper west side of the property by the stream. Have Carol let the Crenshaw's know too. Ricky, will you take a turn up by the stream and follow it down to the cattle to make sure they're safe? Fire a shot if there's trouble." With a few exchanged head nods between the men, everyone split up in opposite directions. And then there were two, *three if you count the horse.* "Is it okay if we ride back?" John asked me. "If not, we can walk. I'd just feel better if we rode, even though I know Ricky is on watch. I'm not sure where the bear is now." He saw the reservation in my eyes. "I'll take care of you this time, I promise."

I took in a deep breath. "I know you will—just like you did a few minutes ago," I said while looking right in his eyes and straight to his soul. "I'll ride, as long as you do too." I was nervous to still be sitting up on the horse, but not nearly as much as when I was alone. Nothing bad would happen as long as John was with me, and I got the feeling that he needed to know that. He mounted the horse and sat behind me.

"Do you want me to take the reins?" he asked softly.

I nodded my head. He slid an arm around me and took hold of the reins. I felt instantly protected and safe. I was also very aware of his arm against my waist, and it made my heart beat faster. He let out three quiet tongue clicks, and it set the horse in motion. I smiled and rolled my eyes, remembering the horse's insistence on obeying only specific command signals.

"John?" I asked softly.

"Hmm?"

"I feel safe with you." My stomach tightened at my boldness.

"Maggie, I—" *Silence.* I needed him to trust me. We had less than a week to see if we thought each other was worth fighting for, and I thought he was.

"I want you to know me," I said. "So, I'm going to tell you everything there possibly is to know."

"Everything?" He said slowly as if I had piqued his interest.

"Down to my shoe size." I smiled and blew out a shaky breath. "My name is Maggie Carver, I'm from California, and I wear a size nine shoe." I heard him laugh a little. "I work in an attorney's office right now as a secretary, so if you ever need a lawyer's joke, I'm your girl."

"I'll keep that in mind," he said. I thought I heard him smile through his words.

"I love Mexican food so much I'm convinced salsa runs through my veins. I've always loved the ocean, but I know once I leave here that I'm going to miss these mountains." My throat started to tighten with emotion, and I dropped my head down. I studied his strong hand holding onto the leather reins for a moment. The thought crossed my mind to reach up and rest my hand on his, but I decided against it and kept holding onto the horse's mane. "I was terrified to get on the horse, but a small part of me is proud that I did it."

"I'm proud too. I just wish it would have been under different circumstances," he said.

80

"Maybe this was the only way. You're the only reason I got up on the horse actually, and I have a feeling that you're the only man who could have convinced me to." I wasn't just talking about horses anymore. I took a deep breath before plunging into the next part. I was nervous to tell him the secret I knew his eyes were searching for when we first met. "I dated a guy two years ago who was secretly seeing someone else on the side the whole time. He would only see me during specific hours, and I was too naïve to question why. I always assumed he was just busy with work…until his two lives accidentally mixed. Since then, I don't trust easily. I'm convinced everybody is living a double life." I took in another deep, shaky breath and tried to keep my voice even. "I struggled for a while. I tried to figure out what was wrong with me—like why I wasn't enough to be someone's only one. It took some time to find my confidence again. There are places in my heart that still hurt when prodded, but I'd like to think that I'm stronger now—or maybe I've just gotten really good at building walls and not letting anyone in." I rubbed my forehead. "I don't know if it's just me, but I feel like you and I have this rare connection. I feel like we can read each other's minds just by looking at each other, even in a crowd. I feel like our eyes have conversations long after the words have stopped. It's crazy." I let my head drop, realizing I had just gone off on a tangent. Those words were more for me, but admitting some of the thoughts out loud was a big deal. John was not getting paid enough to be a therapist on top of being an actor. *He's most likely a seasonal employee, and here I am pouring my heart out. I was starting to forget why Anna and I even came here in the first place.* A moment passed and then another. *What can he even say to all that baggage?* We rode up to the livery, and I knew I needed to escape my embarrassment with as much grace as possible. "Thank you for the walk and for keeping me safe," I said before I pulled my right leg up and over, then slid down the horse. As soon as my boots connected with dirt, I walked toward the livery, trying to hold onto what dignity I had left.

7

"Maggie, wait," John said from behind me.

I slowed down and started to turn back towards John to face him despite my embarrassment, but Devin stepped out from inside the livery first. He took one look at my face, and his countenance changed instantly. "What's wrong?" he asked quietly. I couldn't meet his gaze, but I sensed him look up at something behind me. Something probably wearing a cowboy hat and sitting atop a black horse. "Are you hurt? Was it the bear?" Devin tried to will me to look up at him, but it didn't work. "Was it John?" he whispered.

"No, it wasn't John," I said softly.

"Darn, I'm always looking for any excuse to get in a tussle with him," he joked, but I think he meant it too.

"I'm fine. I need to go."

"Will you let me know if you need anything?"

I nodded, then walked into the livery and out the front doors. I needed someplace to escape...*the bathhouse!* I avoided eye contact with everyone in town. Once I had made it to the bathhouse, I gripped the doorknob and turned it until the door clicked open. An older woman, who I recognized serving dinner from last night, jumped up from a small counter. Soft music cut out abruptly as I stepped inside and onto the wooden planked floor.

"Oh, hello! Maggie, right? I'm Vicky. What can I do for you?" she asked.

"Um, I'm not really sure. What is there to do in a bathhouse?

"We shoeshine, cut hair, and you can also bathe. First water is 25 cents, used water is 15 cents, and soap and a towel is 10 cents." Vicky stared at me, waiting for her words to sink in. *First water...used water...gross!* That did it. She laughed and told me they use clean water nowadays, and everything is free, despite her words and the sign on the wall listing the prices.

"In that case, I'll take one *first water* bath with soap and a towel." I smiled.

"Coming right up!" Vicky disappeared into a back hallway, and a few moments later, I heard water start to run somewhere in the building.

I replayed some of the things I said to John in my mind while I waited for Vicky to come back. I cringed at the words I recalled.

Reading each other's minds through our eyes? Ugh. I rubbed my head and closed my eyes. I was hoping the more I rubbed, the more I could erase the memory. No luck.

"All ready! Come on back!" Vicky called out. I opened the small swinging door that led to a long hallway with five doors on the left side. It reminded me of the changing rooms at the mall back home. I walked down to the only open door, and it squeaked when I opened it further to peek inside. The room was dimly lit by two lanterns. The walls looked like they were made from logs stacked on top of each other. A large metal basin sat in the middle of a tiny room. "Holler if you need anything!"

"Thank you, Vicky."

She peeked back in the door. "Psst. You caught me listening to music when you came in, so as long as you keep it a secret, I'll play some for you. This room is where I spend my time embroidering when the bathhouse closes, so I had a hidden speaker installed. What kind of music do you like?"

"Country, oldies, and…"

"Oldies it is!" she whispered, then placed a finger over her mouth in the "shh" motion.

"Your secret is safe with me," I said.

Vicky smiled, then disappeared. I closed the door and slid the latch into the locked position. Within a few moments, my eyes adjusted fully to the darkness of the room. There were some soap shavings on top of a neatly folded towel on a chair in the corner. I tested the water with my fingers, and it was perfectly warm. I got ready and slid under the water until it reached my chin, then I closed my eyes. My favorite Ricky Nelson song, "It's Up to You" came on softly through the hidden speaker. Vicky had great taste in music. I had soaked for about five minutes before the music cut off mid-chorus. A knock at my door followed.

"Maggie?" Anna said.

"I'm in here!"

"Are you okay? What are you doing?"

"I'm good. I'm just taking a bath."

"A bath?" she asked. I heard her laugh through the door. "I heard about the bear! Are you sure you're all right?" I could tell by her tone she was genuinely concerned.

"I'm fine. I just needed to hideout for a little while if I'm being honest." I hushed my tone a little bit. "I poured my heart out to John, and he didn't say a word, so I'm soaking away my embarrassment. I'm trying to put the conversation behind me, so I can move on and try to enjoy the rest of the week. I'm considering avoiding him forever."

"Maybe he just needs time to process everything?"

"Eh. I'm not so sure."

"I'm sorry, Maggie."

"I'll survive. I'm just embarrassed."

"I understand. I'll be at the post. They're teaching Morse code today. Will you come over when you're done?"

"Yeah."

As soon as the front door clicked closed, marking Anna's departure, the music came back on softly. I closed my eyes once more and soaked until the water turned cold, before hopping out and getting dressed.

I thanked Vicky and told her I'd be back tomorrow. It was a nice and relaxing place to avoid running into John, and I planned to come back every day while we were here.

I walked along the boardwalk until I reached the post. I slid in the door as quickly as I could—knowing the livery was directly across the road. *Click click click.* There were people seated at tables tapping on small machines, making it sound like the building was filled with cockroaches.

"Maggie! Over here!" Anna whispered and waved. I slid into the seat next to her and watched her tap her finger on a little contraption.

An older man approached our table. "Hi, Maggie! I'm Morris. Anna mentioned you'd be joining us today," he said softly. He set a small machine in front of me, then a small piece of paper full of dots and dashes. "Have you ever learned Morse code before?"

"I haven't."

"Very good. We're going to start by learning the diagram, then we'll start decoding simple phrases. The dots are called DITS, and the dashes are called DAHS." Morris helped me understand the diagram and stayed until I got the hang of tapping out the letters. "When you feel comfortable decoding these messages, you and Anna can try decoding a message coming through the line in the backroom. Flag me down if you have any questions," he said, before leaving our table to help someone else.

"How are you doing?" Anna whispered.

"Better."

"Good."

Anna and I went into silent mode and studied the key and coded phrases. Some of the codes I deciphered were: apple pie, Summit Springs, can I tag along, and Monday. As soon as we felt confident in our DITS and DAHS, we made our way to the back room. Anna sat down first in front of the telegraph sounder, and Morris sat nearby, holding a copy of the key.

"Ready?" Morris asked Anna.

"Yes."

The DITS and DAHS started sounding, and I wrote down the pattern. When the message was done, she decoded the dots and dashes before reading it out loud. STEW FOR DINNER. The three of us smiled. Morris congratulated Anna on a job well done. I got situated near the telegraph machine with my diagram and pencil. Luckily, the DITS and DAHS came in at a slow enough pace for me to keep up and write it all down. After a few minutes, the line went silent, and I worked on decoding the message. *ITSNOTJUSTYOU.*

"What does yours say, Maggie?" Anna asked.

I looked up at her and then over at Morris feeling confused.

"I'm not sure I heard mine correctly. It says 'ITS NOT JUST YOU.'" Anna looked as confused as I felt.

"That's a strange message, but I heard the DITS and DAHS too. You translated it correctly. That's the great thing about the line, though, you never know what you're going to get! Well, good job, ladies!"

We thanked Morris before leaving. Anna linked her arm through mine and led me around back instead of down the dirt road through town. We walked over to the orchard, and Anna grabbed four empty baskets next to a fence. She handed me two of them.

"I assume we're going apple picking?" I asked.

"Yes! I saw some people filling these baskets earlier and thought it looked fun!" We walked deeper and deeper into the orchard until we couldn't see anything around us but trees. Anna set one of her baskets down in the grass and hugged the other one to her side as she searched a tree for a good place to start picking apples.

"Okay, so start from the top," Anna said.

"I can't reach the apples up there."

"I meant the story about what happened this morning." She smiled. "I saw you run to John after the shooting lesson."

"He asked me to go to the livery, and I said no. Imagine that," I said. Anna laughed. "I changed my mind and decided to go with him to the livery—as long as I didn't have to get on a horse. We ended up taking his horse for a walk."

"That's cute, almost like walking a dog! I bet you loved that." I gave her and her sarcasm a joking side glare. "Did you ask him if he has a girlfriend?" she asked.

"Yes."

"Yes, he has one, or yes, you asked him?"

"I asked him."

"And?"

"Cue the bear."

"No! Didn't it know that the two of you were possibly having a life-altering conversation? Honestly! Some mammals!"

"My thoughts exactly. Well, actually, that's the farthest thing from what I was thinking, but I agree with you now." I plucked a shiny red apple from a branch.

"So, he didn't answer the question?" she asked.

"No."

"Maybe he'll answer when you two see each other next?" Anna reached up for another apple.

"Maybe, but I'm not holding my breath. I'm also going to try and avoid him, remember?"

"I do, but I don't know exactly why yet. I'm still waiting for that part of the story. Keep going."

"On the way back from the bear encounter, we rode the horse and..."

"Wait. You *both* rode the horse back? That's really romantic," she said.

"To someone on the outside, yes. Except that's exactly where things fell apart. I told him things about me because I wanted him to get to know me, so he'd trust me enough to tell me things about him. I wanted him to break character for me more because we only have less than a week to get to know each other. He never answered the girlfriend question, though. Maybe he has one and felt sorry for me, but didn't know how to break it to me! Ugh! Anna!"

"Keep going with the story."

"I told him about how I was unknowingly a third wheel in my last relationship and what it did to me. I told him that I thought he and I had a connection. I said that I didn't know if it was just me, but that I felt like we could read each other's minds just by looking at each other. I—"

"Wait, you said the line about how you didn't know if it was just you? Word for word? Like out loud to him?" she asked.

"I did."

"The telegraph message, Maggie! The message!"

Then it clicked, literally DIT and DAH'd in my mind...*it's not just you!*

"Anna!"

"I know!"

"Those could have been just recordings coming through the line that they use for everyone, though. What if it wasn't even him?" I asked.

"But Maggie, what if it was?" We stared at each other wide-eyed for a few long moments. My heart rate started to accelerate with hope. I wanted John. "I have a good feeling about the two of you and not the same good feeling you had about the sewing class," she said. I laughed. "Should we take these apples to Carol to see if she needs any of them for pies?"

"For pies? What is your view on pie right now?" I asked while giving her the quizzical eye.

"Pie and I are good right now. Ryan can't rob me of eating buttery, flaky crust my whole life."

"Good for you!" We laughed. I was glad that Anna's ex was being kicked to the curb one day at a time. Anna deserved someone who treated her like a queen—someone like Ricky.

"I'm going to fill up my basket, then I'll meet you back at the hotel for lunch as soon as I'm done," I said.

"See you soon." Anna made her way out of the orchard. I only needed about ten more apples to top off my basket. I took a deep breath and felt my smile widen at the thought of John being on the other end of the telegraph line. After topping off my basket, I noticed the most perfect apple above me. I wanted it. I reached up as high as I could on my tiptoes, but it was still out of reach. I set my basket of apples down and jumped—still too high up. I flipped the extra empty basket over and stepped up to grab the apple. Right as I plucked it from the branch, I heard a cracking sound. The next thing I knew, my foot had broken through the basket, and I toppled down to the hard ground. I was sprawled out with the empty basket still around my lower leg. I didn't escape unscathed either—*ouch*! I looked at the apple that caused me such pain. I was right; it was the most perfect apple I'd ever seen. Rotating the apple, however, revealed a wormhole. The worm was long gone but left its mark on a perfectly good apple.

"Maggie!" Devin's voice sounded. I looked up and saw him running down a row of apple trees towards me. "Are you all right? What hurts?"

"Um…my leg and my pride."

"Let's see about the leg first," he said. Devin delicately examined the basket around my lower leg. I winced as he moved the hem of my dress up slightly to assess the damage. My calf was covered in blood, and it had soaked through my dress already. "Can you still move your toes? Did you hear a pop?"

"Toes, yes. Pop, no."

"Good. Okay, hold still." Devin pried the basket open, and it tore down the middle. He looked closely at my leg and ankle but didn't touch it. "Does anything else hurt?"

"Just a couple scrapes on my hand, but those are fine."

He reached for my hands and examined them briefly. "Do you think you can stand?"

"Yeah," I said. He offered me his hands, and I twisted my hands midair trying to figure out how to best grasp them. Once we locked hands, he pulled me up and held me steady.

"Thankfully, it looks like the boot took most of the brunt," he said. "There are a few scratches in the leather to prove it. I'd feel better if we got a second opinion, though—just to be sure. Can you walk if I helped you?"

"Yeah, I think so."

He slid an arm around my waist and took most of the weight until we were sure I could walk on my own. I could, so he let go. The scrapes stung a bit as the petticoat rubbed against them, so I lifted the skirts just enough to clear the scrapes.

"Okay, so now for your pride. You fell very gracefully. If I'm being honest, I only saw a flash of pink and not the full fall, so

you can rest easy. I'm pretty sure I'm the only witness as well."
He smiled.

"That's a relief!" I truly was relieved there were no other witnesses. "Wait! The apples! Can you grab the basket? I sacrificed my life for those pieces of fruit!" He laughed and went back to quickly retrieve them. "Thank you," I said.

"Of course. We can't forget about the apples at a time like this." I smiled up at him. We walked in silence back to town, and a bench by the bathhouse was our stopping point. "I think the apples need a breather, so take a seat and keep an eye on them," he said. I rolled my eyes and smiled. "I'll be right back." I picked up one of the apples and considered taking a bite, but it was the apple I thought was perfect and turned out not to be. Instead of putting it back into the basket with the others, I just held it in my hands as if it were a crystal ball. What if John turns out to be just like this apple? *Almost perfect.* I closed my eyes and hoped that this wasn't a foreshadowing in our story.

John busted out of the swinging doors of the sheriff's office. He stopped for a split second on the porch, before making eye contact with me from across the road. That's all he needed to determine his destination. He took off his hat as he flew down the stairs and jogged across the dirt road in my direction. I looked down, trying to even my breathing, and when I thought I had it under control, I looked back up at him. The blood on my dress caught his eye as he approached. He didn't show any emotion—minus that his lips seemed to press together in a straight line a little bit tighter. I looked down once more until his boots had come into view. My eyes slowly traveled up until they met his that were staring down at me.

"This whole situation is like a soap opera gone wild—the western kind of wild. This is so humiliating," I said. I brought a hand up to my forehead and shielded my eyes.

"You're just fine, Maggie. Everyone falls through baskets sometimes." He set his hat down on the bench.

"No, they don't," I teased.

"You're right. It's just you." He smiled, and I laughed a little bit. He knelt on one knee in front of me.

"Whoa, John. I don't think I'm ready for that kind of commitment," I said. He looked up at me. Confusion spread across his features for a split second until he saw the mischief in my eyes. His smile grew until that right-sided dimple rivaled the depths of the Mariana Trench. He shook his head to the ground. I bit my lip. I hoped using a bit of shock factor and boldness would mask some of my embarrassment that had been accumulating today. "...but what the heck. While you're down on one knee, go ahead and ask away!" I smiled. I'd be lying if I said I wasn't searching his eyes for deeper feelings underneath the surface. In an instant, his eyes got serious with a hint of mischief in them. He took my left hand in both of his. We locked eyes, and he did the trance thing, and I knew I wouldn't or couldn't look away first.

"Maggie," he said. His voice was low and deep. "Will you..." He tightened his hold on my hand in an enduring way and turned his lips upward into a small smile. "...make me the luckiest man in the world…" My pulse started to race. "…by offering me your leg, so I can access the damage?"

"I will." My smile widened, and so did his. His eyes sparkled.

"Let's get you inside, so I can take a closer look," he said. He offered me his hand to stand before scooping me up into his arms in one fluid motion. My arms wrapped around his neck out of reflex. Despite my squeals and protests, he managed to carry me, petticoat and all, to the bathhouse door. "Hold on a little tighter while I get the door."

Gladly. I tightened my hold around his neck. I could feel the strong muscles on his back flex as he grabbed the doorknob. It clicked open, and his muscled arms held me tighter than before. The door swung open wide. John greeted a startled Vicky, who was near the window.

"Do you mind if we use one of your shoe shine stations for a few minutes?" he asked.

"Of course, not. Can I help in any way?"

"Actually, yes. Would you grab a few clean towels and a bowl of warm water? I'll come grab the bowl when it's ready." Vicky nodded and disappeared through the back door. John lowered me softly and slowly into the raised shoe shining seat. He washed his hands at a small wash station in the corner, then sat down in front of me on a stool. His dark hair had waves throughout—lots of them—like a dark sea that I was in the perfect position to explore.

Look, but don't touch. His dark hair and blue eyes were a dangerous combination. "All right, will you show me the damage?" he asked. I nodded and pulled my skirts up to my knee. John put me through some motion and sensory tests, then he started to unlace my boot, which was surprisingly intimate. "If it hurts at any point, I want you to stop me, okay?" I nodded again because I didn't trust my breathing to formulate even and steady words. John started to slowly remove the boot. It felt like a reverse Cinderella moment, and it made my stomach flutter. The top rim of my sock had turned red from the blood, and John delicately peeled it back. He slipped the sock off my toes and paused with a smile.

"Black, huh? I was so sure they'd be pink," he said softly while looking down at my feet.

I smiled and wiggled my toes that were still painted with black polish. Realizing now that I had forgotten to remove the polish before this trip to 1866. "Don't tell Carol," I whispered. A small smile formed on his lips. *His lips.* They were perfect. Remembering where I was looking, I quickly shifted my eyes back to his—they were reading mine, and his gaze seared right through me. Time seemed to slow as he set my boot down and started to rise—never breaking eye contact. He gripped the armrests on both sides, and I was convinced he started leaning in very slowly towards me. I looked down at his lips again. He had lifted one of

99

his hands off the armrest and was inches away from touching my cheek—

"Water's ready!" Vicky called out from the back.

"I'll be right back," he whispered. I nodded. A few moments later, John came back, holding a white bowl and some towels. I was hoping to pick up where we left off, but no such luck. John felt around my foot and ankle and did a few more of his tests.

"Did I pass, doctor?" I asked.

He didn't move a muscle, but looked up and searched my eyes. He seemed to have found the answer he was looking for in them and responded, "With flying colors." He submerged a small towel in the water and went to work on cleaning my leg. When my leg was clean and dry, he leaned in and took a closer look at the scrapes. "These won't need stitches, but they look like they hurt." He looked up to see if his assumption was correct. I half-smiled. He was right; they did hurt a lot. "I'm going to go grab a few things that should help with the pain and healing. Be right back."

About thirty seconds after John left out the door, Devin walked in.

"Maggie! There you are. What's the verdict?" He asked while walking over to me.

"Just some scrapes, no breaks."

"That's great news!" He looked down my leg and stopped briefly at my toes before looking at me, surprised.

"Maggie, I was wondering—"

"Oh, hello, Devin! I didn't hear you come in," Vicky interrupted. "Would you carry that bowl into the back for me?"

"Yes, ma'am," he said. Vicky smiled at me before trailing after Devin into the back. A few moments later, John came through the door again, and my heart instantly jumped.

"Miss me?" he asked. I responded with a smile. I didn't trust myself with words with all the skipped heartbeats going on. "I'll take your silence as a 'yes,'" he said. My smile widened. John knelt in front of me again, but this time he had a handful of bandaging supplies.

Devin walked back in the same moment John held my leg in his hand and was applying some ointment. "Oh, um…I was…," Devin stumbled over his words.

"Hey Dev," John said while focusing on applying some ointment and bandages. "Thanks for helping her in the orchard. I'm glad you were there."

"Me too," Devin said. John wrapped some gauze around the bandages and rolled my sock back onto my foot. He was just about to slide my boot on when a man opened the bathhouse door quickly. I recognized him as one of the riders who came to our aid with the bear encounter.

"Hey, John. You're needed down the road," the man said.

"I'll be out in just a few minutes."

"Actually, they need you now. I'm sorry."

John let out a deep breath, then looked up to meet my eyes. I gave him a small smile, then let him know through my eyes that it was okay if he went. With that, he stood and reluctantly passed off my boot to Devin. I caught the silent exchange from John's eyes to Devin's—a "take care of her" kind of look. Devin gave a small nod to John before he walked to the door. He turned back to me and said, "Do the apples need to go to Carol?"

I nodded and wished he wasn't leaving. He walked out the door, and I watched him put his hat back on through the window. He picked up the basket of apples before walking across the street with the man.

The removal of the boot was much more romantic than the return, and I knew it was due to the man and not the shoe. Devin did his best to slide the boot back on, but it just seemed to get stuck with every push. I stood up and wiggled my foot in the boot on my own, then he tied it up for me. "Thanks, Devin." I smiled.

"Of course. You hungry?" he asked. My stomach growled loud enough for the both of us to hear. I cradled my vocal stomach. "Say no more!" He walked to the over and opened it for me.

"Thank you, Vicky!" I turned back towards her. She acknowledged my thanks with a smile, but something else shone through as well. *Nervousness? Sorrow? Both? Odd.* Once Devin and I were walking down the dirt road in the direction of the hotel,

I decided to see if he caught Vicky's expression too. "Do you know what was up with Vicky just now?"

He slowly turned his head towards me and gave me a side glance with a hint of a sheepish smile. "I'm not positive, but I think she was worried I was there to fight John for your affections." Devin winked over at me.

"Oh." That thought hadn't even crossed my mind.

"No need to worry, though. I've seen the way John looks at you; only a fool would interfere," he said, then winked over at me. "Besides, I gave my heart away a long time ago."

"What was her name?"

"Cassie."

"What happened?" I asked.

"I don't know." He looked over at me, and I could tell there was a deep internal scar somewhere inside him—most likely on his heart. I could tell the memories playing through his mind were painful ones. I didn't know how to help him, but I had a feeling there was only one person who could.

"I'm sorry, Devin."

"Me too. It happens, though. How's your leg?"

"Much better." I let him change the subject. My heart ached for him.

"I thought you'd like to know that they found the bear and the Division of Wildlife is transporting it into the backcountry as we speak." He whispered as a group of people passed by on the road.

"That is a relief! Thank you for the very modern update." I whispered back.

"You're welcome."

Once we reached the café, Devin helped plate my food. Midway through the buffet table, the kitchen door opened quickly. Carol scanned the room until she found me. There was a look in her eye that made me think she knew I'd be there. *Vicky from the bathhouse.* She used her apron to wipe off her hands as she made her way over to us. Carol said hello to Devin and I before she looked down at my dress. "You look nice, Maggie," she said. "Pink really suits you. I heard you've had quite the day. How are you feeling?" She eyed the hem of my dress a little closer, then asked, "Is that blood?" The look on her face made me think she already knew all the answers. Heat rose to my cheeks from a bit of embarrassment—both from her compliment and the knowledge that she knew about my day. *How much did she know?*

"Um…I took a tumble in the orchard and scraped my leg. I'm all bandaged up now, though. I'm good—just a little tired." I wasn't tired at all, but I knew I could call on that excuse to make a getaway later if needed. I was already looking forward to seeing John again.

"Rightfully, so!" Carol looked down at my dress once more. "The rest of your dresses are blue, right?" Carol asked me with a hand on her hip. Devin looked in my direction, and his eyebrows pulled together with a confused but amused look on his face. My eyes widened slightly. I opened my mouth to explain, but Carol got flustered before I could respond. "Oh, I mean…I thought blue would look wonderful with your hair and complexion, so I hope there's a blue dress in your trunk somewhere. Pink is nice, though." Carol was usually pretty even-keeled, so these few moments were very out of character. "Well, I need to go stir something in the back before it starts stickin'!" she said as she turned and disappeared into the kitchen. I turned to Devin and smiled. He smiled back, knowing there was a story behind the last 30 seconds of conversation.

"How about we find a shady tree outside to eat under?" Devin asked as he balanced all of the food and water cups along his arms and in his hands. He had to have worked in the restaurant business at some point to pick up those kinds of balancing skills.

"Sounds great." We walked around the right side of the hotel and found a large tree that provided a lot of shade to sit under. "What do you do when you're not here because you have some mad balancing skills?" I asked.

"Those came from my high school days of waiting tables."

"Well, that job just paid off." We smiled at one another. "What do you do now during the offseason when you're not playing citizen of Summit Springs?"

"I just accepted a logging job up North this morning actually. I start next month." He took a bite of roll covered in currant jelly.

"Devin! That's exciting! Is that something you've always wanted to do?"

"Nah, but it's a change of scenery, you know?" He took a drink of water. "Anyway, what was my aunt talking about in there?"

"She was referring to my wardrobe for the week. Everything in my trunk is a shade of blue."

"Except for the dress you're wearing?"

"Right. I borrowed this from Anna to change things up a little bit. I didn't think anyone would notice."

"Well, I think there were quite a few people who noticed actually. You look very nice."

"Thank you." Now it was my turn to take a drink of water. He and I ate the rest of our meal in silence as we watched people start setting up the tables and benches for dinner.

"I'll take our plates and cups inside, and be right back." Devin stood and offered me a hand to stand.

"Thank you."

He walked towards the same door Anna and I had run through that first night. I walked in the opposite direction towards the outhouses. Once finished, I opened the moon door slowly, forgetting until this moment about the rooster. *Ugh, where is it?* I poked my head out and looked left, then looked right. *No bird.* I slowly tiptoed down the steps and started walking back to the hotel, trying not to make a sound. I made it about five steps before that strange gargling sound that I dreaded came from behind me. *Not again!* I turned back to see the same huge black rooster strutting out from behind the outhouse. The rooster puffed up its feathers and charged, so I bolted. The cuts on my leg hurt, but letting a rooster eat me would hurt more, I imagine. I saw Devin talking to another guy near the back door of the hotel.

"Devin!" I yelled. He and the other guy looked up in concern until they saw what trailed me and was now gaining on me. Devin smiled and stepped around the guy he was talking to, and I could tell he was trying to gauge what to do next. "You wanted a warning!" I called out to him. "This is it! Catch me!" I sprinted as fast as I could. I didn't slow when I leaped into Devin's outstretched arms. The momentum spun us both around, but Devin never let go. The rooster crashed into Devin's legs. *Victory!* I buried my head into his shoulder as we both laughed. The rooster was clearly irritated and made loud and angry, cawing sounds that I'd never heard before. The sound made me laugh even harder. I noticed a few surrounding people had witnessed the chase and were smiling and trying to suppress laughter. "Don't set me down until we are far enough away from that bird, okay?" I said when I could breathe again through laughing tears.

"You got it. See ya, man!" He called out over his shoulder to the guy he was talking to before I interrupted. Devin started walking back around the hotel in the direction we had come before.

"Thank you! I believe you came to my rescue for the second time today."

"You've had a busy day, haven't you?"

I smiled breathlessly, not because of him but because of the running. Right before we disappeared behind the corner of the hotel, I looked back over Devin's shoulder to see John atop his horse in the distance. He was just far enough away that I couldn't see his expression. By the drop of his hat and the turn of his horse, though, I was willing to bet he had witnessed it all. John started to ride in the opposite direction and over a hill. The situation had lost its humor. I told Devin he could let me down. All I could think about was getting to John and explaining myself. The whole situation started to make me physically ill. I had just jumped into his brother's arms in front of him. Hindsight, I would have rather let the rooster eat me instead. Devin talked as he walked me back to the front door of the hotel, but I couldn't hear a word. The thoughts in my mind were too loud. I nodded as if I was listening intently to what he was saying. I heard something about a poodle and an airplane, but nothing more. My mind was elsewhere, and I knew that's where I needed to be too.

"Do you get it?" He asked as we walked up the stairs to the hotel.

"Get what?"

"The joke. It was a brick! Can you believe it?!" He started to laugh.

"Right! Yeah." I forced a small laugh. We stopped by the front door just inside the hotel in the same place we met. "I think I'm going to go rest and change my dress—as much as I enjoy the attention these blood stains are getting me." I took hold of my skirts and lifted them slightly to scale the staircase.

"If I can guess what color of dress you'll be in next, would you come feed the ducks with me later?" he asked. I laughed a little and looked down at the wood graining on the floorboards. "You're going to be with John later, aren't you?" I felt my cheeks turn pink as I pressed my lips together. "That's okay. I need to go chop some firewood that I've been putting off anyway." We both smiled at one another. "Let me know if you need anything, okay?"

"Will do. Thanks again for all of your help today." He nodded, and then left the hotel.

Once I had made it up to my room, I closed the door behind me. "Hello!" Anna said. I screamed and put my hand on my heart. I was so concentrated on how I would find John that I failed to see

Anna sitting on her bed. "Aren't you jumpy? Who are you hiding from?"

"No one today." I laughed while trying to slow my heart rate. "I didn't see you there. I thought you were going to the assay office this afternoon to learn about gold and such?" A buzzing sound went off. Anna went wide-eyed. "What was that?"

"Nothing," Anna said as she casually slipped something behind her back.

"Anna, what are you hiding?" Without a word, Anna slowly brought her hand back around in front of her. "Your cellphone? How did you get that? So much for playing by the rules while here in Summit Springs! You are sneaky, and I am proud."

"Ricky got it for me, so we could still talk while he was out rounding up cattle."

"Anna!"

"I know what I said, but it's just been nice to talk with him. Before you say anything else—" I smiled as Anna reached under her pillow. She pulled out another phone and handed it to me. "You're welcome. I had Ricky get yours too." Anna made a "shh" motion bringing her pointer finger to her lips.

"Yes! Thank you, and thank Ricky for me. I officially consider him an ally!" I sat down next to her on the bed. "Well, what did he say?"

Anna smiled as she opened the text message. Her cheeks turned a light shade of pink. "Estoy estudiando para ser un maestro."

"That sounds really romantic!"

"It's not," she laughed. "He's just telling me his career goals."

"Romance is in the eye of the beholder! What does he want to do?"

"He's working toward being a school teacher."

"Not romantic, my eye! You're a teacher, and he wants to be one! How is that not the

start of something romantic?"

Anna laughed. "I'm not looking for anything serious just yet, remember?"

"I remember, but I also know that there's no time frame for healing and feelings. If it's right, it's right."

"Is that hope I hear coming from you?"

"It just might be." I smiled and took a shaky breath. "Maybe that last statement was more for me than it was for you. Sorry."

"No need to be. I think it's good to hear those words at all stages of the game."

"And what game is that?"

"The game of looove." Anna smiled. I took another deep breath in, processing what I had just said to Anna about things being 'right.'

"How do you know Ricky is being 'him him' with you and not acting?

"I can just tell by our conversations. We went for a walk earlier today, and he told me about his family and where he grew up. I've also told him about my job and some of my students. I know by his stories and responses to mine that he is being genuine." I responded with a big confused sigh. Anna helped me slide out of my dress and poufy petticoats, before changing into something blue. "Where are you headed?" she asked.

"To find John. He saw Devin and me together, and I just want to make sure he and I are okay." I slid on a solid steel blue dress. The fabric pleated and puckered at the waist, then bloomed out into a full ankle-length skirt. The neckline was scalloped, and the sleeves were long. The dress was simple, but I felt pretty in it.

"Do you want me to braid your hair?" She asked while helping slide my hair out from the inside of the dress at the neckline.

"Nope, but thank you." My voice shook a little bit. My nerves started to set it. If this was just a job for John, would he even care for an explanation about being seen with another employee, even if it was his brother? "Hey, actually, do you want to take a walk through town instead?" I asked Anna while running a hand over the pleats on my dress. They were already perfectly flattened.

"You're stalling."

"I know."

"I'll see you at dinner," she said. "Now, go find your man already!"

I smiled. He wasn't mine, but a girl could dream. "Bye, Anna." I left her smiling down at her phone. Ricky seemed like a good and honest guy. Anna deserved nothing less, and neither did I.

I stepped off the last hotel stair and onto the dirt road. The air smelled like rain. I squinted up at the sun just in time to see it disappear behind a dark cloud. I held on tight to my phone that I had tucked up my sleeve, thinking I'd take a few pictures somewhere along the way to remember Summit Springs by. I decided to walk out through the field behind the hotel in the direction I saw John riding last. I took a deep breath, trying not to let any of my confidence escape before I chickened out. I needed to explain to John why I was seen in his brother's arms. I walked and walked and walked. Every hill I crested, I was sure I would find him—no luck. I was only greeted with another valley, another hill, and lots of field grass and trees. The sky started to darken.

One more hill. If I don't find John, then I'll turn back. Five hills later, I started to hum "The Hills are Alive" from The Sound of Music as I approached the top of another hill. I had the urge to run up it but remembered I had no such lung capacity. After making it to the top of the hill, I stopped to even my breathing and took in my view. The beauty of this place stopped me cold. I just stood still to soak it all in—along with the light sprinkle of rain that started to fall from the angry-looking clouds. Once I had caught my breath, and before the rain picked up anymore, I pulled out my phone from my sleeve. The song, "Cowboy Take Me Away" by The Chicks, started to sound from my lips as I took some panoramic pictures and videos of the view. I wanted to take a lot of pictures of Summit Springs because I didn't want to forget a thing. The rain started to come down a bit heavier now, so I tucked my phone back into my dress to keep it safe and dry.

By the second chorus, my arms were wide open, and I was singing at the top of my lungs to the hills—so many hills and mountains. I knew the majority of the notes I was hitting were off-key, but I didn't care. Tonight, I was the fourth Chick they never knew they needed. I started to spin with my eyes closed, letting the raindrops cascade off my face. I was soaked to the bone. I couldn't remember the last time I let myself just *be* myself. If I couldn't find John tonight, then this moment was the next best thing. I started to slow the spinning, and with each turn, something dark kept catching my eye. I stopped abruptly in horror to find John off his horse, watching the show with amusement. Humiliated didn't even begin to describe how I felt. My mouth dropped open, and I covered it with one of my hands. I just stared at him wide-eyed, too stunned to say anything. I did the most mature thing I could think of, I spun around and started running down the hill in the opposite direction. I knew I couldn't outrun a horse, but maybe I could run off some of the embarrassment, like a calorie, before I had to face him. I couldn't believe out of all the songs I could have sung, I chose "Cowboy Take Me Away!" I slowed down because there was a muddy patch ahead. Slipping in the mud like a piglet would surely cause me to pass away from embarrassment.

Whoosh! That was the sound my wet dress made as I completely wiped out in the mud face up. I didn't even try to get up because I hoped the earth would swallow me whole if I laid there long enough. I closed my eyes for a moment, hoping this was all just a bad dream. I lifted my head slightly and squinted through the rain to see John dismount his horse and slowly walk towards me with all the swagger one could imagine. He was dripping wet from the rain as well, but it suited him—unlike me— the wet muddied piglet. He looked perfect. I let my head fall back down, and my hair squelched in the mud. I covered my eyes with my arms with the if-I-close-my-eyes-you-can't-see-me mentality.

"Hey there, Chick," I heard his deep raspy voice say through the rain. He knew the song. I couldn't take this humiliation; it was too much. John closed the distance until he was standing at my feet. I knew because I could hear his boots slosh through the mud.

With my arms still covering my eyes, I blurted out, "I only jumped into his arms, because of the rooster."

"I know." I sensed him closer to me than he was before.

"You know?!"

"Yeah, I only wish I would have been closer, so I could've been your knight and slay the dragon. Not literally slay, because Bill claims that rooster's bloodlines trace back to royalty. He'd string me up by my toes if I ever touched it, but I have thought of at least 11 different ways to cook that bird. I would've kept you safe is what I'm trying to say."

I laughed. I peeked through my arms to catch a glimpse of him. He was smiling back at me. "I don't think I could possibly be more embarrassed than I am in this moment."

John laughed. "Here, let me help you up."

I reached out and grabbed onto his hands—they still fit perfectly. His hands instantly gripped mine firmly as soon as they made contact, and he pulled me up with ease. I tried to stand up straight, but one of my legs slid out from under me on some slick mud. Down I went again—forward facing this time. John caught me by the waist before the mud reached anything above my knees, though. In one swift motion, he had pulled me up and into him—close and tight. I rested my hands on his shoulders. The brim of his hat shielded us both from the heavy rain. Time, along with my breathing, started to slow. The sound of our inhales and exhales filled my ears. We were both breathing each other in while trying to catch our breath. With the rain pouring all around us, this moment felt so intimate—like we were the only two people in the whole world. I looked in his eyes, and even with the rain and dimming light, his eyes were bright, as if they had their own little flames lit inside. I didn't dare move a muscle. I didn't want anything about this moment to change. I felt the warmth of his breath on my lips, which caused my eyes to shift and focus on his. Gravity started to pull me closer, and I didn't want to fight it. His arms around me slowly started to tighten. His wet shirt clung to his skin, and I could feel every muscle as I slowly started to slide my hands up and around his neck.

The air between us was thick and buzzed with energy. My heartbeat quickened, and I could hear it pulsing through my ears. I gazed back into his eyes, and the look he was giving me was the same one I knew I was giving him. *Kiss me.* We both leaned in until our lips just about touched.

"If I had been next to Devin or any other guy, who would you have run to?" he asked softly. I took in a deep, uneven breath. I wasn't stalling because I was trying to think of an answer; I stalled in an attempt to control my breathing.

"You. Every time," I whispered, before looking down at my muddied boots. I was surprised those words escaped my lips, but I knew now was not the time to be subtle. I wanted John, and I needed him to know that. I looked back up into his eyes and melted like butter on hot biscuits at what I saw there. He looked so happy and content while holding me in his arms. He raised a hand up and curved it around my neck just under my hair. His thumb traced my jaw then softly stroked my neck. "I don't know if I can let you leave, Maggie," he whispered.

"I don't want to leave."

He was thinking hard about something. I could tell from his eyes. "What if I could only afford enough to get by and nothing more. Would you still stay?"

I knew this conversation had just taken a deeper plunge. I wasn't sure how it all fit together and where that put me in his real-life puzzle. "I would," I said. "As long as there's no acting involved."

"I'm not acting," he said softly. My eyes searched his, and I wanted so badly to believe him. He looked and sounded like he was telling the truth, but my insecurity still wasn't convinced. He noticed. Without a word, he brought his hand out from under my hair and raised a balled fist with only his pinky finger raised. *A pinky promise!* I smiled—teeth and all. I held up a balled fist with the pinky raised just like his. We interlocked fingers, both of us never breaking eye contact. There was a spark of mischief in his eyes and smile across his lips—it drove me wild. All I could think about now was kissing him. As if reading my mind, he released my pinky and slid his hand back on my neck under my hair. His warm fingers were a contrast to the cool air the rain had brought with it. John pulled me even closer to him, then stared down at my lips—that's when my heart took off into a full-fledged gallop. "And in answer to your question…" His voice was so low now that I could hardly make out his words through the sound of the downpour going on around us. "I don't have someone waiting on me."

My lips curved upward, and those words gave me the confidence I needed to slowly trace my fingertips along his stubbled jaw. The action caused a deep contented rumble to sound from inside him. I took in one last shaky breath before I leaned in closer, letting my eyes start to close. Our lips were inches apart, and I could feel John start to slant in to kiss me—when a voice carried through the rain. A low, quiet irritated growl sounded from John's chest, and it made me laugh a little. I wanted to kiss him just as bad as he wanted to kiss me it would seem, but he voiced it best for the both of us.

"Joooohn!" Ricky called out. John slowly dropped his hand from my neck but kept his hold around my waist. I took his face in both my hands, and that surprised him in a good way.

"Raincheck?" I whispered.

"Literally. And yes." We smiled at one another. I stared deep into his eyes for one more moment before letting go and dropping my hands to his chest. As soon as Ricky got within talking distance, John and Ricky started talking in what I assumed was Spanish. Hearing John speak in a foreign tongue made him more attractive. I didn't think that was even possible. John started to talk with a little less patience in a funny way as the conversation went on, and whatever he was saying made Ricky laugh and hold up his hands as if to surrender in an apologetic way.

"Bye, Maggie." Ricky smiled and tipped his hat to me. I held up a hand to wave goodbye, then Ricky turned his horse back the way they came. The rain started to slow as John and I both watched Ricky go in silence.

Once Ricky was far enough away, John sighed then asked, "You ready to head back?"

"Yeah." By that response, I really meant "never," but I kept that to myself.

John gave the arm wrapped around my waist a quick squeeze before releasing me and turning to pick up Shady's fallen reins.

Shady. It would seem I was on a first-name basis with his horse now. I wrung the muddy water out of my hair.

The rain had stopped, but the skies were still dark. I walked over to where John and Shady stood. John interlocked his hands and bent over next to the stirrup. I stood staring at him with folded arms.

"What?" He looked up and laughed at my stance.

"Riding a horse twice in one day? Not a chance."

"Maggie," he jokingly growled. I held my ground. "What if I gave you a hint about my last name?"

"Two hints, and you've got a deal."

"All right, get over here." He smiled. I was insane to be getting on a horse again, but I told Anna I'd figure out a way to get us our dresses. *She owes me big time.* I lifted my boot but stopped when I saw just how muddy it was. "I'm not scared of wet dirt. Up you go," he said. I put my boot in his hands, and he lifted me up and over onto the horse's back. John took the reins and slowly walked us up and down all the hills that I had climbed.

"I'm ready for those hints now." I smiled down at him.

"My last name doesn't start with 'Q' or 'X.'"

"What kind of hints are those?"

"Extremely vague ones." He turned and smiled up at me.

"Don't you want me to get to know you and win you over?"

"With all that I have."

The magnitude of what that response meant didn't pass me by. "I don't believe you," I said while giving him a skeptical eye. "Okay, here we go. Is your last name Smith, Wayne, or Appleseed?"

"What kind of guesses are those?"

"Ones that go with your first name."

"Don't you want to get to know me and win me over?"

"With all that I have," I said with a challenging smile.

"I don't believe you at all." He smiled back. *That right-sided dimple of his will be my undoing.* It made me weak. We walked in silence for a little while, and I started to recognize my surroundings. We were only a couple of minutes away from town now. "Why did you come out here?" John broke the silence.

"I...um...wanted you to know why I jumped into your brother's arms earlier."

"That's the real reason?"

"Yeah. I didn't want another minute to pass by with you possibly thinking that there was something between him and I. I wanted to explain myself as soon as I could."

"You don't have to worry about that stuff with me. I trust you, and I'm not worried about Devin. I mean, I'm worried for him as a person, he's nuts, but I'm not worried about him with you."

I laughed a little. "Why did you ask if I would have run to you if you already knew then?"

"I wanted to hear you say it." He smiled up at me once more. I stared up at the sky for a moment and noticed the clouds were starting to disperse. The moon shone bright, and the air was clear and cooler. The horse's hooves sloshed through the puddles and made crunching sounds while walking across the wet dirt and gravel to the hotel. The only light was coming from the moon and the lanterns throughout town. John came around the side of the horse and looked up at me. "I'm only going to let you down if you promise me something."

I gave him a skeptical look. "Let's hear it."

"You have to promise me that you won't go out on your own again. I panicked when I got back to town, and you weren't here."

"I promise. Scout's honor." I held my hand up with my pinky and ring finger touching, and my middle finger and pointer finger touching to form a "V."

"That's Star Trek." We both started laughing. I loved laughing with him, talking with him, looking at him, and just about kissing him. The thought of actually kissing this man sent my pulse into a canter.

"So, can I come down now?" I asked.

"Nope, I'd rarely trust a Vulcan with matters of the heart." He reached up and softly folded my pinky down and put my ring, middle, and pointer fingers together until they were all touching. "That's better. I'd trust a Scout every time," he said. I smiled, and so did he. He cared for me, and I was pretty sure it was more than just as a guest now. I swung my leg over, and he put his hands on my waist. I slid down, and he slowed the descent. I rested my hands on his biceps. That electric buzzy air, like before, was still there between us. A door slammed inside the hotel, and it made me jump and drop my hands. "Well, I need to get Shady dried off in the livery. I'll be back in a bit."

I nodded. John gave me one last smile before turning away to lead Shady through the old lantern-lit town. My footsteps sounded as I went up the wooden stairs to the hotel porch. I could hear people laughing and talking inside the cafe. I smiled as I replayed the evening in my mind until I remembered that John had witnessed my song performance. I cringed for a few seconds, then decided the good moments definitely outweighed the bad today. Luckily, John didn't seem too traumatized by the whole thing. I took a deep breath before quietly opening the hotel door.

"Maggie, there you are!" Anna walked out of the café. I turned around, and the look on her face turned from happy to slightly concerned. "Are you all right? You look…"

"Like a swamp monster?"

"Yeah!" she said.

"All is well. I slipped in the mud."

"Did he catch you?"

"The second time." We smiled at each other. I knew she could tell that all really was well by the look on my face.

"I saved you some dinner," she said, as she looked back towards the café.

"I am the best at picking best friends. Thank you! I'll get changed and get as presentable as possible, then be down. Morse code said stew, right?" I smiled.

"Yep, and I'll make sure yours is hot."

10

After dinner, Anna and I headed up to our room. My spirits were lower than when I had first come down for dinner. John hadn't come back like he said he would, but it had been a long day, and I didn't blame him for turning in early. Anna and I collapsed onto our beds the moment we got to our room. I was relieved to be horizontal after a long day.

"Ricky mentioned that he came up on you and John…um…together?" Anna said through the dark.

"We were like three seconds from kissing! Three seconds!" We both laughed.

"I know! Ricky told me, and he felt horrible."

"It's okay. Well, it's not okay, but Ricky seems like too good of a guy to hold a grudge against." I smiled to myself. "How are you two?"

127

"Really good. I thought the way Ryan used to treat me was the norm or something, but I was so wrong. For once in my life, I'm glad to be wrong. He's taking me on a picnic tomorrow, so I won't be here during lunch. Is that okay?"

"Of course, it is! It's every man, woman, and child out for themselves here in the Wild West—" *Clink.*

"Maggie, what was that?" Anna whispered.

"I don't kn—" *Clink.* "I think it's coming from the window. Do you want to check it out?"

"Nope."

"Darn. Okay, I will." I rolled off my bed and got on all fours to slowly crawl to the window between our beds. I eased my way up next to the desk. *Clink.* I peeked out the window with only my eyes above the window sill. *John.* He smiled and dropped the gravel in his hands when he saw me rise.

"What is it?" Anna asked with a touch of fear in her voice.

"It's John."

"He came back!"

"He did." I smiled.

I unlocked and lifted the window open. "What are you doing here?"

"Do you want to come hunting with me?"

"Hunting right now? For what?" I panicked a little, trying to think of what we could possibly be hunting for at night.

"You'll see. Put these on and meet me on the porch." He tossed up a bundle of something, and I caught it. I closed the window and un-cinched the belt. Unrolling the bundle revealed a thick men's button-up top and wool trousers.

"Should I go?" I whispered.

"You'd be crazy not to. Be home by midnight. Just kidding. I have no idea what time it is. You two have fun."

I squealed before getting dressed in even more borrowed clothes.

Luckily, the descent down the stairs was pretty much silent. I stayed close to the edges to avoid creaking and waking anyone. There wasn't much light by the front door, so I felt my way along the wall until I found the doorknob. I carefully opened, then closed the door behind me and heard soft footsteps up the stairs to the porch where I stood. I turned, and there he was in all his rugged cowboy glory.

"Hey," he said.

Just hearing his voice made me smile. "Hi." My cheeks were pink already, and I was glad he couldn't see them in the dark. Maybe I blushed because I was sneaking out, but it was more than likely because my feelings for the man in front of me were growing. Things were already changing between us, and it made my stomach flutter.

"I brought these other boots for you to wear. I'll help you get them on." He knelt and went to work on untying my laces. I almost lost my balance when I lifted my foot so he could remove my boot, but rested my hand on his shoulder to steady myself. Once I had my balance, I didn't move my hand. "I figured you might need some new bandages, so I brought more. Is it okay if I take a look and rewrap everything?"

"Yeah."

John set a lantern down close to my leg and slid my sock down. He put the new bandages on my leg—which felt better already. I had to take off the old bandages because they were too wet to do any good after my little rain dance earlier. When he was finished, he pulled up my sock, then put a thicker one on over it before sliding on and lacing up a tall, rugged boot. John moved to the other side and did the same thing, adding an extra sock and lacing up a new boot. He set my other boots down next to the hotel door, then grabbed my hand. "All right, let's go!" I could sense the excitement in his voice, and I was excited too. Well, that was until I remembered what we were doing out here—*hunting for something.* A wave of nervousness came over me and settled in my stomach. We snuck around the back of the hotel, and at one point, he started doing dramatic spins around corners like he was a secret spy. His spinning made me laugh, and I could tell he was more himself right now than ever. He took my hand once more, and we walked through the field behind the hotel until we were far enough away for our voices not to carry. Our boots started to squish through some mud.

"Are you going to tell me what we're hunting for yet?" I asked.

"Worms."

"Eh! Why?" I tried not to cringe too much.

"I need to catch some for Bill. He's taking a couple of people fishing up the river early tomorrow morning and needed worms. I volunteered in hopes that you'd come along."

"And the worms come out at night?"

"Yep! You ready?"

"Let's do it!"

We slowed as we approached some trees, then John lowered the lantern and started to scan the grasses.

"Okay, will you hold the lantern right here?" I reached over and held it right where he wanted me to. "The worms can sense the light. If the lantern is too close, they'll slide back into their hole, but if it's too far, then I might not know if I'm reaching for a snake."

"What?!"

"I'm kidding."

"John!"

He laughed. "Normally, half of the worm is in the ground, and half is out. When you grab one, hold on tight. When you feel it start to slide out, pull back slowly."

I was the lantern holder, so I wasn't sure why he explained how to catch a worm in so much detail, but I humored him anyway.

"Here's one!" John said before he bent over and quickly reached in the grass. He grabbed a worm and held on. Within moments, a long worm was dangling from his fingers. *This is so gross.* John looked so proud, and I couldn't help but smile at him despite what he was holding. He put the worm into a small bucket filled halfway with damp dirt. "All right, you can have a go." He held his hand out for the lantern.

"Go where?"

He laughed. "Nowhere. You can have a turn to catch a worm. I'll hold the lantern for you."

"No, thank you."

"No, thank you? Maggie, you're not afraid of worms, are you?"

"I'm not scared. I just think worms belong in the ground more than they belong in my hands."

"You are scared of worms!" he laughed.

"I'm not either!"

"Prove it."

I huffed like a three-year-old. *Great.* I wasn't afraid of them; I was grossed out by them. John challenged me, though, and I have a hard time backing down from a challenge. I silently handed the lantern to him. He laughed as he accepted it. I searched the grass for a worm. *There!* We both bent over. I reached down and tried to grab the slippery little worm. I almost gagged but tried really hard to hold it together. The worm slipped back underground before I could grab it—so did the next worm and the next. "Shoot!" I said as the last one disappeared into the hole. "They know I'm coming!"

"Let's find another one, and I'll help this time."

"Here's one." I pointed one out near a boulder. We both reached in the grass, and he guided my hand towards the worm slowly.

"Okay, grab it on three," he whispered close to my ear. His soft voice made my heart beat faster. "One…two…three!" I grabbed it and held on. John wrapped his hand around mine and helped me know the tension and pace to pull the worm out. After a few moments, the worm was free of the tunnel, and I held it up to John with pride. He was smiling at me again, and it only made me want to forget this hunting business and do something else involving his lips and mine. John held out the bucket. "Atta girl." John and I took turns catching worms until I could do it on my own, then it turned into a game. I don't know how long we ended up worm hunting, but I did know that I was a pro at it now and that worm hunting could, surprisingly, be fun and romantic. We started to make our way back to the hotel after we had enough worms for Bill. We had made it to the middle of the field when John held up the lantern and blew out the flickering flame inside. "Look up," He whispered.

I looked up at the sky and gasped. There were so many stars, thousands and thousands of stars! "I didn't know the sky could look like this! The city lights block out almost all the stars back home. Look!" I pointed up at a shooting star. John pointed out the different constellations and told me stories about them. He tried to explain something called "stellar parallax theory," but lost me from the beginning. From what I caught, though, it all had to do with perspective and relativity, stars that looked like they were moving, but really weren't. As he talked, I started to notice little black things flying back and forth in the sky. "What's up there? Birds?"

"Bats."

"Bats?!"

"Yeah." John laughed.

"Summit Springs is straight-up magic."

"Tonight, it is." He reached over and took my hand in his. I leaned into him and reached my other hand around and held onto his muscled bicep. The chilled air made me shiver. "Let's get you back inside. Tell me a favorite memory of yours while we walk."

"Hmm…okay." I thought for a few moments. "So, one time, there was this really cool guy who witnessed me singing horribly in the rain at the top of my lungs. I was sure that my life was over right then and there, but a favorite memory of mine happened right after."

"And what memory was that?"

"I…well…it was raining. He and I were standing in the rain, and we…"

"You what?" He teasingly pressed.

"Well, you know."

"I don't. Tell me."

"We almost kissed," I whispered.

"Why didn't you?"

"There was an interruption."

"Ah, I see. Well, I think the guy should've kissed you anyway. He must not be as cool as you say he is if he let an interruption keep him from kissing a girl like you."

"Maybe he didn't want to bad enough," I said as I smiled.

"No, I don't think that was it. I think he wanted you and that kiss enough, but I think he got nervous. I bet he likes you a lot, and it scares him just how much."

"No, I don't think that was it," I teased. John quickly wrapped an arm around my waist and pulled me into him, just like when we were standing in the rain. My hands rested on his chest, and I took in a surprised gasp of air and laughed a little.

"What did you say?" I could tell John was smiling, even in the dark.

"I don't think that was…"

John didn't let me finish the sentence. He firmly pressed his lips against mine. His other arm wrapped around me as he leaned deeper into the kiss. I met him with the same force as our lips moved. Kissing John was even better than I had imagined. I slid my hands up his chest and wrapped my arms around his neck—threading a few fingers through his hair along the way. My lips spread into a smile because I was so happy. The kissing stopped, and I instantly regretted smiling. John leaned his forehead against mine, and we both stood there, trying to catch our breaths. When our breathing had slowed until it was in sync with the chirping crickets, I slid my hands down to his biceps.

"So, this guy," John whispered, "do you think I could take him on?"

"I don't know; he's really strong." I gave his arm a squeeze.

"Surely I could outwit him." His voice was low and raspy now.

"It would be hard; he already knows about the stellar parallax theory."

A soft rumble of a laugh sounded from his chest. "There has to be something I would be better at…"

"Kissing," I said. He kissed my lips again softly, then again, and again. I took a deep breath as he pulled away. *If this is all pretend, I might not recover.* "And you're the best at making me happy."

"I think that's the most important thing of all."

"So do I."

"Tell me another one. Another memory." John said, taking my hand in his. We started walking around the hotel to the front door. I looked up at the stars trying to summon down a memory because all I could think about was how perfect this night had been.

"Okay, here's one. My family and I drove to Hermosa Beach one night after dinner. It was dark out, but some lampposts lit up the beach. My brothers played football with my dad, while my mom, sister, and I sat on some swings talking. The boardwalk lamps hit the water just right, and every wave that rolled in was neon blue from the reflection off of the phytoplankton. The weather was perfect; the whole beach was ours, and I was with the people I loved."

"That's a good memory. They're lucky to have your love."

"I'm lucky to have theirs," I said. We quietly stepped up the wooden stairs to the front door.

"If I make it out to California someday, would you take me to see the plankton?"

"I would." We stopped right in front of the hotel door, and John knelt to untie my borrowed boots. "Thank you," I said (a little too breathy) once he stood back up.

"Mmmhmm." He looked down at the ground, then back up into my eyes. It was hard to say in the dark, but it seemed like he was having an inner battle with himself. It seemed that he wanted to say something.

"Say it."

"How did you know?" he asked.

"I can tell from your eyes. Well, what I can see of them at this hour anyway."

John let out a deep breath and looked to his left, then back down at the ground. He slowly sidestepped back and forth a time or two. "You feel this too, right?" He took a step towards me and rested a hand on my waist. He brought his forehead to mine, and my eyes slipped closed as soon as our foreheads touched.

"Yeah. It's not just you," I whispered the same line from his Morse code message. I rested my hands on his strong chest and felt him breathe a sigh of relief after hearing my reply. I kissed his cheek quickly before I lost the courage to kiss him first, then slid through the front door. I turned back around to close the door quietly and pressed my hand to the glass. John touched his fingers on the other side, where my hand was. I smiled, and he did too before I watched him walk away into the darkness. Tip-toeing up the staircase, trying not to make the floorboards squeak, I remembered my boots outside on the porch. *Shoot!* I was already halfway up the stairs, but I had to turn and go back down so no one would question my whereabouts in the morning. I felt around for the doorknob for the second time tonight and turned it slowly, trying not to make a sound. *Click.*

I tip-toed out onto the porch, then reached down for my boots just as John was bounding up the stairs—taking two at a time. In one fluid motion, he softly dropped the boots, lantern, and bucket to wrap a strong arm all the way around the small of my back and reached his other hand up around my neck up in my hair. He pulled me in close, then leaned in with every confidence and kissed me— and he kissed me good. I felt like he was branding me as his own, and my insecurities melted away with every passing second. He wanted me, there was no doubt in his kiss. I reached up and traced along his jaw and rested my other hand on his chest. I could feel his heartbeat. I kissed him in a way that would let him know that I wanted him too. I didn't want this moment to end. I didn't want this week to end. *I want to stay right here, kissing this man who has been tearing down my walls since the moment I met him.* Our kisses slowed and softened until we pulled apart. We were breathless. I was sure my eyes were starrier than the night sky tonight. He kissed me on my forehead, and my eyes closed again.

"Goodnight, Maggie," he said close enough that I could feel the warmth of his breath on my hair.

"Goodnight," I whispered. He brought my hand up and kissed the back of it before putting his hands in his pockets to wait until I made it safely inside. I trekked up the stairs and crept into mine and Anna's room as quietly as possible, then hurried to the window to catch one last glimpse of John. I watched him walk down the road through town until I couldn't see him anymore. I laid in bed for a while, unable to sleep, because I had realized something...*I'm falling in love with John.*

11

The most obnoxious sound started to infiltrate my dreams. *The rooster!* I put the pillow over my head to try and drown out the sound, but it did nothing. I needed to keep sleeping—I felt it in my bones.

"Oh hey, you're up!" I heard Anna say nearby.

I peeked out from under my pillow sideways, but couldn't see her in her bed. "Anna?"

"Yeah?" She sounded from the foot of our beds.

"The bird needs to die."

She laughed. "Here, put this on!" Something weighted draped across the bed over my feet.

"I can't. I'm still so tired!"

"Up late last night, were we?" I could hear the smile in her voice. Last night…*last night!* I sat up in bed super-fast. "Anna!" I started to squeal and my toes got all tingly, just like they always did at the end of a really good chick flick.

Anna squealed too. "Maggie! Look at you! If I didn't know any better, I'd say that you're…"

"Falling in love?"

"Are you?!" Anna looked at me wide-eyed. I nodded, and we both started smiling and squealing again. Anna was so excited she even did a little tap number on the wooden floor. "I'm so happy for you, Maggie!" A loud pound on the door sounded before it swung open fast.

"Ahhh!" Anna and I both screamed.

"Is everything all right?" A red faced and winded Carol stood in the doorway.

The three of us exchanged glances at least three times before anyone said anything. Anna and I couldn't hold back from smiling. Laughter started to bubble up inside me. *Oh no!* "Hahahaha!" I quickly covered my mouth. "I'm sorry, Carol," I blurted out between laughing episodes. "We got a little carried away with the laughing and a tap dance number, but we'll keep it down." I kept looking in Carol's direction, because I knew if I looked at Anna, I would start laughing again.

"Is it John?" Carol asked and her eyes went squinty and tried to read mine. My eyes got wide, and suddenly there was no more air to supply my laughter.

"What?" I pretended not to hear her question.

She looked at me, and smiled just a hint. "Never mind. Carry on." She closed the door behind her and took all the laughter with her.

"The walls are thin, but they're not that thin! There's no way she could have heard our conversation, Maggie!"

"I agree. That was super weird." I was too stunned to say much else. Anna and I whispered the remainder of the time we were in our room. I got dressed in one of Anna's outfits this morning, the one she tossed on my bed earlier. It was a thick wool brown skirt that had pockets, lots of pleats, and a few buttons near the waist in two rows, and the top was a light beige that had delicate lacing around the neckline and around the quarter length sleeves. I smoothed out the wrinkles over my stomach. A stomach that was full of butterflies just thinking about the prior night's events. I was excited, but nervous to see John again. Last night felt like a dream. My heart had to keep reminding my brain that we really did kiss last night—twice! I think Anna noticed my nerves, because she didn't let me stew too long.

"Maggie, we look totally hot! Let's go!" Anna linked her arm through mine with a new flow of confidence surging through me from her. Anna and I sat down to eat breakfast in the café. Just as I took a big bite of a biscuit, Devin flipped a chair around and sat down at the table with us.

"Hey, ladies!" he said. Anna greeted him and I just smiled with cheeks full of biscuit like a happy chipmunk. "I was wondering if the two of you wanted to help me feed the animals after breakfast?"

I opened my mouth to accept the invitation, but Anna spoke first. "We'd love to, but we are actually on our way to make paper this morning!" Anna sounded way too excited than she should be about such a thing. It had to have been her teacher-side coming through. .

I looked at Devin, then to Anna slowly. "Making paper?"

"Yeah!" she said.

I took a deep breath and looked over at Devin. "These animals...I assume they'll need to be fed tomorrow too, right?"

"Yep." He nodded.

"Pencil us in for tomorrow, because there is paper that needs to be made today." I smiled to Anna and she beamed at my agreeing to come along.

"Sounds good. Have fun!" He smiled at us, then spun the chair back around and pushed it under the table.

"We will!" I tried hard to make it sound believable, but the actual event wasn't doing us any favors. He waved and left out the front door. As soon as Anna and I were finished eating, we walked across the dirt road and stopped at a building just to the right of the general store.

"Well, I think this is the place!" Anna grabbed onto the large wooden handle, and pulled open the heavy door. There were groups of people already seated around tables that had piles of white fluff in the middle. Near the back of the room, there were people pressing wooden posts up and down into dark wooden steaming buckets.

"Hi, I'm Richard Lun! Are you both ready to make some paper?" A man asked us as soon as we stepped inside. Anna and I both nodded our heads. *We lead exciting lives.* "Great! Here are some scissors and cotton fabric. Go ahead and pick any table you'd like. We're cutting the fabric as small as it will go. When you're finished, bring your clippings to the buckets in the back." We thanked him, took the offered items, and found a seat. We greeted our fellow tablemates and got to work. The large scissors were made of metal, which made them surprisingly heavy. After about twenty minutes, Anna and I decided to combine our efforts. I held the scissors open, and Anna rubbed the stripes of fabric across the blade. When our fabric couldn't be sliced any smaller, we scooped it all into a bowl and took it to the buckets. Once there, we were instructed to dump the contents into the third bucket down and to be careful because the buckets were filled with boiling water. We were each given a wooden dowel to mash the fabric bits into a pulp. The process was supposed to take about three hours, but they said we could just keep mashing until our arms had had enough. I tried to get Anna to quit after two minutes, but she made us go for fifteen. Next, we made our way into a back room where we helped put a thin layer of pulp (the aftermath of the boiling water and mashed cotton mixture) onto flat rectangular strainers called sieves. We strained out the water, then flipped the thin layer of pulp onto small sheets of leather. We repeated that process about fifty times until we had made a massive baklava looking stack of alternating leather and sheets of pulp. We pressed down on the leather to remove any excess water as we went, and a large heavy rock was set on top to press out any last moisture before the sheets of pulp were hung up to dry. We walked out the back door and saw lots of paper already hung up on clothes lines to dry in the sun.

"You are welcome to go grab some paper from the back row. Those ones have all dried," a woman near the back door told us. "There are dip pens on the tables over there if you'd like to practice or learn how to write with them." She pointed to her right to some tables set up near the apple trees.

"That wasn't as boring as I thought it would be," I said to Anna as I reached up and unclipped a piece of paper from the line.

"Right?! I'm mentally trying to figure out a lesson plan that I can validate teaching my students the process. Things just aren't made like this anymore!" Anna studied her piece of paper up close. The paper was as cool as she was making it out to be, and I really was glad I tagged along this morning. Each piece was thick and soft. We sat down at the tables, and Anna decided to write her favorite quote in elegant cursive while giving me play by play instruction. I dipped my pen nib into the ink well about three fourths of the way in, lightly dabbed off the excess ink from the tip, held the pen at a 45-degree angle, and touched down on the paper. It took a few strokes and dips for me to learn the right applied pressure and when I thought I finally had it down, I decided to try writing a letter or two. I dipped the nib in once more then wrote out the letter "M," a heart, and the letter "J."

"Maggie, you might want to cover that up. The instructor is coming!" Anna whispered. Realizing what I had written, I blushed and stood up. There was no way to hide the paper with wet ink at the table.

"Good call. Thanks! I'll catch up with you later!" I called over my shoulder. Anna gave me a smile, then went to work on another piece of paper with her pen. I walked back through all the hanging pieces of paper while blowing on mine to try and dry the ink quicker. Once the ink had completely dried, I folded up the piece of paper and stuck it in my skirt pocket. Now that my mind wasn't preoccupied with the task of paper making, my stomach instantly started to flutter with butterflies again at the thought of John. I walked around the buildings to the front door of the general store, then walked inside. A colony of cattle bells announced my presence.

An older man at the checkout desk pushed his glasses higher up on the bridge of his nose as he welcomed me in. "Looking for anything specific?"

"Just looking around."

"Well, let me know if I can help you with anything."

"Thank you." Weaving in and out of the small aisles, I saw some gold panning supplies, fishing supplies, oat horse treats, bushels of fruits and vegetables, small sacks of jerky, clothing items, slingshots, and...*other things that I didn't know how I would purchase.* The man must've noticed me pat the sides of my thighs, only to remember that I had no money here in Summit Springs.

"You can pick out anything you'd like in exchange for five minutes of your time to help with a chore. Today's chore is milking Clover."

"I'm assuming Clover is a cow?"

"Nope, goat."

"Aw yes, goats do the milk thing too. I'll pick out a few things and be right up." I picked up a handful of oat horse treats and a few carrots.

"Will that be all?" he asked while sliding the oat treats and carrots into a small gunnysack for me.

"Yep."

"All right; follow me." I followed him to the back of the store, down a hallway, then out the back door. He set down a pail full of hay, an empty pail, and a small stool. "I'll be right back." When he returned, he was not alone. A white goat with brown spots came up beside him and let out a loud and surprising bleat. The sound made me jump. I had never milked anything before and was a little nervous. The man put the pail full of hay down on the ground near the goat's mouth, and Clover immediately started to dig in. The man explained how to milk the goat as he got the empty pail and stool set up for me. I felt the need to introduce myself to the goat before I got started, and told her I'd be milking her today. I gave her a pat on her back and began. After I proved to the man that I could express the milk, he left me to it. By the time he returned, I had only filled the pail with enough milk to barely cover the bottom with a thin layer of milk—a translucent layer really. He took a look at the amount and thanked me for my time. I cringed inwardly knowing it wasn't very much, and said my goodbyes before grabbing my gunnysack. I walked back through the store, out the front door, and headed to the livery.

The smell of hay and dirt greeted me as I walked through the livery doors. I looked around, up in the loft, and in every stall. *No John and no Shady.* A horse whinny sounded outside in the pasture. My boots made small crater-like footprints on the dusty ground as I made my way out of the livery. I squinted my eyes to see if the horse in the distance was Shady. *It was!* Three short whistles sounded from my lips, but they weren't loud enough. I tried once more...no luck. I let out a breath of defeat. *I could just toss the treats and carrots over the fence or—*

"Hey." A deep manly voice sounded from behind me. A smile spread across my face. I knew that voice. I turned around to see John hanking up a rope as he slowly walked toward me. He looked good—really good. He wore dark grey pants, a lighter grey button-up top, and black suspenders today. His sleeves were rolled up to his forearms again—just the way I liked them. He was sans hat today, so I could see his wavy dark brown hair. The man looked like a perfect storm that I was at peace getting caught up in.

"Hey," I said back. I couldn't stop smiling. I got a little nervous not knowing how to greet him after we had kissed last night. He caught it, and took the reins. He wrapped his strong arms around my waist and pulled me in close for an embrace. His hands were splayed across my back, and I could feel the heat from every finger. I closed my eyes and hugged him, pulling him closer to me. He gave me one last squeeze, before releasing me he. He hooked his thumbs on his suspenders.

"How did you sleep last night?" he asked.

"Like a rock. And you?"

John took a deep breath before walking to the fence next to me. I could tell he was wrestling something around in his mind. He rested his arms across the top rung. "I was up early working at…in the mountains rounding up cattle, but I slept really well when I got the chance." He looked over at me and gave me a smile. Whenever that deep right dimple of his was present, I instantly melted into a pool of butter. Which would be handy if I worked in a concession stand with popcorn, but here in Summit Springs it rendered me speechless. All I could do was smile back and try not to kiss that dimple of his to see for myself just how deep it really went. *He's thinking about last night.* I could see it in his eyes. I had a feeling the rest of the week was going to be us trying to pull apart like magnets that just wanted to be as close as possible all the time.

"Want to go for a walk?" he asked.

"Not today." I stared straight into his eyes. He stared right back and held completely still, I think he could've even been holding his breath. "I think I'll ride." I smiled. His eyebrow arched in an instant, and one side of his mouth curved upward into a surprised smile.

"You sure?"

"Yeah."

John's eyes locked on mine. What I saw in them was excitement and something else, but before I could put a finger on it—he gave three loud, short whistles and turned on his heel to grab a saddle. He left so fast it made me laugh out loud, assuming he thought I would change my mind if another minute went by. I turned back around to watch Shady trundle forward in my direction. I couldn't believe I was willingly getting on a horse again, but then again it wasn't just any horse—it was Shady. Getting through the fence was much easier without a really poufy petticoat. I watched John as he strapped on the saddle. He did it with ease, as if he had saddled a horse a thousand times. He looked really rugged and manly getting Shady ready for this ride, and I hoped he still had a few more knots to tie or something so I could keep watching him. I couldn't believe I was risking my heart being broken again, but then again it wasn't just any guy this time—*it's John.* My pulse quickened when he looked up and smiled my way.

"Ready?" he asked.

"Yeah." I stared in his eyes a moment longer, letting my response take on a double meaning. He caught it. He always did. He reached out for my hand and gave it a squeeze, then helped me up into the saddle. This trusting thing was getting easier as each day passed—with the man and the horse. John held the reins and guided Shady out of the pasture in the direction of the duck pond. A few minutes later, John reached up to my waist and caught me as I slid off Shady. His arm caught on the folded paper that was in my pocket and caused it to fall to the ground. He reached down to retrieve it, but I knew what was on the inside, so I grabbed it quicker. He didn't need to say a word, because all the questions were in his eyes.

"I made paper today," I blurted out.

"I see," he said slowly and skeptically. "How did it go?"

"Well." My cheeks started to blush. *Shoot!*

"What else have you been up to this morning?" He smiled as he pressed for more answers, mainly for the one I wasn't voicing willingly.

"Writing…and milking a goat." I tried covering up the writing part.

"Writing, huh? Let's see how you did." He held out his hand for the folded paper in my tightly clenched grip. His eyes were daring me to hand it over. I tried to think of every possible option to get rid of the paper. Eating the paper would be very bizarre and gross. Ripping it would probably be harder than it looked, being as thick as it was. *The pond!* Water should weaken the paper and make it sink! I crumpled the folded paper in my hand and tossed it into the pond. There's no way he would wade out there to get it! I smiled really big at John and he had a very amused smile spreading across his lips. He scooped me up in his arms so fast with ease that I squealed.

"What are you doing?!" I asked in a panic.

"It looks like you lost your paper. Let's go get it!" John started carrying me to the water's edge.

"You wouldn't!"

He smiled, making me think he really would. I looked back desperately over at the floating paper, willing it to sink. "Are you going to tell me what was on the inside?" he asked.

"No way!"

His eyes had fire in them now. I was smiling so much it made my cheeks hurt. He slid off his boots while still holding me, and started to walk into the water. I wiggled and tried protesting, but it was no use; he only laughed and held me tighter. The water was up to John's knees now. I tried calling out for help, which only made John laugh which made me laugh. I saw movement over John's shoulder.

"Anna!" I waved an arm overhead. "Ricky!" They were both on horses and heard my cry for help no doubt! John slowly turned us around to face Anna and Ricky as they stopped up on the bank.

"Everything all right over here?" Ricky asked with a smile on his face. *Why was there a smile on his face?! Why was Anna smiling too?*

"Yeah, man! Everything's good," John said a little too calmly for my liking. He was holding back a smile, and it made me smile even though I was worried for myself.

"Everything is definitely not good!" I half laughed and half pleaded. Ricky and Anna looked at each other before leading their horses back around the way they came.

"Anna! No! Come back!"

"Bye, Maggie!" Anna called out over her shoulder as she and Ricky walked away on their horses, then disappeared. I looked back at John's pleased face. *Man, is he handsome.* I saw the piece of paper just out of our reach, and to my dismay—still afloat. John followed my gaze, then took another step deeper. I squealed. The water was inches away from me now and John was waist deep. I pulled myself closer into his chest by tightening my hold around his neck. I buried my face in his neck. He smelled like pine again, and I loved it. I closed my eyes and breathed him in. His chest was rising and falling beneath me, and I was sure I felt his heart pounding. I slowly lifted my head to look in his eyes. They still had the fire in them, but they were softer now. One look down at his lips was all it took for me to lean in closer and closer. Right before I was going to close my eyes, his attention shifted. I looked to the side and noticed the paper was finally starting to sink. *Yes!* I slid my hand softly along John's jaw, turning his attention back towards me. I tried to keep his focus, but I could tell it was slipping. The corner of his mouth slowly started to turn upward into a sly smile, and the look in his eyes let me know that I had competition. The instant I felt his arm shift to reach for the paper, I lunged too. I lost my hold on him; he lost his footing; and down we both went. I kicked my legs around until my feet found the pond floor. My skirt made it hard to get my balance, but a strong arm was around my waist within seconds pulling me to the surface.

"You dropped me!" I laughed and sputtered at the same time. My mouth was in an accusing, joking, and surprised "O" shape.

"You let go."

"I did not!"

"Well, just don't let it happen again." He smiled. I decided to let him win this one.

"Scout's honor." I held up the Vulcan salute hand sign for a moment, then shifted my fingers into the proper hand signal. He laughed and I did too.

"So, about this piece of paper…" John waved it in front of us both standing there in the water. "I think it's about time we open it to see what's inside."

My eyes went wide with horror, because I really didn't think either one of us would have got to the note in time before it sank. Quickly reaching for the note proved pointless, but not entirely because John had wrapped his arm around me again. He held the paper high above our heads, just out of reach. Our laughs turned to silent smiles, then time started to slow. I watched a drop of water cascade down his cheek, and I swear it fell in slow motion. That magnetic force started buzzing between us again. We stared in each other's eyes, and I knew I'd be giving in this time. I slowly wrapped my arms around his neck, then didn't want to fight it anymore. I closed the distance first and fast. His lips were wet and chilled, but quickly warmed up with the contact. I knew I surprised him for a split second by leaning in for a kiss first, but he quickly recovered. He pulled me in tight, and kissed me back. Time stopped, and it felt like John and I were the only two people in the world again. I could feel his shoulder and back muscles through his wet shirt. I always knew he was strong, but it was nice to feel the defining proof for myself. I slid my hands down his shoulders and biceps, then slowly slid them under his arms. John read my mind and moved his arms up my back, so I could wrap mine around his waist. I pulled him close until we were as close as we could get. His fingers slowly started to slip into my hair. My breathing hitched. In the next second, John pulled back quickly to lift me out of the water. My dress made a whooshing sound, and there I was in his arms again. I let out a laugh, and he smiled. Heat rose to my cheeks, but I hid it by leaning into him.

As soon as John and I had wrung out as much water from our clothes as we possibly could, he whistled Shady over from grazing nearby. While wringing my hair out one more time, I noticed John slowly start to peel open the wet paper. My stomach got a little queasy, but I knew trying to get the paper now would be a losing battle. Once he had carefully unfolded the whole paper, I scrunched my nose and smiled slightly, waiting for his reaction. He looked down at the paper for a few moments, then up at me from the tops of his eyes. My scrunched nose stayed put, but my smile shifted from one side to the other. "Well, what do you think?" I asked, then bit my lip.

"You have some explaining to do."

My stomach dropped and continued to flutter with butterflies. My heart started to beat faster. "What's there to explain?"

He raised an eyebrow and gave me a look that said I should know. I walked forward to see what I had written once more trying to buy myself more time and think of how to respond. Just before I peered over the edge of the paper, John brought it to his chest. I gave him a quizzical look, and he held his ground. I searched his eyes—*he's bluffing!*

"John! Let me see the paper."

He reluctantly surrendered it. To my relief, only a faint heart was left in the center of the paper.

"Right, yes. You wanted an explanation. I practiced some shapes with the dip pen, and would you look at that—only the heart survived the duck pond! You don't think that's some kind of coincidence, do you?" I asked him in a sarcastic coated with concern kind of way. He immediately met my eyes, and I beamed up at him. The wheels were turning in his mind. His eyes were slightly squinted and were studying mine. I broke the eye contact first and walked over to greet Shady before I gave myself away completely. I reached up and stroked Shady's nose until my pulse slowed. John still hadn't joined us yet. Maybe he was still tying up his boot or—nope, he was staring at me right where I left him. He had widened his stance and folded his arms across his chest. His eyes had a hunger about them. John looked like a masculine thunderstorm of a cowboy standing there with his dark hair and wet shirt still clinging to his skin. His muscles pulled against the fabric, and I let my eyes linger a hint longer than I should have. When I met his eyes again, the fire in them had grown even more. He was breathtaking, and just like that, my pulse was racing and my cheeks had colored up again.

"What?" I laughed. He just continued to stare me down. "Well, if we're all finished here, then I think I'll get Shady back to the livery." I turned back towards Shady, but before I could even grab the reins, John's arm wrapped around my waist and spun me back to face him.

He looked me right in the eyes. "I don't think you and I are ever going to be finished."

12

When I got back to my room, I dried off with a towel I had borrowed from Vicky at the bathhouse, then changed into a dress that was the exact shade of blue as John's eyes. My hair dried in a dark wavy mass, and I decided to leave it that way. My pulse hadn't slowed since mine and John's conversation at the duck pond and all the butterflies hadn't cleared out of my stomach either. I was really starting to think that John might reciprocate my feelings for him—real John, not actor John. Even though I didn't know his last name yet, I was falling head over heels for him—which felt strange, but so real. Love calls the shots, though, and I wasn't going to ask any questions. John had asked me to meet up with him after I had changed and eaten lunch. I let out a deep breath that I had been holding. I wished Anna were here to help calm my nerves. *My phone!* I dug to the bottom of my trunk and powered on the phone. I texted Anna asking where she was, and she replied that she was on her way back from fishing. We agreed to meet in the café for lunch in about five minutes.

I had made it down the stairs at the same moment Anna walked through the hotel's front door. We both stopped cold in the doorway to the café because the smell of cornbread greeted us in full force. Anna and I looked at each other and let out a big sigh. There was a silent understanding between us that we wouldn't be leaving until we had eaten our bodyweight in cornbread. We both piled our plates high and only received three judging stares before reaching our table near the window.

"I have no shame," I said. As soon as a big bite of cornbread hit my tongue, my eyes closed out of complete bliss.

"Neither do I. They are all going to be lying in bed tonight, wishing they had eaten more cornbread. I don't want to go to sleep tonight with regrets," she said before diving into her plate. I just nodded my head in complete agreeance. "Speaking of living with no regrets, I saw you riding a horse today. That's a huge deal, Maggie."

"It really is."

"So, things are still going well with your cowboy, I assume?"

"They are," I answered between bites. "How are things with you?"

"Really good. Ricky and I are just enjoying each other's company right now." I raised my eyebrows at her. "…as friends, Maggie. Nothing more. He is such a breath of fresh air, and I'm able to think more clearly. Enough about me, though, what's on the agenda for you for the rest of the day?"

"I caught that quick subject change, but I'll let it slide this one time." I gave her the quizzical eye. "John asked me to meet him at the river after lunch. He's going to teach me how to pan for gold. Do you want to come?"

"No, I'll be okay. I'm going to go upstairs to rest for a little while."

"By 'rest,' you mean secretly text Ricky, don't you?" Anna's cheeks reddened a hint, and she smiled. "You don't have to answer that." We finished off our plates of cornbread and parted ways only after promising to meet up for dinner.

The hike to the river wasn't too far, but just enough to make me feel a little winded. I walked down to the river's edge and put my hands on my hips, letting my breathing even out. I scanned the shore upriver. People were already panning in the shallow water, and I searched the crowd for one specific pair of bright blue eyes. I saw his strong muscled back in a light cream-colored shirt and suspenders first. While his attention was taken, I used the time to admire him from afar. He was helping an older couple sift out their pan. I reached up to sweep a piece of my hair back that had blown

162

astray in the breeze. John stood up and the movement appeared to have caught his eye. When our eyes locked, I smiled and held up my hand for a small wave; he smiled back. Just seeing him made my heart race. When he looked at me, I felt like the luckiest girl in the world. He patted the man on the back and trudged out of the water. He walked down the edge of the river to where I stood, and I enjoyed watching him do it. He was humbly confident and so handsome.

"Hey," he said when he neared.

"Hi, John." I smiled a little mischievously, which made him smile.

"Are you ready for this?"

"Been waiting my whole life."

"Well, let's not wait another minute then." His eyes sparkled before he bent over and picked up a pan and small shovel at the base of a nearby tree. "We're going to go downstream near the bend to my secret spot." He reached out for my hand. I slid my hand in his then tightened my grip. He did too. John led the way and helped me over rocks and fallen logs. We stopped in the shade of a tree just around the river bend. We were in a place where no one else was or could see us. It was just John and me, and that's the way I liked it.

"Okay, so it's easier if we're in the water a little bit, but I can bring the pan to you if you want me to, so you don't get wet."

"I'm okay going into the water because this time, it's willingly." I narrowed my eyes and smiled accusingly at him.

"You could've just told me what was in the love note and avoided the water altogether." He smiled.

"It was not a love note, it was a paper full of shapes."

"…and letters. After the paper dried, I could see the indentation of some letters too."

"I don't believe you." I dared and called his bluff.

"The rearrangement of letters would also be a fact." He winked at me and smiled. "I'll be right back." He waded out into the river and left me there on the bank to decipher what he had just said. There's no way he could've known what was written on the paper—could he? I watched him shovel a few scoops of dirt from the bottom of the river into the pan, then make his way back to me.

"Come on in, the water's not fine at all. It's freezing," he said, and it made me laugh. He smiled over at me, and I knew I was at the mercy of that dimple of his. I did as I was told and waded into where he stood. He was right; the water was freezing. "Don't worry. Your feet will go numb in a few minutes, and you won't be able to feel how cold it is."

"Something to look forward to."

He laughed. "This is my special rock I sit on while panning. Go ahead and take a seat, and I'll teach you how. Normally, I demonstrate the technique, but today you get a hands-on lesson."

"Lucky me." I beamed up at him. I meant it but made sure it came off with a hint of humor. He smiled and handed me the pan full of wet dirt. I held onto it as he sat down behind me and leaned in close. He slid his hands down my forearms until they rested on top of mine, still holding onto the sides of the gold pan. My breathing slowed, but my pulse quickened. The warmth coming from his body pressed against mine was enough to make me forget how cold my feet were.

"You ready?" His deep husky voice sounded softly next to my ear. An "Mmmhmm" was all I could muster with him being as close as he was. John didn't say anything else; he just started to swirl the pan around, picking up little gushes of river water in the process. I watched the light sand filter out with each swirl until only black sand was left. "Now that the light sand is out, I'm going to show you a trick to separate the black sand from the gold." I slid my hands out to let John take over the pan. Without thinking, I slid my elbow up and rested my arm on his knee. When I realized what I had done, I thought about moving my arm—my heart voted against it. He leaned in a little closer to me, and I could feel his soft breaths through my hair. He left a little water in the bottom of the pan, tilted the pan slightly downwards in his left hand, and tapped the raised side against the inside of his right hand. I settled back into his chest a little deeper, and he rested his cheek next to my ear. I started to see specks of gold separate from the black sand. John continued to tap the side of the pan and slosh the water around gently until the gold was completely separated. I closed my eyes and tried to hone in on this moment. I never wanted to forget it as long as I lived.

"Will you hold this?" My eyes popped open, and I took hold of a small glass vial John held out for me to take. He got all the gold out of the pan, put it into the vial that I was holding, put the lid on, and slid it back into his pocket. "Whatever we find, you get to keep. Are you ready for another round?" He asked as he slid out from behind me.

"Yes…but I might still need more help," I said with an extra glint in my eye.

"I was hoping you'd say that." He smiled and waded out in the river to fill up the pan again. John handed it over when he came back and moved in behind me just like before. When his hands were over mine, we swirled the pan around and around. When the light sand had filtered out, John asked if I wanted to try separating the gold.

"Nope." I leaned back into his chest and rested my arm on his knee again. He laughed, and I realized that I liked hearing his laugh and feeling it rumble through his chest at the same time. "Tell me how you got the scar by your left eye."

His hands froze for a brief second mid-sloshing, and I knew that had caught him off guard. He quickly resumed the sloshing and tapping of the pan before responding. "I fell out of a tree when I was young and scraped against a branch on the way down."

"Is that the truth?" I asked skeptically.

"Scout's honor." I laughed when he held up the Vulcan salute with his free hand in front of me.

"Tell me what you're running from when you're riding Shady."

"Are we playing the game of six questions again?"

"Yes. I don't want to leave this rock until I know everything about you—down to your favorite ice cream flavor."

"If that's when we leave, then I don't think I'll ever tell you what it is." He handed the vial to me, and I held it as he emptied the gold from the pan. "Be right back." *He was serious about this gold panning thing.* Once he was seated behind me again, we started swirling the light sand out.

"What's your favorite food?" I asked him.

"Steak. Medium-well."

"A.1. Sauce?"

"Is that even a question?" he asked. I laughed. "Yes." He said softly next to my ear, and I could hear him smile.

167

"Favorite song?"

"My Girl" by The Temptations."

"That's a really great one," I said. He took a turn and asked what my favorite food was. "I thought it was enchiladas until I tasted your aunt's cornbread. My final answer is cornbread."

"It's good, huh?" Knowing our rhythm, and seeing only black sand and specks of gold left in the pan, I took my usual position to let him separate the two. This time though, I leaned my head back on his shoulder. I closed my eyes and felt the light breeze blow through my hair.

"Tell me what you run from," I asked softly once more. A few moments passed, and all I could hear was the rushing river and the leaves blowing in the wind.

"Memories. I have to see a lot of hard things at work. Sometimes I wonder if I made the right career choice."

"What do you do when you're not here?" I asked, hoping he'd answer. *Silence.* I wrestled in my mind whether to let him off the hook or not with the question.

"What do you mean? I'm a livery owner by day and by night."

"Joooohn." We both laughed a little. "At least tell me why you won't tell me." I felt him exhale slowly. I held my breath.

"I don't want anything to change between us." He said softly next to my ear, then handed me the vial. "Here you go." Once the gold was inside, he twisted the lid on, then put it back in his pocket like the other times before. He slid out from behind me, but before he started into the river again, I reached out and softly grasped his wrist. He turned around to face me, and I stared into his eyes straight on.

"Do you really believe I would treat you differently based on what you do for a living?" I didn't let go of his arm, and he didn't move a muscle. We searched each other's eyes for what the other one wasn't saying out loud.

"I don't want to find out." John looked down at the water. "People normally treat me differently once they find out, and I don't want that to happen with you." This was the first time I'd ever seen him this vulnerable—even more so than I had seen him when he wanted to get me to ride Shady away from the bear. I just wanted to pull him close and hold him tight, so that's what I did. I stood up from the rock and wrapped my arms around him, pulling him close. He wrapped his arms around me at the same moment.

"John," I whispered not as a question, but just to say his name out loud as more of a consolation. He buried his face into my hair. I held him tighter, and he tightened his hold on me too. I closed my eyes.

"Please don't make me tell you just yet. I will before the week is up, and I'll answer any questions that you can think of. I promise. I've never known a love like this, and I want everything to stay the same for at least a few more days." He swallowed. "I need to know that you want me for me and not for…anything else."

I slowly pulled back and put my hands gently on each side of his jaw. His 5 o'clock shadow made his jaw feel rough as I stroked the right side softly with my thumb—*a love like this.* A slight smile formed on my lips. "Nothing is going to change," I whispered. "Deep down, you know that too. I can see it in your eyes."

He didn't say another word. Words were no longer necessary to say what we were both feeling. I took a deep breath because I knew I wouldn't be coming up for air for a while. He leaned in as I leaned in, and as soon as our lips touched—we melded. The pressure of his lips on mine was stronger than before, and his hold on me was tighter than before. Everything had just changed between John and me here at the river today. There were more emotions and more of ourselves invested now—whole hearts were involved. It felt like roots were starting to grow between John's heart and mine—as if neither one of us ever planned to let go. I slid my hands and arms up around the back of his neck again, and just flat out kissed him back. *A love like this.* He felt like my best friend already. He moved his free hand across my back and held me close with the arm that held the gold pan. I'm sure my toes would be tingling by now if I could feel them. My breathing hitched, and I pulled away breathless. My eyes opened and gazed into his.

"Four minutes," I whispered.

"Four minutes until what?" His voice was low and raspy.

"That's how long the brain can survive without oxygen."

"They recently changed it to six."

"I like your answer better." I smiled and leaned in to kiss him again. I felt him smile beneath my lips. After a few more minutes, our kisses slowed and softened until we pulled apart, all but our foreheads. We stood in the river holding each other close until both of our breathing had slowed.

"I think we need one more pan of gold, so we have enough," he said.

"Enough for what?"

"A plane ticket for you to come back to Utah."

I pulled back, so I could look in his eyes. He was serious. "No way," I said. I couldn't believe he would think of that and be that sweet. My mouth opened slightly, and I stood there, staring in awe of him. He took my hand and raised it to his lips to kiss softly. I had no words.

"I'll be right back." He waded through the water one last time to fill the gold pan. I took my seat on the rock and waited for him to make his way back. John smiled and handed me the pan. "It's all you this time."

I took a deep breath. "Okay!"

He took his place behind me and rested a hand on my waist. I started to swirl the pan around, picking up river water as I went. The light sand had been carried away within a few minutes.

"Good job."

"Thanks. I liked our rhythm how it was before though. Are you sure you don't want to finish this off?"

"I'm sure. You got this."

I tilted the pan slightly and tried to swirl and tap, but it wasn't working. "This pan is faulty, John."

He laughed and reached his hands down over mine again. He patiently showed me the angle I had to hold the pan at and how to tap it again. He released his hold on the pan, put his hand back on my waist, and watched over my shoulder. It took me a few tries before the gold started to separate from the black sand. Only a couple of taps revealed a large gold nugget. I reached in and pulled the piece of gold out of the pan.

"Whoa!" John said in surprise from behind me.

"It's shaped like a heart! Is it real?" I turned around and handed the nugget to him. He rubbed his thumb over the smooth rounded edges. I looked up in his eyes.

"It is." He was shocked, but then a thought crossed his mind that got him excited. "This is worth like ten plane tickets!"

I laughed. "I think you should have it, though. You're the one who dug it up, so it's technically yours."

"Maybe, but I want you to have it." He held the nugget out for me to take but didn't release it when I reached for it. I looked up into his eyes, and he gave me a smoldering look that made me realize he wasn't just talking about the gold heart we were holding. He was also referring to the one beating inside his chest. I let go of the gold heart, slid my free hand up to touch his cheek, and then leaned in to kiss his other cheek softly. I smiled, then turned around to finish tapping out the gold from the black sand. When I was finished, I put all the remaining gold flakes into the vial and handed the pan to John. He set the pan down on the rock behind us, as I settled back into him. He kissed the top of my head, and we watched the river rush by for a while. The silence was comfortable, and so was the company.

I knew when I signed up for this trip that I would be panning for gold, but what I didn't expect was to be panning for love at the same time. I knew I found one of the things I was panning for today, but as for the second thing—I'd need to have the gold appraised to be sure.

13

After I had changed into a midnight blue long-sleeved dress, I headed down the hotel stairs to meet up with Anna for dinner. The sun had just dipped behind the mountains, and the temperature instantly dropped a few degrees with its absence. I stepped off the wooden plank stairs near the side of the hotel and made my way around back. There was already a large crowd gathered and a few people had already started to form a line near the food tables. As I got closer, I scanned the crowd for Anna and greeted a few familiar faces as I went. My eyes met Ricky's through a group of people and he quickly excused himself and made his way over to where I stood.

"Hi, Ricky! Have you seen Anna?" I asked.

"Yeah, she should be out in a few minutes. She's been helping prepare dinner."

"Sounds good." I smiled. "Thank you for being so good to her."

"She's very special to me. I'm lucky to know her."

"That makes two of us." We both smiled at one another, and I could tell that Ricky truly adored Anna.

"Hi!" Anna came up from behind me with cheeks slightly rosy. "Steer clear of the meat tonight, Maggie. It's venison."

"Thanks for the heads up!"

"What's wrong with venison?" Ricky asked me.

"Not a thing, I'm just not a fan."

"Gotcha," he said. Someone near the kitchen door called out Ricky's name. "Well, it looks like my muscles are needed!" He lifted an arm and flexed his bicep. Anna and I laughed, but Anna also playfully rolled her eyes. Ricky smiled in her direction before heading toward the kitchen to help bring the food out.

"Anna, he adores you," I said.

"I know."

"You know? Oh, is this an unrequited love thing? Poor guy."

"No, it's nothing like that. Quite the opposite actually." Anna and I shuffled our way over to the dinner line, and the whole thing felt a lot like a cattle drive.

"Well, what is it then?"

Anna opened her mouth, but the words seemed to be caught up. "I...I think..." She started to whisper near my ear. "I think that I might be falling for Ricky."

My eyes went wide and I smiled. "Like falling, *falling*?"

"Yes, but I don't want to jinx it. I'm nervous about how recently my last relationship ended, and here I am on the brink of another one. I just want to take things really slow."

"That's the thing with love though, I don't think there are any rules or timeframes." I started to scan the crowd to see if John was here. "If you're ready when the other person is ready, then I think everything is ready to go."

"That was very profound, Maggie. I haven't even told Ricky yet, I'm actually trying to *hide* my feelings."

"An-na." I looked back at her.

"I already know what you're going to say, so you don't need to say it."

"Whoa, we really are best friends, aren't we?"

Anna laughed just as a loud whistle silenced the crowd. Someone near the front of the line started to say the prayer to bless the food. I recognized the voice. I peeked out through a squinted eye and tilted my head until I saw the source of the voice. It was Devin. The instant I looked at him, he opened an eye and looked right at me mid-prayer. He smiled and I knew I had been caught peeking during the prayer. I quickly shut my eye and my cheeks flushed. When the "amen" sounded, the people resumed their conversations and started shuffling up in the food line.

"Guess what?" Anna asked.

"What?"

"I got the cornbread recipe!"

"No, you didn't!"

"I really did." She beamed. "I just need to keep repeating the recipe in my mind until I can get it saved in my phone." Anna and I made it through the food line and sat down at one of the far tables. "I helped make the ash cakes tonight."

I took a bite of one. "You did great! They taste a bit like cornbread."

"That's how I got the recipe! I asked the differences between the two and made mental notes."

"You are a brilliant woman."

"Tonight I am." She laughed. "So, how did panning go earlier?"

"Really well." I blushed immediately. Before we could say anything else, Devin sat down next to me on the bench.

"Hey, you guys. How was paper making this morning?" he asked.

"Thrilling," I said with a hint of sarcasm.

"What Maggie means to say is that it was really neat to be so hands-on with history. The experience made us feel really grateful to have the paper we have today and for it to be so accessible."

"Yes, those were my exact thoughts," I said as I smiled at Anna, then over to Devin. "I'm kidding. It really was cool to see how it was made. I'm glad we went."

Devin laughed then said, "Well, I wanted to come and personally invite you both to the Broken Spoke Saloon after dinner. I'll even be on the tack piano tonight! Will you guys come?"

I looked over at Anna who was staring at her ash cake and tapping something out on the table. *The cornbread recipe.* I turned back to Devin. "We'll be there." I smiled.

"Great!" He stood up to go over to another table.

Anna and I finished our food and went to the wash buckets to clean our plates and cups.

"Maggie, I need to get this cornbread recipe out of my head or I'm afraid I'll forget it!"

"Okay, let's head up to our room really quick."

— —   • —   —   •   • • •

After the cornbread recipe was safely saved in Anna's phone, we headed over to the Broken Spoke Saloon. The sky had darkened, and the lanterns had been lit and were flickering throughout town. I heard some twangy piano music and people laughing from inside the saloon before we walked in. Anna pushed her way through the double swinging doors first and I followed. The big room was warm, lively, and filled with people. There were a lot of small tables throughout with people sitting at them either talking, playing cards, or both. There were a few people over by Devin, who was playing on an old piano. There was a small group that had gathered around him and were clapping along to the tune he was playing. He did a double-take back at me near the door and smiled. I smiled back and gave him a thumbs up. Anna and I weaved our way through the people and tables, then sat down at an empty table in the far corner by the stairs. We people-watched for a few minutes, then I noticed Anna blush and start to fidget with a loose thread on her sleeve near her wrist. I turned around and saw that Ricky had just walked in.

"I think you were wrong by the way." I shifted Anna's attention to me.

"When?"

"At dinner, when you said you knew what I was going to say about hiding your feelings."

"What would you have said?"

"I would've said you do whatever you feel you need to do. If it's hiding your feelings, then I support you. I will say this though. If you're okay losing him, then it wasn't meant to be. If you are happy and can't stand the thought of losing him, then don't let him get away."

Anna took a deep breath. "Thank you, Maggie."

"Hey, ladies! Are you up for a round of cards?" Ricky leaned over the chair between Anna and I. I looked to Anna to respond.

"We are." Anna smiled up at him. She and Ricky had a secret conversation with their eyes, and I allowed them to continue by suddenly taking an interest in the rest of the room. John was on my mind, and I hadn't seen him since we left the river this afternoon. I was starting to become very aware of where he was and right now I wanted him to be here. I saw Ricky grab a few decks of cards and three drinks before he returned to the table.

"Vernors best!" Ricky handed out the drinks before taking a seat. Anna and I looked down at our drinks, then at each other. "It's ginger ale. This stuff was invented in 1866 but didn't start circulating until a few years later. Carol likes us to leave out that last part though, but I, like Carol, like to be historically correct." He winked and we laughed, then he handed us each a deck of cards. I could tell the teacher in Anna was proud of him and his historically correct details.

"So, what game are we going to play?" I asked.

"Do you both know how to play Nertz?" Ricky asked. Anna and I looked at each other and mischievous smiles spread across our lips. "I'll take that as a "yes." We laughed and all of us started shuffling our cards. Little did Ricky know that Anna and I had spent many hot summers in her cool basement mastering the game of Nertz while listening to the Backstreet Boys. We were professionals. I took a sip of the ginger ale and hoped he took defeat well.

Ricky creamed us both, not just once, but every round. After the fifth round of losing, I felt my humility had been restored. The three of us laughed and drank about four cups of ginger ale before the air in the saloon changed—not literally, just in my own personal world. I turned around and looked toward the doors just as John walked through them. He wore a dark brown jacket and looked so handsomely rugged that I had to tell myself not to let my jaw literally drop. I watched him greet a few people near the door, then his eyes flashed over to mine. He knew right where I was the whole time. I smiled and he smiled back. A group of people walked out the door between John and me, and I lost him in the crowd. I turned back to Ricky and Anna and started in on another round of Nertz. I thought John would have made his way over to me as soon as he could, but after a few minutes he still hadn't shown up. I turned around and scanned the room again, and he was nowhere to be found.

"Enjoying yourself tonight you three?" Carol asked as she appeared at our table.

"We are," Anna spoke first.

"What game are you playing?"

Anna and I looked at each other not knowing how to respond, so we looked to Ricky.

"I...um..." Ricky panicked for a split second. "It's that old-time game that John and I told you about that one time. I'm teaching Maggie and Anna how to play."

"Sounds like fun. Carry on." Carol walked away and as soon as her back was turned, the three of us exchanged wide-eyed glances—we knew Nertz wasn't a thing in 1866 and that we had just about been caught.

"I'm going to bow out gracefully while I still can." I gave Ricky the eye which made him laugh and hold up his hands in innocence. I smiled over at Anna. "I'll see you later." I gulped down my last bit of ginger ale and excused myself. I slowly walked the perimeter of the room, scanning as I went. Before I knew it, my path put me directly in front of Devin.

"Hey, Maggie!"

"Hey! You did good tonight!"

He smiled, then whispered. "Thanks. You're going to want to make your way out to the porch within the next 30 seconds if you want a chance."

"A chance at what?"

"You'll see. Trust me."

I gave him a confused look. "Okay, this is me going out to the porch." I pushed my way through the swinging doors and slid around a few people until I had a clear view of the town. I looked up at the sky toward the hotel—not sure what I was looking for. Within 30 seconds, three quick gunshots rang out. I heard Devin from inside the saloon call out that the bank had just been robbed and everyone should try to get a look at the outlaws if they could. Chairs slid out and quick footsteps sounded across the wooden floor like a stampede. I already had a front-row spot just under the overhang as people started to fill in the space around me. Three outlaws bolted out of an alley next to the bank from across the road. They all had bandanas covering their faces, and their hats made it tough to see their eyes. One rider in the back fired a fourth shot into the air, and another rider yelled out a "yah" spurring his horse faster. The outlaw in the front wore a satchel across his chest and rode a brown and white paint horse. As they raced passed the saloon, headed out of town, a glint from a lantern lit up a side of the front outlaw's face. *The scar.* A second later the riders were gone and had disappeared into the night. Everyone funneled back into the saloon, and since I was one of the first out, I was one of the last in. I stopped just outside the swinging doors and heard a man inside tell everyone that whoever could turn in one of the outlaws would receive a $500 reward. Now I had two reasons to track down John—a monetary reward and I missed him. I slipped away and walked down the boardwalk. After a few minutes, I stopped in front of the post. The outside of the livery was lit by two lanterns, and the inside was pitch black. The livery doors slowly opened and John stepped out with a lantern in hand. He slid the doors closed, then locked up. I smiled and stepped onto the dirt road toward the livery. John turned and smiled when he saw it was me.

"Hey!" I said when I was close enough to be heard. John didn't say a word, only held out his hand for me to take. I took his hand, and he led me around the corner of the livery away from town just out of sight. He blew out the lantern, set it down, and wrapped his arms around my waist. I rested my hands on his chest.

"Hey," he said low and soft, "how did cards go?"

"Not well at all. Ricky showed no mercy towards Anna and me during our game of Nertz." John laughed, and I could feel the rumble from his chest through my hands. I breathed in deep and let the air out slowly. All was right in the world when John and I were close.

"Ricky shows no mercy to anyone when it comes to Nertz. The man is an animal," he said. It was my turn to laugh.

"I missed you tonight," I said as I slid my arms up and around his neck.

"Oh yeah?"

"Yeah. Where'd you go?"

"I had to come close up the livery."

"I know it was you," I said a little softer while pulling him a little closer.

"Prove it." I sensed him smile in the dark.

"I saw your scar." I was starting to sound a little breathless. I reached up and softly traced my fingertips across the smooth scar near his left eyebrow. I knew exactly where it was even in the dark.

"That won't hold up in court." He moved in closer until our lips were only inches apart. The warmth from his body mixed with the cold night only made me want him closer—and fast. I couldn't fight it anymore, I took his face in my hands and kissed him. He kissed me back. This kiss was playful and there was a hunger about it. I slid my hands down to his chest and could tell by the rising and falling beneath my hands, that he was in the same breathless boat. I kissed him once more, then burrowed myself into his embrace, letting him just hold me. His strong arms held me tight and close, and I realized being in his arms was my favorite place in the whole world. I was warm enough until the wind picked up and I couldn't hold back a shiver. He loosened his hold on me and rubbed up and down on my arms. "Let's get you inside. I'll walk you back to the hotel."

I didn't protest. He took my hand as we walked out from our hiding place. We stopped near the lanterns outside the livery for a brief moment as he switched out his darkened lantern for one that was hanging up and still lit.

"Weren't you wearing a jacket earlier?" I asked him.

"I...yeah I was. I left it in the livery. Let me go grab it." I nodded and stood nearby as he unlocked the doors. He put a hand on the small of my back to have me walk through first. The inside of the livery was much warmer being out of the wind. I watched John hang up the lantern, grab a ladder to our left, and climb up the rungs into the loft. Within a few moments, he was descending with the jacket over his shoulder. A loft was an odd place to keep a jacket on a cold night, but I didn't voice it. He opened the jacket up and draped it over my shoulders. He pulled it closed, then took my face in his hands, and kissed my forehead softly. My eyes closed and I savored the moment. "You ready?" he asked softly.

"Mmmhmm." I was still a little dizzy from the kissing and being close to him in the low light. John locked up the doors and we walked back to the hotel hand in hand. Only a few people were still at the saloon when we walked by, and the lanterns flickered in the wind through town. A distant tune from the piano sounded throughout the town and this moment felt very surreal—like I really was in a different time period. Our footsteps sounded on the wooden steps of the hotel stairs. I turned to face him and took a deep breath. I didn't want him to go. I didn't want this night to end. I didn't want this week to end. I wanted to stay right here with John in 1866. My heart started to beat faster and louder.

"I don't want to leave," I said quietly.

"We can stay out here a bit longer." John rubbed my arms to warm me through the jacket.

"No, I mean I don't want to leave, *leave*. I want to be here with you in 1866…all the time."

"That sounds very Twilight Zone." He smiled, and I smiled too. His expression went soft, and he looked right in my eyes. "I know exactly what you mean."

"What do we do about it?"

"Whatever we want." His voice was low, smooth, and had a touch of adventure mixed in. The moment made me feel like his hand was outstretched waiting for me to take hold and join him on a flying carpet ride.

"I'm in."

"Me too." He smiled. His eyes sparkled in the lantern's light. The air felt like it was thinning and buzzing. I took another deep breath, then reached my hands out of the jacket and rested them on his hips. He gently took my face in his hands and leaned in slowly. His lips pressed against mine, and we took our time kissing each other, savoring each second as if the night was never-ending and we had all the time in the world. He softly caressed my cheek with his thumb and wrapped his other arm around me to pull me close. When I deepened the kiss, he moved the hand on my neck through my hair and kissed me back with the same hunger. After a few minutes, he pulled back. My eyes opened slowly and a smile spread across my lips at the same speed. He looked deep into my eyes, then wrapped both of his strong arms around me in an enveloping hug. He held me so close that I was sure every last piece of my heart had been pushed back into place.

"Goodnight, Maggie." He whispered through my hair in a deep scratchy tone before releasing me.

"Night, John."

He waited until I was safely in the hotel and had made it up the stairs. I crawled in my bed and stared at the night sky out the window. *I don't think I'm falling in love anymore—I think I'm already there.* With that thought, I fell asleep fast with stars in the sky and stars in my eyes.

14

Anna and I sat down at our table near the window for breakfast. We had eaten a few bites of our biscuits and gravy when Devin walked through the front door. I watched his eyes scan the whole room before they found mine. He smiled and made his way over to us.

"Hey, guys! Are you still up for helping me feed the animals this morning?" he asked. I had forgotten that we agreed to it yesterday in this very same spot. "Don't tell me you forgot." He held his hands to his heart in an exaggerated way.

"Of course not! We were starting to wonder if *you* were going to show." I smiled. "We just need to finish eating really quick. I'm useless unless I'm fed—it's an oxygen mask thing."

"What?" he asked, confused.

"Like on an airplane. I can't help anyone else unless I've helped myself first…" I stopped mid-tangent. "We'll just meet you outside in five."

"Deal." He laughed. Once he was outside, I saw him load a few crates into a wagon. I bit into a fresh peach slice. "We'll do this quick, and I'll fake some form of distress if needed. I want you to have plenty of time to freshen up for your picnic with Ricky later."

"Thank you. That's a sign of a true friend—one that can fake distress at any given moment." We both laughed, then the two of us finished our food in comfortable silence. We walked outside to meet Devin. When the hotel door clicked closed, he looked up at us and smiled. He offered a hand to help Anna up into the wagon, then to me. There were crates full of fruits and veggies near our feet. I weaved through them and made my way to the front of the wagon where the bench was. There was a pile of ropes on my side of the bench, so I attempted to scoot them over as far as I could to make room for myself next to Anna.

"Oh, I'll take those," Devin said with his hand outstretched over the side of the wagon. "John had the wagon before and must've forgot them. We'll drop them by the livery on the way out of town." Devin hopped up and sat on the bench in the front of the wagon (the spot intended for the driver). There were two horses already harnessed in, and Devin held the reins at the ready. "You guys ready for this?"

"Onward!" Anna threw a fist in the air—surprising us all. I laughed until the wagon lurched forward. We bumbled along the dirt road through town. My heart started to beat faster and faster as we approached the livery.

"I'll be right back," Devin called out over his shoulder. I smiled and nodded to him, then something white caught my eye on the bench beside me. There was an envelope that had been hidden under the ropes. I heard Anna talking to someone on the other side of the wagon as I picked the envelope up and pulled out a folded paper from inside. I wasn't sure if the paper needed to stay with the ropes and go into the livery too. My eyes quickly skimmed over the words written in blue pen.

John,

I know the service isn't very good there, and I don't want to wait any longer to see you. I'll come by Wednesday night at 8!

Love Always, Kelsey

Nausea started to sink into my stomach. I flipped the envelope over and saw that she had sent it through the mail at the attention of John to Summit Springs. *This can't be happening—not again.* I closed my eyes. When I picked up the piece of paper only moments ago, I had no idea that a skeleton in the closet was about to make itself known. The whole world seemed to be in slow motion, and not in the good kind of way. My heartbeat started to sound in my ears, and all other sounds blended together. John wouldn't have acted the way he did and said the things he said if he had a girlfriend. *Would he?* I stared down at each word over and over, hoping that I had read it wrong. *I didn't.* The words didn't change, no matter how long I stared at them. The wagon started to roll forward, and I hadn't even noticed Devin climb back into the driver's seat. I quickly folded the note back up and slid it into the envelope. The rest of the ride was a blur. My mind was racing and replaying every conversation that John and I have had. *What about yesterday at the river while we were panning? What about last night?* My eyes started to burn, so I looked down in my lap at my deep, emerald green dress. My vision started to go blurry because of the tears that were threatening to fall. A large flock of chickens surrounded the wagon, and I knew we had made it to our destination.

"The chickens get the two crates and the three cans in the far-right corner," Devin said while guiding the horses directly through the mass of chickens. I couldn't focus.

"You ready, Maggie?" Anna looked over at me with questioning eyes. I nodded. We lifted and tilted each crate over the edge, then poured out the three cans. Devin then steered the wagon to the kitty-corner side of the field.

"To the mammals!" Devin called out.

"He is so strange," Anna mouthed, then laughed. I forced a smile. "What's up with you?"

"I'm not feeling very good."

"Should we go back?"

"I'm not sure yet. Maybe."

We pulled up to a gate a few minutes later, and Devin hopped down to unlatch the lock. "Anna, I was wondering if you wanted to steer the wagon along the fence while I pour out these next crates into the troughs?" he asked.

"Sure." Anna agreed with a little hesitation, then looked to me. I nodded to let her know I'd be fine. Devin talked to Anna for a couple of minutes, then we were in motion again. Devin stood and emptied the first crate into a trough. I could see pigs hustling over muddy mounds towards us.

"Hey, Devin?" I asked as he lifted and poured out a crate into a large metal trough. "Is there another John that works here?" *Please say yes.*

"Nope. Just my brother. Why do you ask?"

"I…um…" The pit in my stomach started to grow even more. I slid my fingers over the edge of the envelope. He looked down and saw what was in my hands, then looked back up to my eyes.

"Is that from a girl named Kelsey?" he asked. I took a deep breath and nodded. He dumped the next crate out with a little more force than the previous one. "I saw that letter come through the mail at the employee cabin on Monday. I wanted to give you a heads up, so that's why I sent the message."

"What message?"

"Through the wires on Monday at the post. You got it, right?" He looked over at me to see if I recalled it.

"I didn't get one from you. What did it say?"

"It's not just you." My head started to spin. No, it couldn't be. *The message was from John—definitely not Devin.* He couldn't have overheard mine and John's conversation on our way back from the bear encounter—unless the message had nothing to do with that conversation. *Devin did know about the message—word for word even.* Dread started to seep into every part of my mind.

"Devin, there was no way I could've known the message was from you—it was too vague."

"After I sent it, I went out looking for you in the orchard to explain, but that's when you fell, and I didn't think it was the right time anymore. I spaced bringing it up since then. I realize now that I should have just let you and John work that out. I'm sorry, Maggie." He took a deep breath. "I'm sure John can explain everything. This was my bad, and I was in the wrong."

"No, thank you for trying to help," I said. I took a deep, shaky breath and numbly looked out in the direction of where the town should be through the trees. I swallowed hard and tried to swallow

194

any rising emotion with it. "I think I'm going to walk back to town." I tried to stand, but forgot I was in a moving wagon and lost my balance. Devin caught me.

"Maggie…" I heard the pity in his voice, and I knew he was trying to will me to look up at him, but I couldn't.

"Where's the employee cabin?" I asked quietly when I regained my balance.

"Through the corn," he said, then let out a deep breath. I nodded and asked him not to tell anyone about our conversation. He still held onto my arms to help me keep my balance, and I made the mistake of looking up into his eyes. I could see John in Devin—they were glaringly similar. The same blood ran through their veins, and it was too much right now.

"Hey, Anna?" I called to her over my shoulder, "will you stop the wagon for a second? I'm going to hop off and head back to town."

"Yeah, do you want me to come with you?" she asked.

"No, I'll be fine." I smiled back at her. I knew she knew it was forced. I slid off the wagon as soon as it stopped and ducked under the pig's fence. As soon as I was far enough away, I let the tears that I had been holding back flow freely. *Why didn't he just leave me alone if he had somebody else?* Soon, my surroundings of thick brush and trees started to look familiar the more I walked. I was close to the duck pond. While pushing the branches away from my face, the sobs turned to a few hiccup intakes of air. The tears slowed, then ceased all together until there were no more left. Feathers were scattered all around in the mud where I stood at the water's edge, but there wasn't a duck in sight. Which was a relief because I didn't want an audience while I tried to pull myself together. I opened the envelope one more time. Each time I read the letter, it broke my heart a little more—until there was nothing left but pieces. John would be meeting another girl tonight. I could feel my eyes start to burn again, so I folded the paper back up.

Closing my eyes, I let the sun warm my body and dry the last of the trails of tears on my cheeks. I wrapped my arms around my middle and just stood staring out at the water for a while, listening to the water lap up on the shore. *I've survived the double life thing before, and I can do it again.* At least that's what I told myself, but half of my heart wasn't convinced. I thought this time would be different. *John* was different. This time hurt more than the first time—unbearably more. I had to try and shut off the emotions, or the hurt would be too much. I tried to place all the blame in John's court, but half of it stayed on my side. *I know better than to let myself trust and fall for someone this fast or at all.* I shook my head at my stupidity. There was no more heart left to break. The sadness slowly turned into a numbing. The numbness is what I would have to hone in on to get me through until Saturday. I would have to do my best to try not to let John sense a change, until I saw for myself that John was not who I thought he was or maybe exactly what I thought he was, but hoped he wasn't. My breathing evened out a bit. I wiped away any remaining traces of tears on my sleeve and took a deep breath. I breathed in every memory of John: *The first time I saw him; the moment in the livery when I confided in him and what he said back; the proud look on his face when I hit all the bottles at the shooting range; when he bandaged up my leg; when he found me singing at the top of my lungs; the way he kissed me; the way I kissed him back; the worms, those stars, panning for gold, last night—all of it...wasn't real.* With that thought, I exhaled it all out. I covered my mouth and closed my eyes, forcing myself not to cry out.

A duck landed in the water in the middle of the pond, and I turned around and headed back through the bushes before it could call out and tell the others that I was there. I didn't have any bread, and I didn't want to get their hopes up. The ground beneath my boots turned from damp dirt from the pond shore to field grass within a few moments. I pushed the last branch away from my face, and when I looked up, I locked eyes with John's blue ones. Pain surged through my heart, and my stomach dropped at the sight of him riding towards me on Shady. I didn't think I would have to face him so soon, and I didn't feel prepared. Seeing him was agonizing. The realization that he wasn't mine and never was made me feel physically ill.

I tried not to let my pain show, so I avoided eye contact. I knew he'd be able to tell something was wrong just by looking in my eyes, so I looked at the ground as long as I could until he was close. Instead of looking directly at him, though, I walked up to Shady and stroked his nose with my body slightly turned away from John's questioning eyes. I could tell he knew something was up already—so much for not letting him sense a change. He was silent as he dismounted on the opposite side from where I stood. He walked over and stopped on the other side of Shady's head, and I let my eyes flit up to his. We just stared at one another. Holding eye contact this long with anyone else would have been awkward, but never with John—not before and not even now. I hated that this rare connection between us—was between us. Why couldn't it have been with someone else? *Anyone else.* Someone not as wonderful as John or at least the man I thought he was. I could tell that John could read me. The backs of my eyes started to sting again. *We're too close—mentally and physically.*

"I'm fine," I said calmly, breaking the silence and the eye contact—answering the question I saw in his concerned eyes.

"Say it again while looking me in the eye, and I'll believe you." He said softly, too softly. Things were falling apart between us. I had to push that thought aside quickly. I took a deep breath and honed in on the numbness. I looked up into his eyes and held his gaze while trying to exude a confidence that I was far from feeling.

I needed him to believe whatever I said next, so he wouldn't be alarmed enough to cancel any plans tonight—specifically the ones he had at 8:00 p.m. I needed to see for myself that he would leave me to be with her so that I could push away any shred of hope that might trickle into my mind while I tried to heal from this.

"I haven't been feeling well today, but I'm really okay." I held his gaze with a false sense of poise that I'm sure would make any actress proud.

"Do you want to go for a ride?"

"Not today." I didn't meet his eyes. Before John could voice the question I knew was on the tip of his tongue, and one I didn't want to answer right now, I turned to walk away.

John grabbed my wrist quickly but softly. "Maggie."

I looked in his eyes—the same eyes I put so much trust in. *They were so blue. Why? Why would you do this?* I needed to get away before the tears started up again. I started to pull back on my wrist, and he released it immediately. "I'll see you later," I said, trying to sound more chipper than I felt. My goal was not to see him later...well not until 8:00 p.m. tonight. I turned and walked in the direction that would take me back to town.

John didn't call out for me or try to convince me to stay, but I didn't think he would after the look I saw in his eyes in that final moment. He looked genuinely hurt. He was a great actor; I'd give him that. Somebody get that man an Academy Award pronto.

Luckily, the distance I needed to put between John and I wasn't too far. People were walking up and down the street and in and out of the buildings. Stepping out into the middle of the dirt road made me realize just how far away from home I really was. *None of this was real.* My eyes darted wildly around me. *What am I even doing here?* I thought about going back to my room, but I wasn't ready to face Anna just yet. She was probably with Ricky—*John's best friend.* At least I think they were best friends. I didn't really know what was true and untrue at this point in this town. My mind felt kind of chaotic, and I couldn't seem to slow it down. *The bathhouse.* It would be the perfect escape and would hopefully give me enough time alone to put myself back together.

I crossed the dirt road with haste and tried to avoid any eye contact. Relief spread over me as I reached for the doorknob to the bathhouse and clicked it open. I put on my best actress smile and asked for a bath to be drawn as soon as Vicky looked up from the small desk.

"Of course, Maggie! I'll be right back," she said before disappearing into the back and turning the water on. I couldn't wait to be alone in a dark room for a while. I avoided looking at the shoe-shining chair where I had sat while John bandaged up my leg, which had healed surprisingly quickly—thanks to that ointment, no doubt. *I don't even know what his real job is.* I shook my head and gave out a puff of air. Letting myself fall in love with an actor went down in the books for being one of the most reckless things I'd ever put my heart through. "Ready! Come on back!" Vicky called out. I walked into the back hall and toward the only open door as Vicky stepped out. "Towel and soap are on the chair. Any requests today?" she asked with a wink.

"Stop! In the Name of Love."

Vicky nodded before I even finished the title. "The Supremes."

"That's the one."

"Coming right up!" she turned and started to walk down the hall, but she turned back before she crossed the threshold. "Everything all right today?"

"Yes." I forced a smile and hoped I sounded convincing.

I slipped into the warm tub and tipped my head back. The music started out soft then increased in volume within seconds. Between the warm water, dim lights, and music, my aching insides were easing up. I was proud of all the progress I'd made...getting back on a horse, but I don't think I wanted to ride ever again. Halfway through the song, the music cut off abruptly. When the music stopped, I was sure it was Anna coming to check on me like last time. Nobody came into the back, though, and I was relieved. A few moments later, "My Girl" by The Temptations faded in through the speaker instead. *I'm nobody's girl.* I let myself tune out the lyrics and decided to go Zen. Long after I had turned into a prune, I got dressed, thanked Vicky, and went back to the hotel as quickly as possible. I made it safely inside the hotel doors without any confrontation from anyone. I let out a sigh of relief as soon as I clicked the door closed behind me. I knew I had missed lunch, which I was fine with me because I wasn't hungry. However, my stomach loudly protested otherwise. I decided to go into the cafe to see if there might be something left over to silence my vocal stomach. Anna and Ricky were sitting at the table near the window. I tried to turn around before Anna saw me.

"Maggie!" she called out.

Shoot. I didn't want to interrupt their alone time, and I wasn't ready to face Anna yet. Luckily, Ricky was there too, so I knew Anna wouldn't probe with her words—just her eyes.

"Hey, you guys!" I said, trying to sound natural. Ricky stood and slid out a chair for me, major brownie points in my book. I liked him for Anna—they fit. "Weren't the two of you supposed to be going on a picnic soon?"

"Carol won't let us leave until the pies are done cooking. She insists we take one with us," Ricky said.

"Pie, huh?" I looked over at Anna. She smiled and nodded her head. She must be in a good place right now, and I was happy for her.

"Do you want to come with us? I heard the morning was—" Ricky stopped mid-sentence. I looked to Anna and saw that she was subtly shaking her head in Ricky's direction before smiling at me. She knew she had been caught.

"No, thanks. I was actually going to see if—" The front door opened, and the movement caught my eye. *John.* I needed more time to build up the walls around my heart again, but he wasn't giving me the chance. I looked down and fiddled with something imaginary between my fingers. Ricky turned around to see what had taken my attention away. He and Anna greeted John first. As soon as they finished, I could feel his gaze on me.

"Hi." I forced a smile up at him.

"Hi." His eyes carried on the conversation. He wanted to talk; I didn't want to talk.

"What's that?" Anna said as she squinted out the window at what looked like a car coming up the road. The car was going pretty fast and stirring up a dust cloud in its wake. Some surprised townsfolk hurried to the boardwalk to get out of its way.

"I'll be right back," John said as we all stared at the approaching car out the window.

"Wait!" Anna called out to John. I looked over at Anna and noticed the color had drained from her face.

"What is it, Anna?" I whispered.

"It's Ryan."

The men were silent and unmoving, waiting for more answers to the questions that were no doubt formulating in their minds.

"No, it couldn't be." I looked back outside at the white mustang with a familiar red stripe down the side. *It was Ryan.* "Should we go upstairs?" When Anna didn't respond, Ricky asked if everything was okay. His voice was full of concern and protectiveness on Anna's behalf.

"Um, yeah. That is my ex-boyfriend out there. I'll be right back." She tucked a loose tendril of hair behind her ear and swallowed hard.

"Do you want me to come?" I asked her.

"No, I'll be fine." She stood and went out the door. Ricky was trying to decide what to do, and I could tell John was just waiting to see where he was needed. I stood and went to look out the window. Ricky followed suit. John didn't come stand next me, but I could feel him close by. Anna stood out on the porch with her arms folded. Ryan's voice was a little muffled through the glass, but I was pretty sure he just asked what she was "even" doing here. He looked around the town in disgust.

"What do you want, Ryan?" she asked him.

"I want you back." He started to walk around the front of his car slowly. "These last few weeks have got me thinking, and I realized that I was wrong to end things between us. I know, me, wrong? Hard for me to admit too."

I puffed out some air and rolled my eyes. *Typical Ryan. What a moron.*

"It's over, Ryan." Anna shook her head.

"Are you crazy? Do you really think that someone better is going to come along?" He lifted his arms and looked around. Ricky made a move for the door. I'm sure he planned to bust out of the cafe blazing. I turned to see John put a hand on his shoulder. "Hold on. Just watch her, and she'll let you know when she needs you." I could hear Ricky let out an impatient exhale, and I didn't blame him. I was ready to go give Ryan a piece of my mind too. "You want me to beg, is that it?" Ryan started to walk towards the stairs. Ryan's eyes were wild, too wild. I saw Anna look around and took a step back.

"That's your cue—" John said, but Ricky was already pushing the front door open. John moved up closer to the window next to me with his arms folded. His sleeves were rolled up, revealing his muscled forearms again. I let out a long silent exhale.

"Well!" Ryan smugly stopped in his tracks at the sight of Ricky.

"Get out of here, man," Ricky said.

"Gladly. Come on, Anna. Let's go." Ryan turned to leave but turned back after a few steps to see Anna hadn't moved from her place on the porch. "Oh, I see. You think you've found all you've ever wanted in this farm boy, have you?" Ricky stepped down the stairs slowly. "What are you going to do?" Ryan asked Ricky. "You know what, Anna? You're not worth this trouble. You know what they say, one man's trash—" Ricky did what we all wanted to do from the moment Ryan opened his mouth. His fist connected with Ryan's face.

"I liked Ricky for Anna before, but now I really like Ricky for Anna," I said without looking away from the window.

"Some might say violence isn't the answer," John said quietly beside me.

"But if it's the only way…" I smiled and looked up at him. He smiled back, and I let out a small laugh. I missed John even though he was standing right next to me.

"You'll be hearing from my lawyer!" Ryan cowered back to his car.

"I'll be waiting by my phone and will make sure they know how you trespassed on private property, drove on the wrong side of the road, and harassed a lady. We have cameras all over this place, so let me know where to send the footage." Ricky turned and made his way back up the stairs to Anna.

"Are there cameras here?" I asked John.

"Nope, that was a bluff. A town full of witnesses would suffice if needed, but that guy isn't going to do anything though—I could see it in his eyes." Carol opened the kitchen door holding a fabric wrapped something that could only be pie. She took one look out the window at the retreating car and told us to cover our eyes in a panic. "You missed the fireworks, Aunt Carol."

"You saw it already?" she asked.

"It?" John asked in a teasing tone, obviously referring to the car.

"Don't make me say it."

John smiled, knowing Carol liked to stick to the 1866 script as much as possible. She would not say the very modern word "car" no matter how much John teased. I smiled at him, and he curved half of his lips upward. Our eyes locked until I remembered where he'd be tonight. He caught my mental shift.

"Carol?" I turned her attention to me instead of delivering the pie out to Ricky and Anna. "Can I have that?"

"Well, this one is for Ricky. There will be more out in just a few minutes." She tried to head towards the front door again, but I needed to let Ricky and Anna have this moment. Anna sure didn't need pie right now. I wasn't sure what else I could do.

"Great, then she'll take this one," John said. "Ricky won't mind waiting for the next one. You snooze, you lose, I always say." He reached out a hand for the pie, and Carol reluctantly handed it over. "Thanks, Aunt Carol." John handed the pie to me.

"There's a whole pie in there, dear," Carol said. "Are you sure you can eat a *whole* pie?"

"I'm always up for a challenge. Someone should time me."

"I'll do it," John chimed in.

"Well, okay. I'll get a fork." Carol turned, not knowing how to handle my sudden sarcasm and John's insistence to come to my aid. She did seem at peace with the fact knowing that John and I would be together, though.

"Forks," John corrected.

Carol turned to smile and wink at him.

I handed Ricky and Anna's picnic basket to John. "Will you take this basket to Ricky and tell them to be on their way? They need to be gone before another pie comes out." He gave me a questioning look, and I knew what it meant. *I always did.* "Ryan loved pie."

"Say no more."

Looking out the window, I could see John ask Anna something and her nod in return.

"Here you are." Carol set two forks and two small plates down on the table near the window and retreated into the kitchen. *I can't sit down and eat this pie with John.* Time away from him is what I needed. The more time alone I spend with him, the more time I spend playing with fire. John walked through the door the next second, and my heart skipped a beat. *Why did it have to be him? Why did I have to fall in love with someone who was committed to someone else? It's cruel.*

"Anna's okay. She's more embarrassed that it even happened," John said as he walked towards me.

"Thank you for checking up."

"Mmhmm. Well, shall we?" John pulled out a chair for me to sit, then pulled one out for him. He cut a piece of pie and slid it onto a plate. He held it back, though, when I reached for it. "This one's mine, and this one..." He slid the entire pie, minus one piece, in front of me. "...is yours." He stuck the fork right in the middle and held up his pocket watch. "Your time starts... now!"

"Do I get a free t-shirt or my picture on the wall if I finish this?"

"I'll arrange it. I wouldn't mind a picture of you on the wall." He took a big bite of pie while I blushed. I wasn't fishing for a compliment, but he found a way to give me one anyway. I dug into my first bite. The crust was golden and flaky, and the spiced apple inside was warm and not too sweet. Just the way I liked it. "Good, right?" he asked.

"Mmmhmm. Thank you, by the way."

"For what?"

"Getting Carol to hand over the pie."

"Of course. You're a good friend." *A good friend to him or Anna?* "To Anna." He read my thoughts through my eyes, no doubt, and smiled before taking another bite. "So, are you going to tell me what happened this morning?"

Not sure how to respond, I took a really big bite of pie to give me more time to think of what to say while I chewed. "I received some news that I needed to process on my own. That's all. I'm better now." I forced a smile. He wasn't convinced, but he didn't question further. We ate in silence for a little while. Before I knew it, I had eaten half of the pie. So much for not being hungry. I blame the nerves.

"I'm impressed," John said, leaning back in his chair and folding his arms.

"You should see me on Taco Tuesday."

"Are you implying you want to see me after this is all over?" he asked. I looked in his eyes and mentally reminded myself to breathe. He was trying to read me as he kept his expression emotionless.

"I…I'm still figuring that out." Before I divulged too much, I thanked him for the pie and excused myself.

I hurried up to mine and Anna's room and flopped across my bed. I grabbed my phone out from its hiding place and powered it on. I wanted to try and do some background work on John while I had a few moments to myself. Facebook and Instagram were my go-to social media outlets, but I didn't even know where to start with a name like John and no last name. Hoping to find Ricky through Anna's Facebook friends list, I searched until I found him. Ricky's friend list was hidden though, along with his wall posts and anything else that might've helped me find John. *Nothing. Ugh.* A piece of me was really hoping to find John on social media and learn that Kelsey was just a sister or cousin. *No luck.* I stared at the ceiling until my eyelids got heavy, and I slipped into a deep slumber.

15

"Maggie! Wake up!" A familiar voice sounded in the distant corners of my mind. I didn't want to surrender to the voice, so I buried my head deeper into my pillow. My sheets flew off in the next moment. "Maggie!" Anna said.

"I'm awake! I'm awake!" I yawned and rubbed my eyes. "What is it?"

"Ricky and I just got back, and I wanted to come find you before dinner!" She sat on the edge of her bed, and I scooted up in mine and leaned against the headboard. "Ricky told me that John confided in him a little bit this morning!" Anna excitedly whispered. "John really likes you, Maggie! Like he *really* likes you. Ricky told me not to say anything, but I would expect you to tell me if the roles were reversed!"

"Thanks Anna. I don't think it's true, though. The actor side of him might feel that way, but in real life, the one that counts, I think there's somebody else."

"What do you mean?" Her eyebrows pulled together.

"I found this under the ropes in the wagon this morning. The same wagon John was in before we had it." Anna opened the envelope, read the letter, then looked up at me, confused and waiting for more details. "That letter is why I left this morning. I didn't want either of you to see me cry while I attempted to pull myself together. He's meeting someone tonight." We both let out big slow sighs.

"I'm sorry, Maggie." She handed the envelope back to me. I shrugged my shoulders, forcing myself to feel nothing—nothing but a tightness in my throat. "Does John know you know about the letter?"

"No."

"What are you going to do?" she asked.

"I want to see him and her together for myself before I do anything."

"Are you saying you're going to sneak away from town?"

"That's exactly what I'm going to do. Devin already told me where the employees stay."

"Do you want me to come with you?"

"No, I'll be all right," I said. "I'm not going to interfere. I just want to see what I need to see for closure's sake, then I'll be back."

"It just doesn't make any sense. Why would Ricky tell me about John's feelings for you if it wasn't true? Ricky wouldn't just make it up."

"I believe you. I don't doubt what Ricky said, but maybe John is living more than just a double life, and Ricky doesn't even know."

"Maybe." Anna's mouth shifted to the side as she stared out the window. "I can't believe this is happening. Even a fool would have been able to see the connection between you and John. I really was hoping for the best, and I still am. Let me know if you need anything, okay?"

"Will do."

"I hope she's his sister or something," she said.

"You and me both."

We went downstairs and outside for dinner. Anna ate pork, green beans, and fried potatoes, while I mostly just pushed my food around the plate. We went to the dreaded outhouses after dinner. I creaked open the wooden moon cutout door and looked over at Anna. She didn't look frightened at all. She even stepped off the wooden step like she didn't have a care in the world.

"Anna! What are you doing?!" The black rooster strutted out from behind the outhouses. *This is how it ends.* "Anna! Run!" I yelled as I took a flying leap off the stairs and ran in the direction of the hotel. Looking over my shoulder, I saw her toss the crazy bird a handful of something. The rooster let out a gargling sound and started to peck at whatever Anna had just tossed on the ground. I slowed to a stop and waited for Anna to catch up. I was shocked.

"Ricky told me the secret is to take a few berries, apple slices, or whatever is in that bucket over there to distract the rooster." She pointed to a bucket under a tree near the back door of the hotel. "They fill it each day with random things for that purpose."

"How come nobody told us sooner?"

"I think they liked the entertainment."

"Traitors! All of them!" I shook my head, and we both laughed. We noticed a group gathering to our left out in the field on our walk back to the hotel. We decided to go check things out, but I quickly regretted it as we neared the group. John was building a fire, and people were gathering tree stumps and benches to make a circle of seats around it.

"Do you want to go?" Anna whispered nonchalantly. The sun was setting now, and the clouds had all turned a pretty peachy pink color. I saw the first star start to shine, and it instantly caused a pit to form in my stomach. *The stars.* This is right where we kissed for the first time. The pit in my stomach shifted into a sickening feeling. I needed to find out the truth and quick.

"No, we can stay," I said. Anna and I took our seats, then others quickly filled in around us on both sides. The fire started to rise until I could feel its warmth from where I sat. The sunset started to fade, and the sky began to darken a little bit. Out of my peripheral vision, I could see John and Ricky sit down on the opposite side of the fire from us. Anna smiled and waved, no doubt at Ricky. I couldn't look over at John. My heart ached, and I knew it would only ache more if I looked into his eyes.

"John keeps looking over here," Anna whispered. "I've already smiled awkwardly at him twice."

"Keep up the good work." I smiled at her.

"Maggie!"

I laughed and made the mistake of choosing that moment to glance over at John. My big smile turned into a small one. John and I just stared at one another. I could tell he was not thrilled by this distance between us—literally and mentally. *Just a little longer.* I let out the breath I had been holding. The more I looked at him, the sicker my stomach felt. *I was so in love with you.* My eyes must have given the sadness in me away, because he leaned forward and put his elbows on his knees, then looked down at the ground. I swallowed the emotion rising in my throat. He usually was never the one to look away first—*until now.* I was struggling to know when John was acting and when he wasn't anymore.

"Hello, folks!" Old Tom addressed the large group circled around the fire. "Thanks for joining us for some poetry reading tonight. Who wants to go first?" He didn't really want a volunteer, because he immediately turned and looked at me. I looked down at some field grass near my shoes, blowing in the light breeze. *No, no, no, no, no.* "Maggie!" *Shoot!* "Here you go." I reached out and took the small worn leather book he was offering me. "This is one of my favorites," he said.

I stumbled my way through the poem titled "Blackbird." I assumed it was about a blackbird. I wasn't completely sure, though, because I was too nervous trying to say the words right and make them sound flowy. When I finished reading, I handed the small book back to Old Tom. Nobody clapped or made a sound. I expected at least some snapping of the fingers or something—none sounded. I blushed a little bit. I looked up to meet John's eyes that were already on me. He smiled a reassuring and apologetic smile my way. I gave him a that-was-completely-horrible wide-eyed look. His smile grew a little bit. About three more poems later, John stood up and excused himself. *This was it. It must be almost 8:00 p.m.* I waited until John had rounded the corner of the hotel and disappeared before I excused myself as well.

"Good luck," Anna said. I nodded and took a deep breath. My heart hurt, and my stomach felt queasy, but I still held onto the smallest bit of hope that the letter was just a misunderstanding. I held back behind the corner of the hotel and watched John walk down the dirt road to the livery. A big part of me didn't want to know the truth so that John and I could keep going as if nothing had happened. Another piece of me knew it wasn't fair to my heart to carry on like normal, knowing there was a big wedge keeping us from progressing. I had to find out the truth, and I would know soon enough. A few minutes later, I saw John ride out of town on Shady in the direction of the cornfield. He took off in a trot, and I took off in a speed walk in the same direction, but behind the buildings near the orchard. John headed to what looked to be a pathway through the corn. He cut left and disappeared. I picked up my skirts and started to jog. I went straight into the corn. Slowing down a little bit to keep my bearings, I made my way through the thick tall stalks of corn. I pushed the big green leaves away from my face while trying to hurry. The sky had darkened to the time of evening when everything seemed to be a shade of blue and grey. I realized I wore the perfect camouflage today without knowing it; the emerald green dress matched the corn stalks perfectly. It's as if the universe knew I would need to sneak through a cornfield for the worst of reasons tonight.

The cornfield was huge, so I tried to pick up my pace. I didn't want to miss the moment I needed to see—the greeting. The greeting would tell me all that I needed to know. Treetops started to come into view, letting me know that I was almost there. I quietly walked to the edge of the cornfield with caution, but full of adrenaline. My heartbeat sounded in my ears. The employee cabin was huge and made from large logs. Lanterns illuminated the porch. I scanned the grounds until my eyes found what they were looking for. John was brushing down Shady near the stairs that led to the front door. As if on cue, car lights started to shine down the road, and I backed up in the corn so the light wouldn't give me away. I snuck closer toward the cabin to get a better look. I needed to be sure about whatever I was about to see. Once I was close enough, I peeked out of the corn once more just as a girl with bleached blonde hair stepped out of a sleek SUV. *Please let her be a cousin. Please let her be anything else but a girlfriend...John's girlfriend.* I tried not to go there in my mind. John was on the opposite side of Shady when she closed her car door but immediately walked around to meet her. John's back was toward me. *A quick hug. A quick hug is what cousins do.* I saw her arms wrap around John. *My John. He's not mine. He never was. This cannot be happening.* My throat constricted, and my eyes started to burn, letting me know that tears would soon follow. I watched her reach up, and just as her hands were about to rest on either side of John's face, she looked over in my direction. John turned around. He had no doubt seen me before I could retreat completely into the corn. *Oh no. This was not part of the plan!* I picked up my skirts again and ran as fast as my boots would carry me. A rhythmic pounding of boots sounded behind me. He was closing in. I was sure John couldn't tell in the darkened light who was peeking out from the corn, but he would find out soon enough if I didn't come up with a plan. I knew I wouldn't be able to outrun him. Darting to the right, I crouched down into a ball on the ground and held perfectly still. *Silence.* I would stay here all night if it meant I didn't have to face John right now. Holding my breath, I waited and waited. Footfalls started to sound nearby again, and they headed in my direction and fast. *Thud!* I winced from a new kind of pain in my side before remembering I needed to get away. I stood and tried to run once more, but the pain caused me to stop to take a breath and cry out for a split second. As John was running, his boot had connected with my side. I'm pretty sure he tripped but would be up and going again within seconds.

"Hey!" John yelled from behind me. *Nope.* I tried to run again. Strong familiar arms wrapped around me in the darkening field, and we collided with another "thud" on the ground. John rolled me over quick with a stern, impatient, and tired look on his face until his eyes adjusted. His expression had turned into complete shock. He instantly recoiled back and let go of his grip on my shoulders that had been pinning me down. "Maggie?" he asked in disbelief. I didn't say anything. Now that I had been caught, the emotions had time to catch up to me. Tears welled up in my eyes and threatened to spill out if I dared blink. I swallowed hard and pulled my arms over my eyes to avoid his gaze. "What are you doing here?" he asked in disbelief. I didn't respond again; I couldn't. "Maggie?" he asked in a softer tone. I wish he hadn't taken that tone, it unraveled me, and the tears started to slip down the sides of my face. He gently took hold of my wrists and pulled them away from my eyes. "Maggie," he whispered. I opened my tear-filled eyes and looked right into his.

"I trusted you." I tried to keep my shaky voice as even as possible.

"Come back with me. Come back to the cabin, and I'll explain everything," he said. "Let me fix this."

"I can't. I need to put some distance between you and me right now, and we both know you already have somebody waiting on you."

He shook his head. "No, I don't." He tried to convince me. I couldn't tell the actor from the real man anymore. I reached in my pocket, pulled out the letter, and held it up for him to take.

"I already know the truth," I said. "I just wish I would've found out from you instead." He didn't even look at the piece of paper, because I could see in his eyes that he already knew what it was. I tried to lift myself up but laid back down in pain. John moved off of me quickly and started to ask all sorts of medically related questions. I had no desire to answer any of them right now. The only thing I knew was broken was something he couldn't fix right now—my heart. "I need to go," I said. He let out an exhale in defeat. I powered through the sharp pain in my side and sat up. John quickly helped me rise. I turned to go, but he quickly, but softly, grabbed my wrist.

"Maggie," he said. There was more emotion in his deep raspy voice now. "Please don't go." I made the slightest tug on my wrist, and he released it.

"I trusted you, John." He looked pained by my departing words, and I felt pain saying them. I turned and disappeared into the corn. It was over. It was all over between us. The tears flowed freely now, and I didn't even try to brush them away. That numbing that I was telling myself that I'd need to try to hone in on today had taken over me completely, and I didn't need to try anymore. I covered my mouth to keep from crying out as I walked in the darkness through the cornfield. The pain in my side was almost unbearable and caused me to slow way down.

The time it took to get out of the field seemed to have tripled the amount that it took to come into it. I started to question if I was headed in the right direction until I heard distant laughter and the old piano playing at the saloon. A few minutes later, I emerged from the corn and was walking through the orchard in the direction of the hotel. That perfect apple I reached for the other day came to mind—the parallels between it and John were hauntingly similar.

I tried to stay in the shadows and make it inside the hotel unseen. I quietly opened the door and crept upstairs to my room. Anna hadn't come up yet, which I was grateful for. The tears fell again in full force as I sat alone on my bed in the dark. The pain in my side throbbed, but my heart hurt more than my side ever could. I didn't even bother getting ready for bed. I curled under my covers in my dress and cried until it started to lull me to sleep. Right before my eyes closed for the night, I heard small tapping sounds on the window. I was too tired and broken to get out of bed to see if the sound was just my imagination. With that thought, sleep overtook me, and tonight I welcomed it taking away the pain.

16

The sunlight lit the way out from the depths of my dreams. I was in a peaceful state of mind and let my body and mind wake up slowly. The sun warmed my eyelids and cheeks. *Click.* My mind started to recall where I was, and that click must've been Anna coming or going from our room. I heard a floorboard squeak—*she was coming.*

"Hi, Anna," I said groggily.

"Shoot. Did I wake you up?"

"No, I was already awake. Did I sleep through the rooster?"

"You did. I brought you some breakfast. I wasn't sure if you'd be up before they put it all away."

"Thank you." I opened my eyes and tried to roll over to face her, but a sharp pain in my side stopped me cold. Anna set the plate down quickly and rushed to my bedside.

"Maggie, what's wrong?"

"My side. It hurts." I tried to catch my breath.

"What can I do? What happened?" Last night's events slowly started to seep into my mind, and a sick feeling grew in my stomach with each memory. I wanted to be sleeping again instead of dealing with this reality.

"I think I just need some pain medicine or just anything for the pain. Can you ask Ricky?"

"He's out with the cattle and doesn't have service, but I'll go find someone!"

"Anna, wait! Not John!" I paused, trying to think of anyone I could possibly trust in this town. "Find Devin."

"Okay." Anna's tone turned from worry to sorrow. She didn't need to know the details of last night to know how it went. She closed the door, and I heard her footsteps sound down the hall. I painfully adjusted myself in bed until I was on my back.

A soft knock sounded at the door a little while later. "Hey, Maggie. It's Devin. Can I come in?" Devin said.

"Yeah."

He opened the door and let Anna through first, then came over and sat near the foot of my bed. "Hey, Maggie," he said softly. "What hurts?"

"My side." I hovered a finger over where John's boot had surely left a mark. Devin asked me questions about dizziness, my breathing, the pain, memory loss, and a few other things. "You sound like John." I let out an exasperated sigh before he could ask another question. "Devin, I'm fine. I just need whatever you're holding in your right hand." He smiled and opened his right hand that revealed one large white pill.

"I have a feeling you're always this stubborn." He handed the pill to me, and Anna laughed a little bit before handing me a cup of water. "I'm sorry for all the questions. I was given specific instruction before coming up here, and I knew I'd need to report back." Once the pill was down, the questions started again. "So, how did this happen?"

"I went to see for myself if John was meeting somebody last night, and he was. He ran; I hid; he tripped, and that's all."

"Maggie! He wears steel toe boots!"

"You're telling me."

"What did John say?" he asked.

"About what?"

"About why she came here."

"I'm not sure."

"He didn't tell you?" I saw a flash of frustration pass through his eyes before he shook his head slightly. "What about—" he started, but I closed my eyes and faked a few snores. I didn't want to give too much of myself away. This was my humiliating and horribly painful story that I now had to bear. Despite what happened, I had enough respect for all involved parties to not give all details away. "Okay, okay, I can take a hint—even the subtlest of hints," he said. I heard him smile through his words.

I smiled with my eyes closed. "Thank you, Devin. Thank you for everything."

"Of course, Maggie. Let me know if you need anything else." As soon as Devin closed the door, Anna sat down on my bed and was ready for details about last night. I still didn't want to tell anyone every detail, so I held back most of the story.

"I got there, and they were in each other's arms."

"Was it like a quick relative hug?"

"I don't think it was."

"So, then you ran, and he tripped over you, and that's it? How did it end?"

"I don't know. It just ended. I think the relationship, if that's even what it was called, is beyond repair. I saw him with her, and I can't erase that from my mind. I was too emotional and hurt to stand there and possibly hear him say that there was somebody else—just like the first time two years ago. I want...wanted him so much that I didn't want to hear him say that he wouldn't be choosing me. It feels like history is repeating itself, except this time, it's like 100 times worse because of the connection I thought we had. Normally, when it's too good to be true, it *is* too good to be true. This week with John was perfect." I shook my head in disbelief.

"I was hoping for a different outcome. I'm really sorry, Maggie. I trust your judgment, but I can't help but feel like there's more to the story—like there's still some important words on his end left unsaid."

"Maybe it's better that way."

"Maybe. I'll let you rest. Text me if you need anything."

"What if you don't have service?"

"Yell really loud." She smiled, then left the room. My mind replayed last night's conversation with John over and over. The ending didn't change, no matter how many times I replayed it. Tears started to silently fall out of the corners of my eyes. I really thought it was all real, and that I could finally trust someone again. I knew better than to fall for an actor.

A little while later, the medicine had taken away the majority of the pain. I eased out of bed slowly and changed out of my green dress. When I pulled a navy-blue dress out of the trunk, the small vial full of gold rolled out across the floor. I picked it up and stared at the gold flakes swirling around the gold heart in the water. I let out a deep breath and a few more tears. *This thing with John, or the lack thereof now, was going to take some time to heal—a long time. I've never had a connection this strong with anyone until John—the actor side of him.* I slid on the dress and decided to go soak in a tub. I still didn't have an appetite, but I drank the rest of the water. Just as I set the cup down, Anna came back through the door.

"What's up?" I asked as she closed the door behind her.

"John and Devin are having a discussion just outside the front doors on the porch, making it so I can't leave. It would be extremely awkward to interrupt. I waited on the stairs for a bit for them to finish because I didn't think they would be long. I was wrong. They're still at it, so I've decided to wait up here instead." Both of us walked over to the window, but couldn't see them down below because of the balcony. She opened the window quietly, but we could only hear their voices—not any words.

"Did you hear what they were saying while you were downstairs?"

"No, but they both didn't look too happy." Movement on the road caught my eye; it was John walking away. He was wearing the same clothes he wore yesterday.

"He's wearing the same clothes he had on yesterday. You don't think he..."

"...stayed out there all night?" Anna said. "I'm thinking that's exactly what he did."

"I don't know why he's trying so hard. He must really want five stars on a comment card or something." It pained me to make light of the situation, but I felt like I had to so no one would know just how hard I had fallen for John and how much I was hurting.

"I don't think it has anything to do with a comment card, Maggie."

"He got caught, though. I saw them together, so I don't know why he wouldn't just admit to it and give up."

"I know, but something is off. John doesn't seem like that kind of guy."

"Neither did the last one."

"True, but there were signs with the last one—like avoiding you during business hours. John is different. There haven't been any red flags."

"Until the letter."

"I don't know," Anna said deep in thought. "Well, it would seem that the coast is clear now."

"I'm going to go soak in a tub, so we can walk down together. Will you do my hair first, though?"

Anna braided my hair into a loose braid, then I draped it over my shoulder before leaving our room and descended the hotel stairs. When we stepped out onto the dirt road, a horse whinny sounded off to our right in the pasture. My heart skipped a beat at the thought of seeing Shady—as if Shady was connected to John and me somehow. He knew some of our secrets. The horse in the pasture wasn't Shady, though. It was a brown and white paint horse. There was something familiar about that particular horse, and I couldn't put a finger on it. The wheels started to turn in my mind. *The same one from the heist the other night!* Anna and I parted ways on the dirt road. I opened the bathhouse door and greeted Vicky. When she asked what song I wanted today, I told her to surprise me. I slid down into the tub and let the warm water soothe my aches. I closed my eyes and started to think about John and what he could possibly say to make this situation better. I was coming up short. An old love song played through the speaker, then another love song after that...*and another*. I tuned them all out because they didn't apply to me anymore. The thought of turning John in for the reward money crossed my mind. *He's the livery owner, so he has free rein to use any horse he wants. The horse he rode is in the pasture now. He wore a jacket to the saloon, not during the heist, but it was in the loft at the livery a few minutes later. There could be more evidence up in the loft too. The scar.* I remembered when it was normal to be close enough to John to see the scar up close, to look into his blue eyes, to run my fingers through his hair, and to kiss him. I swallowed hard and shut my eyes. *I can do this.* I only have to hold it together for two more days. I decided to treat the rest of my stay here as a challenge. *If I can prove that John was one of the outlaws, then I'd make back some of the money I spent on this trip!* I dried off, got dressed, and thanked Vicky on my way out of the bathhouse. I crossed the street to the sheriff's office and slid through the swinging doors.

"What can I do for you?" said a man sitting at a large wooden desk. He wore a white long-sleeved top with a brown vest over it and matching brown pants. He stood to shake my hand when I walked across the wooden floorboards towards him.

"I need to talk to the sheriff. I think I know who robbed the bank Tuesday night."

"I'm the sheriff of this town," he said. "Who do you suspect it was?"

"The livery owner."

"John Hudson?" he asked in disbelief.

"Yep," I answered confidently.

"Let's hear the evidence." He leaned back in his chair.

"His face is on a wanted poster in the cabin at the end of the road. The outlaw who carried the money rode a brown and white paint horse, and that same horse is out in the pasture as we speak. A livery owner would have access to any horse. I believe there is a satchel full of money in the livery right now, and possibly the bandana the outlaw used that night too."

"Where in the livery do you think these things are?"

"The loft."

"Why the loft?"

"I...I saw the livery owner up in the loft after the heist."

"What were you doing in the livery late at night?" he asked. This conversation had suddenly taken a turn I was not prepared for. I blushed. The sheriff had a smirk on his face, and it made me think he knew more about the situation than he was letting on. He clearly enjoyed this part of the job.

"I plead the fifth."

He leaned forward on his desk and interlaced his fingers. "Fair enough. If the stolen money is up in the loft, then John will be locked up, and you'll be rewarded five hundred dollars. You can take a seat, and I'll go take a look." I nodded and sat down. Once the sheriff had left, my mind started to race. *Locked up?* That wasn't part of the plan. I thought I was just supposed to prove that John was the outlaw, and I'd win the money. I sighed deeply, and my pulse started to race. A part of me didn't want the sheriff to find anything, because he'd be bringing John back here if I was right. I leaned my head back against the wall. I still didn't feel ready to face John yet. The doors swung open just as I had mentally decided to leave and forget about the money. My stomach dropped, and I quickly looked down at my navy-blue dress and brushed off some imaginary dust until they passed me by. I watched John's boots walk across the floorboards, then into one of the jail cells. He was wearing grey pants now, which meant he must've just changed while I was at the bathhouse.

"Well, Maggie, it looks like you just got five hundred dollars richer," the sheriff said as he locked up John's cell. "I'll be right back with your reward." The sheriff disappeared into the back. Out of my peripheral vision, I could tell John was sitting on the chair inside the cell. I looked up at the same time he looked up at me; his eyes bored into mine as he leaned over in the chair with his elbows on his knees. He looked stressed and tired as if he hadn't slept all night. "When are we going to talk, Maggie?" His low and slightly pained voice broke the silence as I broke the eye contact. Looking down at my hands in my lap, I tried to think of what to say back. Hearing his voice and seeing him stirred up dust that I had been trying to settle all morning. I reminded myself to keep breathing. "Maggie, I—" He cut off as the sheriff walked back into the room. I stood and walked over to his desk.

"Here you are." The sheriff pushed the bag of money across his desk towards me. "Good work. One less outlaw out on the streets will help me sleep easier tonight," he said. I had nothing to say. I forced a smile and picked up the bag of money. "Is there anything else I can do for you today?"

"No, that was it. Thank you," I said. I raised the bag slightly before heading out the door. As soon as I had made it outside, I inhaled deep and exhaled slow. I could breathe again. Once I made it back to the hotel, I planned to be a recluse for the rest of the afternoon in my bedroom. Just as I reached out for the doorknob to the hotel, a woman's voice called out to me.

"Maggie, right?" a woman asked. My determination to get back to my room kept me from noticing the older couple packing things into a bag near the front door.

"That's me. I don't think we've met yet."

"We haven't, but we've heard about you," the woman said. *Oh, man.* "We're the Hansens. We were just on our way to go pan for some gold! Would you like to come with us?"

"Thank you for the offer, but I already have plans for the afternoon."

"Well, we go every day, so feel free to join us tomorrow if you'd like! Mr. Hansen believes there is still lots of gold in these mountains—something about a "lost Rhoades Mine," she said. Her eyebrows rose before she winked at me. "We come here each year in search of it. We only live about an hour away, but he is convinced that this mountain is filled with gold."

"Now, let's not tell all of our secrets before we know she can be trusted," the man next to her said. Mrs. Hansen and I smiled at each other.

"Well, I have to be on my way, but I hope both of you strike gold!" I said.

"Eureka!" Mr. Hansen shot up a fist to the air. I smiled and raised my fist slowly into the air to support him in his excitement.

I trekked up the stairs thinking I'd be alone, but Anna was in our room. She looked up from her phone when I walked through the door.

"I put him in jail."

"Like the dog house cliché? Like he's in trouble?" she asked.

"No, like I literally put him in the jail," I said. Anna's eyes went wide with horror. "He was the outlaw from the robbery Tuesday night, and I proved it to the sheriff. So, he locked John up in a cell and gave me five hundred bucks." I forced a smile and held up the bag of money.

"Maggie!" Anna looked shocked with her hand over her opened mouth.

"What?"

"You're in love with the man! You can't put him in jail."

"I'm in love…was…in love with the *actor*." I held up some of the money. "Inflight movie is on me on Saturday!"

"Maggie," she sighed. *This was it. This was the moment I had no choice but to listen to Anna's wisdom, and possibly make me feel even more guilty for putting the man who broke my heart in jail.* "You're hurt, and you have every right to be, but you don't have to hide it from me. We're best friends, remember? This isn't about inflight movies. This isn't even about this trip. This is about your heart, Maggie. That's not something to be taken lightly. You may have signed a form saying you'd try to stick to an 1866 mindset—"

"Technically, you signed mine."

"Well, good, because now you don't have an excuse not to figure things out with John. You can get to the bottom of everything on a modern level with no contracts holding you back. We may not know his last name, but the feelings are real. You opened your heart up for John, and John alone, after spending two years kicking everyone else to the curb. There's a reason for that." She gave me an I-dare-you-to-tell-me-I'm-wrong look. She was right. "I don't think it was a coincidence we ended up here in Summit Springs. An actor can't fake some of the things you've told me about you and John—not even the best of actors. You need to look him in the eyes, because that's how the two of you do things, and you need to let him try to make this better. You need to know the truth before you make up your mind. You have to face this and tell him how you feel, or he will be the "what if" guy for the rest of your life. John would make a tormenting "what if" guy too. Have you seen his biceps?"

"Anna!" I blushed instantly.

"So, you have seen them…" Anna smiled. I laughed. My mind was still processing everything. "I think if you don't see this through, it will haunt you more than that sweater you didn't buy."

"Ugh! Anna! Why did you bring that up?" I laughed because I knew the exact sweater she was referring to. It still made me sick, knowing I didn't buy it before it sold out; I waited too long. "It took me five years to forget it the last time you brought it up!"

She laughed. "Here," Anna said, as she pulled out a picture from her trunk. She handed it to me, and I stared at the younger version of myself. The picture was taken on the beach a month before I had met the last guy. I was so happy. Tears started to form in my eyes. *I just wish I could be this happy again and go back to before I was hurt.* I missed the girl I used to be—one that laughed more and trusted easily. I wished that I had met John before my heart had been put through so much. I closed my eyes and took a deep breath. "I didn't know why I felt the need to pack and smuggle this picture of you into Summit Springs, but now I do. I wanted to remind you of yourself before everything went down two years ago. This girl was happy." Anna pointed to the picture in my hands. "...and this week she came back. Whether it works out with you and John—I don't know, but I think this week has been more than worth it just to know that the girl you used to be is still inside. John was able to pull her out, and no matter what happens, I will always be grateful to him for that. It's time to figure out what really went on last night. You owe it to John and to yourself. I don't know how you're going to make this right and get him out of jail, but I have a feeling you'll think of something. Off you go now. Quick quick!"

"An-na!"

"Go, Maggie. You're not allowed to come back up here until you've made up with John, or until you've got the closure you need to move on. Good luck."

I let out a defeated puff of air. "You just want me to go, so you can get back to texting Ricky, huh?"

"Don't bring me into this." She smiled.

"Byyyye, Anna."

I found myself out on the dirt road again, unmoving and staring in the direction of the sheriff's office. I took a deep breath and let my feet carry me there. Taking one more deep breath, I pushed my way through the swinging doors. Before John looked over at me, I glanced at him first. He was leaning back in the chair with his feet propped up against the jail cell door. He had his arms folded, and his black long sleeves rolled up his forearms like always. My heart skipped a beat, and I forced myself to take another breath. The sheriff and John were talking about something, but as soon as they saw me step inside, the conversation ceased. I kept my focus on the sheriff even though I could feel John's eyes on me. My footsteps on the wooden floor were the only sound to be heard, besides my heartbeat pounding through my ears. I walked over to the sheriff's desk and set the money down.

"His bail," I said quietly.

The sheriff just stared at me, clearly at a loss for words. I turned around with my eyes cast down and quickly left the building. The air was too thick to breathe in there, and the elephant in the room was too large for the four of us. I needed to get away for a while. The emotion started to constrict my throat, and the tears started to well up again. Anna was right. This town and everyone in it appeared to be acting—but it was real. All of it was real, especially my feelings towards John. I rubbed my forehead. *I need to be alone, so I can think clearer.* I walked down the road, through the livery, and out to the pasture. Shady was grazing with the other horses when I whistled three short whistles to call him over. He lifted his head at the sound and started walking in my direction. It was a strangely intimate thing to know the secret to John's horse and to call him over to ride him without John this time. *If you ever want to outrun something, this is the horse to do it on.* Hearing John's voice in my mind wasn't nearly as undoing as the real thing, and it's all I could handle right now until I sorted out my thoughts. The plan was to outrun all these emotions and clear my mind enough to think straight. I asked a guy who was brushing down a horse near the livery if he could saddle up Shady for me. He agreed and did it quickly—which I was grateful for. John coming to the livery would foil my plan, so I had to hurry. The man moved a stool near Shady, so I could climb up in the saddle.

Once there, it hit me what exactly I was doing. *I am riding a horse again—on my own*. I took a deep breath, thanked the man, gave Shady a quick rub on the neck, and then let Shady know I was ready to go by clicking my tongue three times. I started trotting in the direction of the duck pond, then cut right into the fields and trees behind the pasture. I slid the small strip of cloth out of my hair that had been holding my braid in. I deserved to feel free from everything that had no right to hold me back—past fears and current fears. I needed to figure out what I really wanted. To do that, I needed to outrun the insecurities that I'd been holding onto for so long. I knew how to ride a horse once, and I could do it again. *This is my story, and I get to choose how it ends.*

17

Galloping was a lot smoother than trotting, and a lot faster. Before I got thrown from the horse long ago, I remembered that I used to crave the speed. Riding Shady now helped me remember that I still did. I felt like I was the heroine on the cover of a romance novel. My hair was blowing wild in the wind, and it was freeing. My heart raced, and I couldn't hear anything besides the wind in my ears. I felt happy. I smiled but quickly closed my mouth, remembering a joke my mom told me about bugs in teeth and being able to tell a happy motorcyclist. I reined in Shady to a stop, then loosened the reins to let him graze.

My mind was still buzzing from the adrenaline. I took a deep breath in and let it out slow, taking in my surroundings. This small valley looked familiar. I noticed a patch of dried dirt, and that's when it clicked—*this is where John and I stood in the rain together after my song performance.* I smiled, but my heart ached at the memory, and my stomach felt queasy thinking back to how off-key I was. When my pulse had slowed, my thoughts started to align. John didn't care that I sang off-key; he wanted me anyway. Well, at least a part of him did. I'd be crazy to downplay the mental connection he and I had. I couldn't just act like nothing happened between him and me this week. Too much had happened to just leave on Saturday and never look back. *I need to hear him out.* I took a deep breath. I couldn't think of a way that he could make everything better without twisting the truth, but I hoped he would find a way if there was one. A piece of me was grateful that I had been hurt two years ago to the extent I had, or else there was a chance that I would've never met John. A pit formed in my stomach at that thought—*no John.* I closed my eyes, and the next breath I took in was a shaky one. *What do I really want?* A light breeze blew through the valley, and Shady stood up tall from grazing and held completely still. It caused my eyes to open. His ears shifted in all directions before freezing in the direction of the river. The wind carried the sound of a woman's scream over the hills. Without another thought, I clicked my tongue, and we took off in a gallop as if he understood the urgency.

A few minutes later, Shady rounded a wooded area, and in the clearing up ahead, I saw someone. The closer we got, the more details I could make out. It was Mrs. Hansen. She was running in the direction of the town until she saw me. She waved her arms over her head to make sure she got my attention. Shady and I closed the distance. Once we were close enough, I could tell Mrs. Hansen was out of breath, scared, and looking more pale than a person should. The look on her face was that of terror.

"What's wrong?" I asked.

"It's Mr. Hansen! He went off the trail." She gasped for breath. "Rattlesnake!"

"Where is he now?"

She pointed back the way she had come near a small canyon. "The tree with the white bark."

I squinted until I saw it. "I'll go find him!"

"Thank you, Maggie." She said as tears started to fall down her cheeks. The sight of her made my eyes sting, but I knew I had to hold it together and keep calm for her sake.

"Do you want to ride back to town instead?" I asked.

She shook her head, then turned and started to run again towards town. I sent Shady into motion as fast as he could fly until we reached the tree Mrs. Hansen had pointed to. I swung my leg around and slid off Shady, then tied him up to the small tree with the white bark. I started to jog in the direction that I hoped led to the river, climbing over a few boulders and fallen logs as I went. With each stride and climb, I could feel the pain medicine wearing off. My side started to ache, but I kept going even though the pain made it harder to breathe. The sound of rushing water sounded in my ears before I could see it with my eyes. Rounding a bend, Mr. Hansen came into view. My EMT training kicked in as I ran as fast as possible while trying to recall what needed to be done for a rattlesnake bite. He was lying on the ground and not moving. As I neared, I stopped short. There was a snake coiled near Mr. Hansen's head.

I took a few moments to process the situation and make a plan. *I need a stick.* Searching the area as quickly as I could, I came across a long stick that should work. I moved slowly and tried to get as close as possible to Mr. Hansen and the snake. I pulled out my phone to snap a picture of the snake in hopes that it would help the doctors know which anti-venom to use, then inched closer with the stick raised outward and toward the snake. My hands started to shake no matter how hard I tried to keep them steady. I held the stick down low, and the snake started to make a loud, rattling sound similar to the sound of a sprinkler. Knowing I had to act quickly, I held on tight to my end of the stick and put the other end into the middle of the coil. I lifted with all my strength, as the snake started to strike in my direction. Luckily, the stick was long enough to keep me safe. My quick flinging motion made the rattlesnake go airborne and away from Mr. Hansen. The snake sailed through the air, clearing the riverbank and into the water below. I watched the snake swim downstream for a few seconds, then slither out on the opposite side of the river. I ran back to Mr. Hansen.

"Mr. Hansen, it's Maggie! I'm an EMT. Can I help you?" Nothing but a mumble sounded from his mouth—*I'll take that as a "yes."* His eyes were glazed over, and he looked exhausted. I undid the buttons on his shirt and loosened the belt around his waist just in case he started to swell. There was a small dark stain on his lower leg. I carefully rolled up his pant leg to take a look at the bite. *Bites. He was bitten twice.* Blood from the bites dripped down his leg, and I hoped some of the venom would come out with it. I knew doctors could sometimes test the venom in the blood to check for anti-venom compatibility too. I slid one of his boots off, so I could get his sock to tie a restrictive band. I tied the knot a few inches above the bites to hopefully slow the spread of the venom.

"Wa…." Mr. Hansen's slurred speech trailed off.

"What is it?"

"Water," he whispered.

"Soon," I said, knowing I couldn't give him any while he was going in and out of consciousness—most likely due to shock. "Are you having any trouble breathing?"

"No, I'm just tired, and my eyes can't seem to focus. My leg feels like it's on fire." His eyes closed in the next moment. I pressed down on his toenail to see how quickly it refilled with blood to check circulation. *Normal.* I found his pulse when movement caught my eye. *John.* Seeing him made me sigh in relief. Relief that someone had come, and relief that it was him. He ran over to us, closing the distance quickly. I could tell there was panic in his eyes. I looked up at him, and we stared at one another for a brief moment. I missed those eyes. I remembered how things were between us, and it caused me to look away and back to Mr. Hansen.

"He was bitten twice," I told John. He knelt next to me to scan over Mr. Hansen, and then looked back at me. He took a gentle but urgent hold on both of my shoulders. The look in his eyes was similar to the look he gave me with the bear when he was trying to convince me to ride Shady. There was more fear this time, though.

"What about you?" he asked as he searched my eyes.

"What do you mean?"

"Were you bitten?"

"No." I shook my head, slightly confused. John dropped his head down and took a deep breath before meeting my eyes again. I could see there was extra moisture in them. *He thought it was me who had been bitten.* "Didn't Mrs. Hansen say what happened?" I asked.

Before he responded, he released his hold on my shoulders. He began doing a quick but thorough assessment of Mr. Hansen. "She only said the words 'rattlesnake' and 'river' before she went into shock. Bill is taking her to the hospital to be checked and monitored. Do you know where the snake is now?"

"In the river." He briefly glanced over at me, then turned back to Mr. Hansen—never stopping his assessment. I saw the confusion in his features. "I flung it into the river."

"You flung it?" He was surprised. "With what?"

"That stick." He looked at the stick on the ground next to us, then to the river. "It got out on the other side of the river downstream a bit. I took a picture of the snake too. I can send it to you if you want."

"Yeah, that'd be great." He looked over at me with a shocked expression on his face mixed with pride, just like when had I shot all the bottles. I didn't know how to handle the look he was giving me, so I kept talking.

"He said he felt tired, that his eyes couldn't focus, and that his leg felt like it was on fire." John was silent, but I could tell he was listening to my words as he checked Mr. Hansen's ribs. "I let the wound bleed just in case the doctor's wanted to—"

"Test it for anti-venom compatibility."

"Yeah," I said, surprised. A few moments passed, and I just watched John in awe. He was already almost done with the assessment, and he didn't miss a thing. He got to the restrictive band I had tied and put a finger underneath it. "It's a restrictive band to slow spreading of the venom."

He nodded once as if he knew what I was going to say before I said it. "It looks great, Maggie." John took a deep breath. "You promised me you wouldn't go out on your own again," he said, still focused on Mr. Hansen.

"I wasn't alone; I was with Shady."

He looked over at me out of the tops of his eyes, tilting one side of his head down slightly. He wasn't thrilled by my loophole. "I'm adding a clause to our agreement," he said, as he slid off Mr. Hansen's other boot and checked for a pulse. "Animals don't count."

"Noted." My lips curved upward into a small smile. I felt like I had been caught passing notes in class. "You thought it was me. You thought I was the one who was bit, didn't you?"

"Of course, I thought it was you." He paused. "You're my person." He didn't look up at me.

"Your person?"

"You're the person I think about when I'm not with you. You're the person I care about more than anyone else. You're the one…" Emotion got caught in his throat, and I instantly found it in mine as well. He paused for a brief second to look me in the eyes. "You're my only person." I couldn't breathe or respond in any way. The look in his eyes held no sarcasm. He wanted me to know he meant every word. He glanced behind me, and I turned to see a group of men running around the bend.

"He's ready to go. Backseat on the driver's side," John told them as they neared. The group of men lifted Mr. Hansen with ease and hustled down the trail. Mr. Hansen's boots had been left behind. I bent over and picked them up, but winced when I stood up straight. John held out his hand to take them from me.

"Thank you," I said.

"When we get to the hospital, will you let me have an x-ray done on your ribs?"

"John, I'm fine."

"Please." I exhaled slow and gave him a look that let him know he was overreacting. "I'm not overreacting," he said.

I smiled. "An x-ray will be fine."

"Thank you." We turned and headed down the side canyon. John held out his hand for me to climb over logs and to help me down if the incline was too steep. Once we had made it down to the valley, I noticed a big black truck parked next to Shady.

"Yours?" I asked.

"Yep. Here you go." John pulled some keys out from his pocket. I looked down at them in his hands; he sensed my hesitation. "I need you to drive to the hospital. He's in shock, and I need to monitor him. He should be okay as long as we hurry. I'll help you get there."

I took as deep of a breath as the pain in my side would allow. "Okay."

The men had already buckled Mr. Hansen in the backseat. John was handing Shady's reins over to one of the men, as I opened the driver's door to climb in. I turned the key, and the engine roared like a monster truck. *Oh dear.* I had never driven anything this big before; I felt like I was in a tank. I adjusted the seat and mirrors quickly as John slid into the middle of the backseat next to Mr. Hansen, who had regained consciousness.

"We're ready back here when you're ready. Straight ahead and to the left."

I shifted the truck into drive, and it lurched forward. "Sorry!"

"You're just fine." We neared the dirt road into town, and John started asking Mr. Hansen some medical questions. It seemed that everyone in town had been warned we'd be coming through because they were out of the road and watching us pass by from the boardwalk. I picked up the pace as soon as we made it to the cornfield. I passed the cabin we checked in at—*that felt like eons ago.* "Turn right, then take another right at the stop sign," John said as soon as the tires connected with the pavement. The whites of my knuckles were visible because I was holding the steering wheel so tightly. "Drive as fast as you feel comfortable, and don't stop until you reach the freeway." I pressed a little harder on the gas, the truck accelerated, and it felt like an airplane was taking off. We were whizzing by fields, hills, and trees when John's voice broke the silence. "Yes, I'll hold." We made eye contact through the rearview mirror. "Hi, this is Dr. Christensen from ER. I'm headed your way ETA 15 minutes with a rattlesnake bite. Are there any ambulances available? Okay. Would you be able to transfer me up to Dr. Brown, please? Thank you."

He's a doctor. The gears in my mind started to spin. Once John finished talking with Dr. Brown, we drove in silence for a few minutes. "Nothing would've changed between us," I said softly and looked in the rearview mirror to briefly meet his eyes. I wanted to make sure he knew I was referring to the occupation conversation we had while panning for gold. *He knew.* "I get why you didn't want to say anything, though, but for the record, I'm not that kind of girl." I paused for a few moments. "You owe me like 50 dresses, by the way, *Dr. Christensen.*" I met his eyes once more with a glint in mine.

"Send me an address." He smiled with his eyes. I turned my focus back to the road.

"How is he?"

"He's hanging in there. He lost consciousness again when we passed the cabin, but his breathing is normal, and his heart rate hasn't climbed much more. We're almost there. Stay in the middle lane and go straight through. The road will curve left, then take your first right on Round Valley Drive."

"If the doctor thing doesn't work out, I think a GPS company would hire you in a heartbeat to record their voice navigation instructions."

"Because you like the sound of my voice?"

"I think you have a good sense of direction." I smiled with my eyes through the rearview mirror one last time before pulling up to the hospital's emergency room entrance around back.

"Your destination is up on the right," John said a little robotically. I smiled as I put the truck in park.

"I'll be right back," he said, as he jumped out of the truck and ran through the sliding doors into the hospital. I turned around and checked on Mr. Hansen. He was starting to gain consciousness again.

"Hi, Mr. Hansen. We're at the hospital now, and they're going to take care of you."

"Where's my wife?"

"She should already be here, but I'll make sure John finds her and lets you know for sure." About a minute later, John and another guy dressed in grey scrubs were there with a gurney. They had moved Mr. Hansen on it and were just finishing up with the adjustments when another man in scrubs came outside to help wheel him in. Once the two other men had Mr. Hansen inside, John came over to the driver's door and helped me down. I handed him the keys.

"I'll hand these off to the valet. You did a great job driving," he said.

"You gave great directions."

"So I've been told." We smiled at each other, then started to walk to the sliding doors.

"And your voice was pleasant," I added.

"Pleasant?" he asked. I sensed that he was hoping for a bigger compliment, and it made me laugh a little bit.

"What's your number?" I asked as I pulled out my phone and held my fingers at the ready.

"Are those the lines you use on the other guys?"

"Only you," I said as I smiled.

He smiled back and seemed satisfied. "8...0...1..." I typed his number into my phone and saved it, not knowing if I'd be using it past Saturday. It all depended on how our story unfolded during the next couple of days, but I still held onto a small glimmer of hope. He did say I was his *only* person today, and there was nothing but truth in his eyes when he said it. "I'll be down in about an hour. Are you going to be okay?" he asked once we had made it into the waiting room.

"Yep." I turned to find a seat but remembered I was supposed to relay a message. "John!" He turned back towards me, and it took me a second to remember what I was going to say. He looked really handsome in fluorescent lighting—all lighting really.

"Um…I…Oh! Mr. Hansen wanted to know where his wife was. He was worried about her."

"That feeling is something he and I have had in common today." He winked at me. "I'll be sure to tell him. Thanks, Maggie." I smiled at him right before he disappeared behind two large doors. I found a seat near the fish tank. The people who were already in the waiting room stopped what they were doing to look over at me. They all had confused looks on their faces, and I wasn't sure why. I smoothed my hair down that was surprisingly not all over the place, then ran my hands down my thighs to smooth out my…*dress*. I looked very out of place—about 150 years out of place. I avoided their stares and looked down at my phone to send John the picture of the rattlesnake. I got nervous right before I hit send. By the time I had texted John, everyone seemed to have gotten back to what they were doing before I had walked in.

"Hi, are you Maggie?" an older woman in dark purple scrubs asked as she approached me.

"I am."

"Dr. Christensen wanted me to bring you these." She handed me a cup of ice water and one large white pill.

"Thank you so much."

"Let us know if you need anything else." She smiled.

I thanked her once more before she turned and disappeared through the large doors. I leaned my head back and closed my eyes for a little while until the medicine kicked in.

18

A little over an hour later, John came walking through the large doors. During that time, the waiting room had filled up almost completely. John weaved his way through the people standing in line waiting to be checked in. I took in the sight of him before we made eye contact. His dark wavy hair was tousled a bit, and his black button-up shirt still had the sleeves rolled up exposing his muscled forearms that always seemed to hold my attention a little too long. That's as far as I got before his blue eyes found mine. He smiled before taking a seat next to me.

"Hey," he said as he sighed, "how are you doing?"

"I'm good. Thank you for the pill."

"Has it kicked in yet?"

"Yeah. How are the Hansens?"

"Stable. Both of them. Julie was treated for shock. She is back to normal and sitting right next to Mark as we speak—right where she belongs." He looked over at me and his eyes told me that last bit wasn't just about the Hansens. I wanted to believe him. "We got him the anti-venom just in time. The picture you took shaved off waiting time that could have been critical. You're trained in something medical, aren't you?"

"EMT."

He nodded his head. "You did a great job, Maggie."

"Thank you. You did too." We looked into each other's eyes. There was still so much left unsaid. I was ready for him to make everything better, so we could get back to how it used to be between us. His eyes seemed to tell me that he wanted the same thing. A nurse searched the crowd and quickly made her way over to us.

"Dr. Christensen, someone just came in and said there's a woman outside who is in labor. All of the rooms are filled over in Labor and Delivery and we don't have any open in ER either. All of the doctors are with code blue patients. Are you able to go?"

"Yeah, will you find the next available room, grab the kit, and grab a lot of towels." The nurse nodded and disappeared in the crowd. "I need you, Maggie. What do you say?" John locked eyes with mine, smiled, and held out his hand.

I took it. "Let's go!" John grabbed gloves and two masks before we ran out the sliding doors. John and I looked around searching for the woman, then heard someone call out in pain down the sidewalk. She was lying on the ground in the fetal position but looked up at us as we approached.

"Hi, ma'am, my name is Dr. Christensen and I'm a doctor here in the ER. This is Maggie, and she's an EMT. Can we help you?

"What kind of hospital is this?" she wheezed looking down at our clothes. John and I smiled at each other.

"Our clothes may be outdated, but our training is the opposite. I'm the on-call doctor and haven't had a chance to change yet. Is it okay if we help you?"

"Yes." The woman said between breaths. "I think the baby is coming now."

The nurse from before wheeled out a wheelchair with the delivery kit and towels. "There's a room opening up in Labor and Delivery and will be ready in five minutes," she said.

"Thank you," John said as he took the kit and towels. "I don't think we'll make it up in time. We're going to get things ready here. Will you let them know?"

The nurse nodded and hustled back into the hospital. John got everything ready for the delivery and explained everything he was doing as he went. As I watched and listened to him, it felt like I was seeing him for the first time. His mask was on, but I could *see* him. He had that cool confidence like before, but this time everything felt real. *This is him. This is who he really is.* I snapped out of it when the woman rolled over to her back. I heard John ask her name, which was Shannon, so I picked up where he left off as he did the final delivery prep.

"How far along are you?" I asked as I pulled out my phone to watch the clock, then slid on my gloves and mask.

"38 weeks."

"What pregnancy is this?"

"First." Shannon bore down in pain from another contraction. I looked down at my clock and mentally marked the time in my mind. I couldn't do anything for the pain, so I encouraged her and reminded her to breathe. The contraction passed.

"How far apart have the contractions been?" I asked.

"Three minutes."

"Have you received prenatal care?"

"Yes, from Dr. Wilson," she said.

"Have they mentioned any concerns that might affect you or your baby during delivery?"

"No."

"Very good." I looked over at John, he met my eyes. His eyes smiled and he gave me a small nod as if I had done well.

"Shannon, you are dilated to a ten, and the baby's head is crowning," John said through his mask. "Are you ready?"

"But my husband! He's supposed to be here! He was on his way. We had a plan! Can we wait?" Shannon bore down with another contraction.

I glanced at my clock. "One minute between contractions now." I looked over at John to let him know. He nodded.

"We aren't able to wait. I'm sorry. Your baby is in the birth canal now and will be coming out within the next minute." John calmly explained to Shannon. "When the next contraction comes, I'm going to need you to take a deep breath in and hold it. Maggie will help you sit up a little bit, okay? Push hard as you can, okay?"

She nodded, and I could tell she was nervous.

"You got this. You're going to have a baby right now!" I squealed as she let out a labored laugh. "Wait, are you having a boy or girl?!"

"I don't know. My husband and I wanted it to be a surprise." She closed her eyes as a few teardrops started to fall.

"He'll get here, Shannon. Are you ready?"

"Yes. Here comes the contraction. Ah!" She bore down once more.

"All right. Here we go. Deep breath." I encouraged her as I helped her roll up into a crunch position.

"Great job, Shannon," John said. "Baby is almost here. Keep pushing. You're making this look easy—you can let out a battle cry or something." John smiled, I could tell because his eyes crinkled a little bit near the corners.

Shannon let out an "ahhhhh" sound.

"I'm the husband! I'm the husband! I'm the husband!" A man was yelling to no one in particular running from the parking lot.

"Husband!" John yelled. The man bolted over to us. "Whose husband are you?"

"Hers!" He smiled while breathing heavily. I stood quickly and let the husband take over the support role. He knelt next to Shannon and they grasped each other's hands tightly. It was a special moment to witness the love that they had. I quickly scooted down towards John and grabbed a clean towel.

"Here comes the baby," John said. I could hear the excitement in his voice. With a whoosh, John guided the baby out. Shannon laid back down in exhausted relief. The littlest cry sounded, and we all watched in amazement. While all eyes were on the new baby, I watched John. He held the baby on his arm while he suctioned out the mouth and nose with a bulb. My throat started to constrict a little at the sight, but I tried to swallow it down. John smiled up at me. I held out the towel when John was ready to hand the baby off. I started to dry and clean the baby...*boy!* John clamped the umbilical cord twice and asked the husband if he wanted to do the honors. John showed him where to cut, and talked him through it. John was an amazing doctor. I was so proud of him. Shannon did so well too, the husband showed up just in time, and the baby was perfect. *Birth is nothing short of a miracle.*

I looked over at John and whispered, "Can I tell them?" He smiled and nodded. I swaddled up the new baby and handed him carefully to his mom.

"It's a boy!" I softly squealed.

"Really?!" They both said in excited unison. I nodded. John congratulated them both.

Three nurses found us and had a gurney in tow. Once Shannon and her new baby were all settled on the gurney, the husband came over to thank John and me before heading into the hospital. John updated the nurse who was holding a clipboard, then he and I got everything cleaned up—including ourselves. Once we were back inside the hospital, John grabbed a pair of green scrubs and a pair of black scrubs before we headed down a long white hall.

"You ready?" He asked.

"For what?"

"It's x-ray time."

"Oh right, I agreed to that earlier, didn't I?" I smiled over at him.

We stopped outside a wooden door and John gave two quick knocks. He handed me the pair of black scrubs. "To match your toes," he said as he smiled. Once the x-rays were done, I met John back out in the hall. He had his arms folded, legs crossed, and was leaning against the wall in his green scrubs. He looked good. When I emerged, he pushed off the wall. "Hey, how'd it go?"

"I survived."

"Good. You look good in black." He smiled and I blushed. We walked up to each other, then stopped abruptly, remembering the air between us hadn't been cleared yet. The next few minutes would determine our future, and a piece of me didn't want to know the truth and have it possibly end things completely between us. I took a deep breath and he did too.

"Well, I think I'm ready to talk about the many lives of John Christensen now," I said. John didn't say anything. He just looked at me briefly from the tops of his eyes with a slight smirk on his face. I could tell he appreciated my sarcasm but wasn't completely thrilled it was directed towards him this time. He held up a card to a small grey box on the wall. A little light went from red to green, and something unlocked nearby. John opened a door for me, then closed it behind him. He took his place against the wall on one side of what looked like a supply room, and I took my place on the opposite side facing him with folded arms. We stared at each other for a few moments, and I knew I needed to let him tell his side of the story.

"I'm really sorry about your ribs," he said. "I know it was an accident, but I still feel horrible. Horrible enough to where I've been physically sick about it since it happened."

"Yeah yeah."

"Maggie!" He said in a jokingly exasperated tone.

"I believe you."

He let out a stressed breath of air and ran a hand through his dark hair. He was nervous about this conversation. I was nervous too.

"It wasn't what it looked like," he said.

"Living a double life, but this time you got caught?"

"That's what it looked like, but I'm not that kind of guy. She's an ex-girlfriend who came on her own despite my efforts. She wanted to try to rekindle something that went out a long time ago, and after meeting you this week, I'm convinced it never really was there in the first place. I thought if I handled things on my own, then that was my way of protecting you, and protecting what you and I have." He took two slow steps towards me. "I know you've been burned before in a big way, and I didn't want you to doubt me had she just showed up in town. There was nothing to hide, but I hid it anyway with good intentions. I should've told you, and if I could go back I would have. I'm sorry, Maggie," he said. I sighed. He couldn't just fix everything with a couple of lines—too much damage had been done. I was relieved and confused at the same time. I looked up at him, and he took a couple more slow steps in my direction. "Why are you scowling at me?" He smiled with his eyes.

"Because I don't want to let you off the hook so easy, and I'm thinking of something to say," I said. His lips spread into a small smile. "I saw you two together. If there was nothing there, then why were the two of you in each other's arms?"

"I didn't hug her back." He shook his head. "My thumbs were hung on my suspenders, and she hugged me anyway. The moment she touched me, I was already backing away. I told her there was nothing between us and that it was time for her to leave."

"You were going to let her reach up and touch you like I have so many times though…had she not seen me first." My head dropped down. I didn't want him to see me cry again, but all the emotions came flooding back all at once. I felt the hurt all over again. He instantly had his arms around me.

"I would've never let her get that far," he whispered next to my ear.

"I believe you."

The door buzzed and gears shifted. John released me and went to the door. He opened it and poked his head out.

"Oh…hi Dr. Christensen. I just needed a few things." A voice from the outside said.

"Right on, I've got a few carts that I'm filling up in here, so it's a little full. What do you need?"

"One pack of large gloves, Coban, antibiotic, gauze, and steri-strips."

"Coming right up." John quickly moved from one side of the supply room to the other searching for the items as quickly as possible.

"Gloves. Gloves. Gloves," he whispered to himself while searching the opposite wall.

I turned around and found the gloves behind me. "Here you go," I whispered and tossed the box to him. He gave me a small smile and mouthed "thank you." John opened the door and handed off all the supplies, then let out a sigh of relief when he walked back to where I stood. I took a deep shaky breath in and folded my arms again—more for comfort this time.

"Maggie." He reached up and gently placed a hand on my cheek. "Every word I've said to you, every kiss between us…" He looked me right in the eyes "…has been real. My name is John Christensen, I'm 29 years old, and I was born and raised here in Utah. My shoe size is 12.5." I smiled up at him. "I'm an ER doctor, and I also work at Summit Springs as a favor to my parents a few weeks out of the summer. I love baseball. You already know I love steak, but I also love pizza—every single kind. I refuse to eat mushrooms, though." I laughed a little, and he smiled. He stroked my cheek with his thumb. "And," he said in a daring way that implied that this next confession was the most important part about him, "I know how to build remote control cars, and I know how to make them go fast." He smiled proudly.

"That's an important skill to have," I said. His smile was contagious and I couldn't help but smile back.

"It really is." He paused for effect. "Especially, when I race them each July with my brothers behind an old warehouse on the outskirts of town. There's a trophy for the winner and everything."

"You don't."

"I really do," he said. I laughed. "Maggie." His voice took on a more tender tone. He raised his other hand to take my face softly in his hands, then looked right into my eyes. "It's not just you. That connection that you mentioned a few days ago when we were on the horse—I feel it too. I was nervous at the time. I was trying to find the right words, and I wasn't quick enough. I realize now, that I should've told you what was on my mind and not have tried to get all the words right the first time." He took a deep breath. "I have a lot of different sides, but I want you to know every one of them. I'm not like the last guy, and I promise I will never break your heart. I—" A beeping sound started going off and it made me jump. John reached down without looking away from my eyes to silence the sound. "Maggie, I—" The beeping sound went off again. He dropped his head down and pulled away to look at his pager. "The images are ready and the tech can't find us. That's probably because we're *hiding.*" He smiled down at me, then looked at the watch on his wrist. "We have to go now too if we're going to make it there in time."

"Make it where?"

"You'll see," he said. I moved towards the door, but he softly took hold of my wrist before I reached the knob. "Hold on." He gently took my face in his hands once more. "I need you to know one more thing...my heart is all here and it's all yours." He said in a quiet raspy tone, then leaned in to kiss my forehead. I forced myself to breathe. He pulled back slowly and we just searched each other's eyes—until his pager went off again. John didn't reach down to silence it for a few moments, because we were having a silent conversation that couldn't be interrupted by anything. When we were done, John opened the door and we walked across the hall. John knocked twice, and the same x-ray technician came to the door and handed over the images. John thanked him before the technician went back into the lab. John flipped through the images and studied them carefully. He held two images side by side, then started to squint at the last one.

"What is it?" I asked. The look in his eyes started to stir up concern in me. "What do you see? What's wrong?"

"Oh, there it is! You do have a heart. So, does that mean you forgive me?"

My eyes went wide in shock, and my hand went to my heart. "John! You can't...You scared me!"

"Is that a yes?"

"Yes. Yes, I forgive you for last night, but not for this." I pointed at the images in his hands. He smiled big enough so I could see that dimple of his.

"Well, there are no cracks, which is a relief," he said. He let out a relieved sigh to back up his words. "I'm sure you have a lot of inflammation though. I have a feeling that you're in more pain than you're letting on—just like your leg. You don't have to be so strong all the time." He looked straight into my soul. "Not with me."

I swallowed hard and nodded. Our eyes carried on a silent conversation. Two days ago, I would've met him halfway with what his eyes were saying right now, but instead, I still felt guarded. My feelings for him hadn't changed, and I had forgiven him, but I needed time to process everything and let my heart rest. John had just put mending sutures on my heart, and it was up to me to decide how fast I would let the wound heal.

Before we left, John stopped at the pharmacist's counter to get me a small orange bottle filled with more pain medicine as a souvenir. Once the valet had pulled John's truck around, he helped me up into the passenger seat. The sky had already darkened, so I couldn't see the mountains and get my bearings. I had no idea which way we were facing or where we were headed.

"I do have a question for you," John said as we merged onto the freeway. "Why did you bring the reward money back this morning? They would've let me out eventually."

"You know why I brought the money back," I said.

"I want to hear you say it."

"I didn't think they'd literally put you in jail, and even if you didn't want me—"

"But I do want you."

"Okay, but I didn't know that this morning. So even if you didn't want me—"

"But I do want you," he said. I looked over at him and gave him a smirk with "the eye." "Okay, okay. Go ahead." He smiled.

"I couldn't let you sit in a cell all day. I cared about you too much to wait for "eventually" to roll around. Even if you didn't want me, I still wanted you. It will never be about the money when it comes to you...even in a fictional town."

"Cared...wanted...those are both past tense," he said.

I looked out the window at the stars. His words caught me off guard. I was still struggling to sort out my thoughts. He pulled up into a parking stall next to a building covered in neon lights.

"I'm sorry I borrowed Shady without asking you today."

"You can ride my horse anytime you want to. You don't need permission," he said softly without meeting my eyes. "What were you trying to outrun?"

"It started with running to stop thinking—then it turned into just…running." I smiled a little bit remembering the feeling.

"I'm really proud of you, you know." He looked over at me. "I don't know everything you went through, but I know enough to know that it's a big deal you got back in the saddle again and rode on your own."

"Thank you." I looked down at my lap. His praise meant more to me than anyone else's. There was weight in his words, and he always meant what he said. "Speaking of outrunning things," I said softly. "You questioned if you had made the right career choice, and I think you're right where you need to be. You are an incredible doctor, and I feel really lucky to have watched you shine in that way tonight."

We made eye contact, but he didn't say a word. His eyes looked like they held a little more moisture in them than usual, but it was hard to tell for sure in the dark and before he turned away. "I'm still on the past tense thing," he said. His voice was lower and raspier than normal.

I took a deep breath as I stared out the window. "Of course, I care about you, John. A lot."

"What about the "want" part?" he asked. I looked over at him and thought he could have been holding his breath.

"I…" A few moments passed. I still didn't know how to put my thoughts into words.

"It's okay," he said softly, then forced a smile. "I'll be right back." He reached for the door handle.

"Wait!" I scooted over on the bench seat until I was right next to him. I reached up and held his face in my hands. "I can't let you go to bed tonight or whenever it is that you sleep, not knowing how I feel right now, or at least the parts I can put into words." I took a deep shaky breath. "Of course, I want you. The connection you and I have is the kind of stuff people write novels about. It's once in a lifetime, and my heart knows that. I'm waiting for my mind to catch up to my heart, and I just need a little bit more time." I searched his eyes for understanding.

He reached up and took hold of one of my hands and brought it to his lips. His eyes closed when he kissed my fingers. "You have until I get back." The look on my face was probably something of panic. "I'm kidding," he said. A small relieved laugh sounded from my lips.

"Where are you going?" I asked.

"If I remember right, I think I owe you something." John winked over at me before he got out of the truck. I let out a nervous sigh of relief to have finally gotten those words out. I watched him until he disappeared into the building. The word "cantina" was blinking in yellow neon above the door. Some upbeat music played through outdoor speakers, but I couldn't understand the words. A few minutes later, John opened the door with a big brown bag in hand. He held the door open for a man pushing a cart. They approached my side of the truck, and it made my heart start to beat faster. I rolled down the window to ask what they needed, but my question was answered as soon as I realized what was on the man's cart—*guacamole ingredients*. My eyes went wide, and a huge smile spread across my face. I looked at John who stood right outside my window as the man scooped a bunch of avocados into one of those big black molcajete bowls.

"John. No. Way!" He didn't say anything but just smiled at me instead. When the man finished making the guacamole, he put it in a container and handed it to me through the window. I thanked him like five times, and I knew I was blushing from all the attention. When John got back in the truck, I gave him a this-would-have-been-funny-if-it-wasn't-me look. He laughed, which made me laugh. "That was almost as bad as being forced to wear a sombrero while the entire staff claps and sings for a birthday. Thank you for this, though." I smiled and held up the freshly made guacamole. Now that the embarrassment was wearing off, I was starting to appreciate the gesture more. "I have a feeling that was their first request to have the guacamole made curbside rather than tableside."

"It was," John said, looking very pleased with himself—still smiling. He pulled things out of the bag until there was nothing left, then handed me a container and four small cups of...

"Salsa!" I opened up the container. "Enchiladas! John!"

"I had a feeling you haven't had much to eat today."

"You're right, but I haven't been that hungry." I looked over at him.

"Me neither. Until now." He smiled and I smiled back. "We would've gone inside to eat, but I don't have very much time. I'm the on-call doctor tonight and have to go back to the hospital when we're done."

"I understand." We both devoured our food in silence, except for me saying "this is so good" every three bites. "Thank you for dinner. I'm glad I went over to greener pastures, petticoat and all." We locked eyes.

"That makes two of us." He gave me a look that made me think we weren't just talking about literal pastures. "So, Bill will be here any minute to take you back to Summit Springs." My heart sank. I think he felt it because he took my hand in the same moment. "I want to take you back to Summit Springs myself more than words can express right now, but I have to go back."

"How late do you work tonight?"

"I'm not sure, but from the looks of it, I'll be working into tomorrow. I'll be back tomorrow night though."

"Promise?" I extended my free hand with only the pinky raised.

"I promise." He smiled as we interlocked pinky fingers. Headlights shined through the truck right before another truck pulled up next to us. "That's Bill. You ready?" he asked. I shook my head. I didn't want to leave until everything was back to how it was before the cornfield incident, even though I didn't know how to get us there. I saw his chest rise, then fall. He pulled me close and kissed my head through my hair—letting it linger. I swallowed the building emotion in my throat. He pulled back and looked in my eyes as he stroked my cheek, then said, "I'm going to fix this." I nodded, hoping it was possible.

John helped me down from his truck and into Bill's. He stopped at Bill's window to talk for a minute and made eye contact with me before he left. The look in his eyes was something fierce, and I knew in that moment he was handing me over reluctantly— very reluctantly.

"Bye, Maggie," he said.

"Bye, John."

19

I never thought I would've felt this way, but I think I might actually miss that noisy bird when we leave tomorrow. I laid in bed, staring at the ceiling for a while longer after the rooster had sounded. Today would be our last full day in Summit Springs. The thought made my stomach feel a little sick. It wasn't enough time. *Time for what? To fall in love? No, I was already there. Not enough time with John? Yep, that was it.* My stomach dropped and had doubled in queasiness at the thought of leaving. I let out a stressed sigh. I didn't know how our story would end, but all I knew was that I didn't want it to.

Anna was still asleep. My side started to ache, which was my cue to take more pain medicine before it got unbearable. I slowly rolled out of bed, hoping not to make any noise in the process. I looked down at my scrubs, and the memories from yesterday started to filter into my mind. I wrapped my arms around my middle and felt a little closer to John by the gesture. *I miss him.* I tiptoed across the floorboards, stepping in all the right places to not make them squeak. I opened my trunk and grabbed a pill from the orange bottle before changing into one of my blue dresses. Today's shade de jour was powder blue. It had more ruffles than any of the others. I felt like a pretty éclair. After I laced up my boots and brushed my hair, I slowly made my way downstairs. Every muscle tensed, trying to compensate and brace for the pain that came with each step. A few people were up and about when I walked into the café. I searched the buffet table for a water pitcher, but none had been brought out yet. Opening the kitchen door slowly, I peeked my head through. Carol was working at a table near the door and looked up at the movement.

"Hi, Carol, I was wondering if I could grab some water?" I asked.

"Of course, dear. I'm running a little bit behind schedule this morning, so come on in and help yourself. Cups are on that shelf over there." She said as she tilted her head back towards the far wall. I grabbed a cup of water, and discreetly took the pill. I definitely did not want her to know where the pain came from.

"What can I help with?" I said as I started to wash my hands at the sink.

"Thank you, Maggie. Will you come help me peel these eggs?"

"Of course." I grabbed a boiled egg from the bowl and went to work.

"I see you're back to wearing blue again."

"Yes." I looked down at my dress.

"It's his favorite color, you know?"

"Whose favorite color?"

"John's."

"Oh." Heat immediately rose to my cheeks. I wasn't used to talking about John to anyone but Anna and sometimes Devin—especially not to John's aunt. The gears started to turn in my mind...*my entire trunk is blue.* "Would that have anything to do with my trunk being filled with blue clothes for the week?"

"We thought it might help."

"We?"

"His mom and I."

"His Mom?" I sputtered.

"Yes."

"Does that happen each week? A girl is chosen to wear blue for the week in hopes of catching John's eye?"

She laughed a little. "No, you are the first and the last. We would have never meddled, but John showed interest in you before he had even met you, so we decided to do what we could."

"Before we met?"

"Yes. We read through a little background information at the beginning of the week about each guest. When I got to yours, John laughed out loud at some joke you had made in your "medical history" section. No one else got the joke, but him." I smiled at their reasoning in thinking John and I would be compatible and also recalling the joke. "John has to work at the hospital all the time—even during the weeks he works here. He's never been in town this much, though. When he is here in Summit Springs, he normally volunteers to be out with the cattle."

"So, the blue dresses worked then?" I teased.

"I don't think it had anything to do with the color of your dress, dear. He would've chosen you anyway." She smiled over at me, and I smiled back. Reaching into the bowl, I pulled out the last egg to peel.

"Is there anything else I can help you with?"

"No, that was the last of it. Thank you, Maggie." Carol said as she wiped her hands on her apron. Somehow, I got turned around and went through one too many wrong doors. My mouth opened wide as I took in the room that stood before me. The newest models of washers, dryers, dishwashers, ovens, microwaves, toasters, fridges, and other appliances lined the walls and counters. There were at least three of each appliance. It was strange to see all the modern appliances in such an old mining town. "Maggie!

Oh no!" Carol called out from behind me. I closed the door and turned around to smile at a speechless Carol.

"My lips are sealed. I won't tell a soul." I made a locking motion near my lips.

"Thank you." She said breathlessly. "I try to keep things as time period appropriate as possible, but some weeks I have more help than others. I just..."

"You don't have to explain a thing to me, Carol. I support everything in there. By the way, if you ever need any extra help, let me know."

"Does this mean you'll be coming back to Summit Springs?"

"We'll see." I smiled. Sliding out of the pantry and kitchen proved much easier the second time around. Carol let me sneak an egg and piece of cornbread before I left. I felt restless this morning and couldn't stay in one place for too long. John kept crossing my mind, and I had to keep busy. I walked out onto the hotel porch and saw that the door to Sutter's General Store was open. When I finished my makeshift breakfast, I headed over to exchange some of my time for carrots. The same older man as before was restocking some shelves when I walked in.

"Hello, again. Can I help you find anything?" he said as he turned towards me.

"I just need a few carrots."

"That'll be fine. Today's chore is milking Buttercup."

"I'm assuming Buttercup is a goat?" I smiled, remembering our last encounter.

"Nope, cow."

I cringed inwardly as he quietly led me out the back door. He got me all set up to milk a brown cow tethered to a post and eating hay, then left me to it. When he came back out when my time was up, he was surprised and possibly even pleased at the amount of milk in the bottom of the pail this time. He nodded, and I smiled. I grabbed the carrots and headed to the livery. The large doors had already been opened. My heart skipped a beat, thinking about the possibility of John already being back. I hurried across the road and stepped inside the livery. No one was there. I walked out back to the pasture and whistled—even though I couldn't see Shady. I whistled again, but louder. After a few minutes, I saw a dark horse in the distance walking toward me. *Shady!*

Once he had made it across the pasture, I smiled up at him and stroked his cheek. "Hi, boy." I wanted to be with Shady if I couldn't be close to John right now. After giving him all the carrots I had, I stroked his nose until he walked away, ready to graze. Watching Shady made me think back to all the memories the three of us made. I took a deep breath in, then slowly let it out.

"Hey!" A man's voice came from behind me. I startled and held my heart. I turned around just as Devin was walking out of the livery in my direction.

"You scared me!"

"Sorry." He smiled.

"No, you aren't."

"A little bit. How's your side doing?"

"Better," I said. Devin came up next to me and rested his arms on the fence post. "You're in big trouble, you know."

"I'm sure you have me confused with someone else; I have one of those faces."

"I know about the rooster."

"Oh, that." His eyes went wide for a second before he smiled and looked back out at the pasture.

"Devin! How could you not tell me? I was almost eaten alive like 24 times this week."

"But you weren't."

"But I could have been!"

"Fine." He surrendered. "I'm sorry for not telling you about the bucket and the rooster."

I smiled and glared at him at the same time. "I do want to thank you for everything this week. You've been a really great friend. I hope everything goes well with your new job. I'll be cheering you on."

"Thanks." He held out an arm and squeezed my shoulders in a side hug.

"Do you think you'll ever come back to Summit Springs?" I asked.

"I don't know." Devin looked out into the distance.

"Well, whatever you decide, I just want you to be happy wherever you are."

We smiled at one another before saying our goodbyes. I walked back through the livery and out onto the dirt road. Anna walked into a building near the Broken Spoke Saloon, so I headed that way too. When I opened the door, a large group stood around four tall narrow wooden buckets with sticks poking out of the tops of them. I scanned the room to find Anna.

"Hey!" I said once I made my way through the small crowd.

"Hi! I was wondering where you were. I didn't hear you come in last night."

"I was at the hospital late."

"I still can't believe Mr. Hansen got bit by a rattlesnake! How were they doing when you left last night?" Anna asked.

"John said Mr. Hansen was stable and that Mrs. Hansen was back to normal."

"So, did the two of you smooth things over?"

"Mrs. Hansen and I never had any bad blood."

"Mag-gie."

"Um, yeah. John and I smoothed things over," I said.

"Good."

"Okay, everyone! I think we're going to get started," a woman's voice called out over the crowd. It hit me that I wasn't sure what I had just walked into and what we were all about to do. "All right, I need five people to gather around each of the plunge churns to start." A few people dispersed in front of Anna and me to be guinea pigs. "We've let some fresh milk sit in a cool place until the cream separated, then scooped it off into these four plunge churns. It is called a plunge churn because we will be pulling up and down on this stick like a plunger. The stick has a flat plate-like piece at the bottom with holes that will help separate the butter from the buttermilk. I will now demonstrate with this group." She grabbed onto the stick, raised it like a sword in a stone, then pushed it back down again. "Everyone who is not near a plunge churn will be making butter using the shaking method, then we will switch." Anna and I shuffled with the others to the back of the room, where the woman handed each pair of people one jar. As the people took the jars filled with cream, the woman was spouting off random facts "The Mason jar was named after and invented by John Landis Mason. He patented the Mason jar in 1858." After taking a jar, Anna and I found two chairs, and I took the first turn shaking the jar.

"How's your side feeling today?" Anna asked.

"The medicine kicked in, so I'm doing well, but probably not plunge churning well."

"We'll sneak out when she calls for us to switch then."

"Sounds like a plan. Your turn," I said as I handed her the jar. "How are things with you and Ricky?" Anna smiled and turned the deepest shade of red. "That good, huh?" I smiled at her and turned my focus toward the plunge churners to give her a minute. "Thank you by the way."

"For what?" she asked.

"For making us come to Summit Springs."

"I did kind of make you, didn't I?"

"Yes, and you deserve an award. I'm sure pulling teeth would have been easier." We both laughed.

"I was hoping this trip would give us a chance to spend more time together like old times, but we haven't really been in the same place for too long," she said.

"I think our friendship has morphed into this really great thing where we can pick up where we left off at any given moment—no matter how long we've been apart or how long we get to be together. I feel like we've bonded in a different kind of way. I've enjoyed this week a lot."

"Me too, but I can think of another tall, dark, and handsome reason why this week might have been enjoyable." She smiled. "Did you enjoy the week enough to have it be an annual tradition?" I could hear the excitement in her voice.

I laughed. "That is still up in the air," I said. Anna handed me the jar, and I frowned. "I will never take the bricks of butter we have back home for granted again." Once our arms had turned into jelly, that's when we knew we had officially made butter. We took our jar back up to the woman who then separated the buttermilk from the butter for us. She smooshed the contents of the jar into a piece of cloth to strain out as much of the buttermilk as possible. She was just about to add our hard-earned butter into a bowl with all the other butter that had been made—before I intervened. "Could we actually keep that? We need it."

"For what?"

Anna and I gave each other a side glance before I spoke up. "Eating?" I said with slight hesitation.

She eyed us both before she said, "That'll be fine. Here you go. Good job." She handed us our labor of love in a jar. "Okay, everybody, let's switch!"

"That's our cue," I whispered. Anna winked. We slowly walked around the perimeter of the room until we were out the door. We both let out sighs of relief, and once we were out in the middle of the dirt road, I pushed the jar of butter in the air as if it were a gold medal. We both laughed, but Anna's laugh was cut short. I followed her gaze to see Ricky standing on a nearby porch smiling in our direction. "Go. I'll make sure to keep our butter safe."

"Thanks, Maggie." She smiled a nervous smile and took a deep breath. I walked back to the hotel and ate some lunch. When I finished, I asked Carol if I could help with something in exchange for a few square inches of fridge space for our butter. I helped clean a few dishes, then slid the jar of butter into one of the fridges when the job was done.

I headed over to the bathhouse one last time. When the door clicked open, Vicky's head popped up from behind the desk, just like always. *I'm going to miss her.*

"Hello, dear! How are you feeling today?"

"I'm good. I'm ready for one last bath."

"Coming right up!" She disappeared just like she always had before. The water started to run, and a few minutes later, I heard her call out to me that everything was ready and to come on back. "Any song requests today?" she asked.

"Nope. Today it's all you."

She smiled, and I could tell she was excited as she walked away. The room was dimly lit, and the water was the perfect temperature; it always was. "Annie's Song" by John Denver softly sounded through the speaker. *I love this song.* A tear slipped down my cheek as I sunk deeper into the warm water. *I didn't want to leave.* I closed my eyes, soaking in this moment—literally. I let my salty tears mix with the dark bathwater and stayed until the water had turned cold. My mind was at war. I wanted John, but I was still so afraid of getting hurt. Feeling no less confused than when I walked into the bathhouse, I emerged from the tub and got dressed. I thanked Vicky for everything this week on my way out, then said goodbye. I hoped I would see her again. We had bonded over our love of oldies, and she had become a friend. Vicky's eyes got a little misty when I waved myself out the door, and it made emotion rise in my throat. *I hate goodbyes. There's nothing "good" about them.*

Taking my mind off John was easier when I was out in public—this fictional kind of public anyway. I headed back to the hotel when I saw people loading things into wagons for the Pasture Party. When I got upstairs to our room, I was relieved to see Anna.

"Hi!" I said as I closed the door behind me. "Can I borrow one last dress from you tonight?"

"Of course! Come pick one."

"Thank you! You look really pretty, by the way." She wore the cream-colored lace dress that she had reserved the whole week for tonight, and I'm glad that she did. I was pretty sure Ricky would agree with me too. I smiled to myself, sifting through Anna's trunk. At the bottom, I found the perfect dress. It was black with intricate lace around the neckline, and it fit like a glove. This was my favorite dress of them all.

"Maggie, I know you love black, but are you sure about that one?" She had a concerned look on her face. "You're going to a party…not a wake."

"I don't care, I love it." I smiled and swished my skirts back and forth. Anna and I brushed each other's hair. Once my natural waves had been tamed, I decided to leave my hair down for the night. Anna wore her strawberry blonde hair up in a pretty braided updo. Bending over to close my trunk, I noticed the vial filled with gold specks and the one nugget shaped like a heart. I rubbed my thumb across the smooth glass. My mind drifted back to the day John and I panned for the gold that I held. I wished I could go back and do things a little differently. I would've just asked John about the letter I found in the wagon instead of trying to take care of things on my own. I really did think that he would have told me the truth, and we would have figured it all out together. Instead, I tried to do it my way, and everything got messy. I breathed in deeply and let it out slow.

"You ready?" Anna's voice called me out of my daydream.

"Yeah." I stood, and we closed the door behind us.

Anna and I walked out to the pasture behind the livery where everyone had already started to gather. The horses had all been moved, and tables and benches were already set up. We got there just in time to hear the blessing on the food. After we had done our time waiting in line, we had finally made it to the front.

"Anna, there's cornbread!"

"Yes!"

"It wasn't on the menu tonight." Carol overheard our conversation and joined in. "A little bird told me that you love the cornbread and convinced me to whip some up for tonight."

I blushed. "Where is that bird?"

"I haven't seen him yet." She smiled.

I let out a sigh and thanked her for making the cornbread and for everything else. The food tasted as delicious as it looked and included: baked chicken, mashed potatoes, corn, green beans, and cornbread. Through the entire meal, I found myself looking around for John. When just about everyone had finished eating, people started to scatter to all the different games and events throughout the large pasture. There were people using slingshots to hit targets, and others were throwing balls to knock over bottles. There were also pairs of people stick pulling (like tug of war, but with only two people and the stick was turned sideways). Groups played horseshoes over by the trees, and others nearby were flinging disc-like objects into the air as far as they could. Ricky joined us just as we were trying to decide what to do.

"Hey, you guys!" he said. Anna and I greeted him. Loud cheers sounded over by the flinging object group, and it caught our attention.

"What are they throwing over there?" I asked while squinting, trying to see what the objects were.

"Cow pies," he said.

"What are cow pies?" When I was given silence instead of words, I looked back at Ricky and Anna. They were exchanging glances. "Wait, like literal cow pies?" I asked.

Ricky nodded his head. "Yep!" I cringed and looked back at the group. "You'd be surprised how far they can fly. Do you guys want to try?" he asked.

"I'm okay skipping that," I answered a little too quickly, and Anna agreed. "What about we go try the slingshots instead?"

Ricky laughed, and we all made our way across the pasture to where the slingshots were. Anna and Ricky were hand in hand, and it made me miss John even more.

20

The sky was darkening quickly. Everyone was helping load things from dinner and the games into wagons. There was a group of men setting up tall posts and anchoring them in the ground. Others were stringing lanterns from post to post until a large area in the pasture had been illuminated. I heard instruments being tuned somewhere through the crowd too. Ricky had left for a bit to help with the posts. Anna and I helped gather horseshoes and put them into a gunnysack. The whole evening, I searched the crowd for John, but he hadn't come yet. He pinky promised he'd be here, which was even more binding than a regular promise. I started to feel deflated. *This was our last night.*

A little while later, after everything had been cleaned up, Bill thanked the crowd of people for a great week. When he started talking about the checkout process and how everyone would depart tomorrow afternoon, my stomach dropped with every word. He finished and introduced the band, who immediately began to play a lively song that got everyone skipping, twirling, and dancing. I hung back on the outskirts and convinced Anna to go ahead without me. I knew I couldn't move too much with my side just yet. After a few songs, I somehow got pulled into a synchronized dance that everyone picked up quickly. The motions and steps weren't too strenuous, so I was able to hold my own. When the song ended, everyone clapped for the band, and I laughed with the people near me. I promised them I'd learn my left foot from my right before we ever did that dance again. The sky had darkened completely, and I couldn't see anything beyond the glow of the stringed lights.

The tune slowed way down, and couples started to form around me. I smiled, seeing a dad pick up his young daughter and start to spin her around. I turned around, planning to be a wallflower for this song, but the handsome man standing in front of me stopped me in my tracks. *John.* My lips couldn't help but curl up into a smile. He smiled back. His eyes smoldered, and the look in them made me feel *very* wanted. He closed the distance between us quickly and wrapped his arm around my waist. I put one hand on his shoulder, and the other rested on his chest. He pulled me in close with such confidence, and I couldn't look away from his eyes. He was relaxed tonight, and it helped me breathe easier. I slowly slid the hand that rested on his chest up around his neck. We stared into each other's eyes. Without a word from either of our lips, we started to dance, and it felt so natural being in his arms again.

"You look beautiful," he whispered through my hair. "Black is my favorite color."

I looked at him quizzically. "Isn't it blue?"

"Nope." He shook his head. "It's black…like my truck, my horse, your scrubs, your dress tonight, and let's not forget about your toes," he said quietly, then winked.

"Well, that's not what your mom and aunt think."

"My mom?" He looked surprised.

"They think your favorite color is blue, and apparently, they secretly selected my wardrobe accordingly. I think they thought if I wore blue, then *maybe* I'd catch your eye."

"Catch my eye, huh?" He raised an eyebrow. "I think you caught a whole lot more than just my eye, and it had nothing to do with the color of your clothes."

My heart started to beat faster. "I thought you were going to go back on your promise tonight."

"I never go back on a promise, especially not one I've made with you." He slightly tightened his arms that were wrapped around my waist. "I would've been here this morning if it was up to me, and I would have been here sooner if not for traffic. Have I told you how beautiful you look tonight already?"

"You have." I blushed.

"Okay, good." He smiled because he knew he had. My arms started to slide down his slowly. When I corrected them, a questioning look crossed John's eyes.

"I made butter today," I said.

"Say no more." He smiled and pulled me in even closer until my arms rested completely on his shoulders. I stroked my thumb along the back of his neck. We were only inches apart, and my dress was brushing against his legs. When I looked up into his eyes, they started to reel me in slowly. We were so close that I could feel the warmth of his breath on my parting lips. My eyelids started to slowly close, but right before our lips touched, loud applause erupted, and it startled me. The band immediately started into an upbeat twangy tune next. I pulled back and smiled up at John. "Let's go get a drink," he said before taking my hand to lead me through the crowd. He and I stayed close to one another for the rest of the night and only went out on the dance floor during the slow songs. When the party ended, I stayed behind with John. When all the posts and lanterns had been taken down, everyone left—leaving John and me in the middle of the darkened pasture. He wrapped his arms around me, and we stood there looking up at the stars. He broke the silence first. "Last night, you said you thought I was right where I needed to be, but I don't think that's true."

"What do you mean?" I asked.

"If you're in California, that's where I want to be. If you come to Utah, then this is where I want to be."

"You have a life here, John. You can't just pick up and leave for a girl you just met."

"Is that a challenge?"

I smiled and swallowed. This conversation was going deeper and deeper by the second. "I would never ask you to leave what you have here for me."

"Maggie," he said. "I'm trying to tell you I want to be with you...I want to *be* with you. I know that you've been my missing piece."

"John." I could feel the emotion rising, so I didn't say anything else—I couldn't.

"What's on your mind?" He softly reached up and held my face, stroking his thumb along my cheek.

I closed my eyes. I took three deep, shaky breaths until I allowed myself to speak. "John, you don't know me, and I don't know you."

He leaned in until our foreheads touched. "Maggie, you do know me," he whispered, "you may not know all of my likes and dislikes yet, but you know *me*—and that's the most important part." He kissed my forehead. "And I do know you. I've seen your soul. You're it for me. This is real, Maggie—all of it. Especially my feelings for you. I have felt more for you in a week's time than I could with anyone else in a lifetime. I want to make this work, not just here, but after tomorrow too. You're my person." I was hearing his words, but focusing on my breathing. I was one more declaration away from coming undone completely. We stood in silence for a few minutes, and I know he was waiting for me to say something…anything. The wind started to blow, and it chilled me enough to make me start shivering. John pulled me into a tight enveloping hug, and I leaned into his warmth. He kissed the top of my head through my hair. "I'll walk you back," he said softly. I took his arm and stayed close to him the whole way back to the hotel. I was trying to find the words to say as we walked, but my mind was fuzzy and racing. I couldn't seem to focus. I was thinking about all the worst-case scenarios if I moved forward in the relationship. The lanterns' flames flickered throughout the town, and it was easier to see John in their low light. He walked me up to the hotel door, then turned towards me. He gently took my face in his hands again and willed me to look up into his eyes. As soon as I did, he softly spoke, and his tone made my throat tighten. "If you're going to trust one more time, let it be with me. I promise to not let you regret it. Maggie…" He gave me a look that bored straight into my soul. "I love you." His voice was low and smooth, and his words made time stop altogether. I searched his eyes and knew without a doubt that he meant every word. This declaration made tears start to well up in my eyes. I rose on my tiptoes and wrapped my arms around his neck to pull him close and hold him tight. He wrapped his arms around me, and we didn't let go. He rubbed my back as I let silent tears fall. I buried my face into his strong chest, and he rested his head against mine. The wind started to pick up and howl. "Say something, Maggie. Anything," he whispered. I could hear his voice shake, and it made my heart physically ache. I pulled back and opened my mouth to speak, but the words weren't there.

"Tell me." He pleaded.

I closed my eyes tighter, not allowing any tears to escape. I took a deep breath—so deep that my shoulders rose slightly. "I'm still guarded, and I know it's coming from my past. I wish I wasn't coming to you broken." My voice cracked. I started to back away as the first tear slid down my cheek. I couldn't suppress the emotions anymore.

"Wait," he said softly and pulled me back quickly into a close and strong embrace. "I want you to know that this love I have for you won't change, and I will wait as long as it takes. I don't think you're broken, but if you were…" He pulled back and held my face softly as he looked into my eyes. "…I'm a doctor, and I'm good at putting pieces back together." His lips curved upward a hint, and I could see his dimple—even in the dark.

"That's kind of gross."

"I know," he said. His smile widened, and mine did too. I blinked away a few more tears, and his thumbs wiped them away before they could get very far. The cold wind blew my hair all around. John tamed as much of it as he could before repeating his words from last night, "I'm going to fix this." He kissed my forehead, then let me go. "Goodnight, Maggie."

"Night, John." I gave him a small pained smile as I closed the door. My footsteps up the stairs felt weighted, and my mind felt heavy too. The pain in my side started to throb. I opened the door quietly to our room and saw that Anna was already sleeping. A plate of cornbread, the jar of butter we made, a glass of water, and my bottle of pills sat on the desk next to our beds. *Thank you, Anna.* I wasn't hungry, but I was relieved to see the water and pills. Leaning against the door for support, I stood in the dark as my mind raced, my heart ached, and my stomach churned. I could feel myself pushing John away. Tears started to stream down the sides of my cheeks. *He's my person—like the one I'm supposed to be with. The one I want to be with.* If I was ever going to love someone in a long-term kind of way…it would have been with him.

21

Old Tom and the rooster started their rounds to wake up the town, but I was already awake and had been for a while. My mind wouldn't let me sleep, so I stared at the wall and gave my mind free rein to think about everything that had happened this week instead. When the rooster's calls had stopped, my mind and my heart started to race. Panic began to take over. It was Saturday, and Anna and I were supposed to leave Summit Springs today after lunch. However, I didn't think I could wait that long. I know if I stayed, I would talk myself out of leaving early which would ultimately end up hurting John in the long run. I was still guarded and I just couldn't waste John's time while he waited for me to undo the past's damage on my trust issues. *I care about him too much.* I had spent the early hours of the morning figuring out a plan, and it was just about time to set it in motion. I started to roll over in my bed, and realized my side didn't hurt nearly as much as before. I turned to face Anna, and let out a little scream of surprise. She was sitting on her bed facing me, already dressed for the day.

"Sorry. I had to talk to you the moment you woke up. It took everything I had not to wake you up like we used to wake our parents on Christmas morning."

"What do you want to talk about?" I asked.

"Plans for the day. Ricky and I are taking our last ride together this morning, but I won't be too long."

"Take your time. Really."

"No, it's okay. I wanted to come back and eat our last lunch together," she said.

"It won't be our last lunch. We'll eat another lunch tomorrow."

"Maggie." She looked at me with worry in her in eyes. "I knew something was up when you didn't touch the cornbread I left for you last night. What's wrong?"

"I don't know. I didn't sleep much, so I'll probably just try to rest some more before we leave."

"Okay. I'll be back soon."

As soon as Anna had closed the door, and I'd given her enough time to go down the stairs, I flung off the covers, got dressed quickly, and slid on my boots. Once I was ready to go, I sat down at the small desk under the window and pulled out the dip pen, ink, and paper. Two letters needed to be written before I left, and I chose the easier of the two to write first. I dipped the nib into the inkwell and tapped off the excess ink before writing. I had come a long way regarding writing with a dip pen in a week's time. I wrote Anna a quick explanation for my leaving, I knew she'd understand why I had to do it this way. I didn't wait for the ink to dry, so I just placed the letter on Anna's bed when I had finished. I took a deep breath and dipped the pen into the inkwell again. My hand shook, and I waited until I was still enough to write legibly. *Dear John.* I shut my eyes tightly and pushed through the emotion building inside me. I needed to let John know how I felt about him, but that I needed to go. He deserved someone who wouldn't hold back. I didn't think he would support my motive for leaving, but I thought he would understand later in life and probably thank me for it too. I blew on the ink until it had dried and I wiped away my tears until those had dried up as well. I folded the letter and wrote his name on the outside, then sifted through my trunk to find my phone. I powered it on and sent a request for an Uber driver to come pick me up. My stomach felt sick when I clicked on the submit button, but I did it anyway. Right as I was about to close the trunk lid, a glimmer of gold caught my eye. Instant tears formed in my eyes and fell just as quickly. I picked up the vial that seemed to feel heavier than it did before. I watched the flecks of gold swirl around the gold heart—John's heart. I didn't stay long enough to watch the flecks settle.

Looking at our room one last time before leaving proved to be harder than I thought it would be. I closed the door for the last time behind me, and reminded myself to keep breathing or I would fall apart. I couldn't think about what I was doing and what I was giving up or I would fold, but I knew it was all for the best. *The best for who?* I ignored the question, and started to walk down the staircase. John will find someone else who can be what he needs, and I'll just be that girl from that one week—at least that's how I validated it. *Someone else.* The thought made me so nauseous I had to stop mid-flight of stairs to focus solely on my breathing. People were coming and going from the café during breakfast, and I tried not to make eye contact with any of them. I slid out the hotel door and quickly walked on the side of the road near the sheriff's office, trying not to bring any attention to myself. I made it to the livery, and slowly peeked around the large doors to make sure no one was there—to make sure John wasn't there. When I was sure it was only me inside, I placed the letter on the worktable. I had to force my fingers to let the letter go. I swallowed the emotion, and had the thought to leave the vial too. A tear fell, then the flood gates opened. I thought I was strong enough to follow through with the leaving plan, but every step was breaking my heart a little more. I decided to take the vial with me, so that a piece of John's heart would always be mine. I wiped away as many of the tears as I could, then turned to leave.

"Maggie?" I stopped cold in my tracks and my stomach dropped. *Anna.* I turned around to face her. "What's up?" she asked.

"I can't do it—I can't face John again. I wrote you a letter that explains everything. John's a great guy…the best kind. I just can't hurt him, so that's why I have to leave like this." The tears started to fall again as I dropped my head.

"You're leaving? You said you smoothed things over…"

"We kind of did, but my trust issues came creeping up again. I can't keep hurting him. I can't be what he needs even though I wish so badly that I was."

"What do you think he needs, Maggie?" she challenged me.

"Someone who won't hold back."

"No, he doesn't. He just needs someone to love him like only you can do. He wants you, Maggie, exactly as you are. Just go talk to him. Let him be there for you right now." Movement from behind Anna caught my eye and caused her to turn around. It was Ricky, but he took one look at the situation and backed out of the livery with his hands up. Anna and I let out a small laugh, me through my tears. *Smart man.*

"I sent for an Uber that will be here soon. I need to go, but I'll meet you at the airport later," I said.

"Where are you going to go until then?"

"I don't know."

"I think you're making a mistake," she said.

"Only time will tell." I shrugged my shoulders and shook my head as if I wasn't even convinced my excuse for leaving was valid.

I hurried down the road to the check-in cabin to change and get my bag. With Anna, and probably Ricky, knowing my escape plan, I needed to be quick. It took a little longer than I had planned to walk to the cabin, but I finally made it. I opened the door and called out to see if anyone was there. *No reply.* My boots clunked across the wooden floorboards and into the dressing room. I changed back into my normal clothes and got my bag from mine and Anna's trunk. As I headed back out towards the front door, a familiar wanted poster willed me to turn back around. I slowly walked over to John's poster near the flickering fireplace and stared into his eyes. *He is so handsome.* I remember wondering at the beginning of the week what he would look like when he smiled or what his laugh might sound like—*now I knew.* He had the best smile with a deep right-sided dimple. His laugh was, and forever would be, my favorite sound in the world. I took a deep breath in, and felt a sinking feeling in my stomach. *What am I doing?* A few tears fell. I reached out and touched his jaw. "I was so in love with you," I whispered to the outlaw on the wanted poster. My heart ached, because it wasn't the real thing. I wanted the real thing. *I have to go back!*

"Past tense?" John's voice broke through my thoughts. My eyes went wide as I turned to face him. He stood just inside the cabin's front door.

"Did you read the letter?" I asked.

"No, Ricky told me where you were headed, and I came straight here from the cattle. I've never pushed Shady as hard as I did just now."

"Why?"

"I don't want to lose you. You're running?" he asked rhetorically.

I took a deep breath. "Not literally, that sounds exhausting." I smiled with my eyes. His eyes narrowed, and I knew he thought my reply was funny but wouldn't show it.

"Why are you leaving?" he asked.

"I panicked. A couple nights ago, you broke my heart into more pieces than I ever thought possible, and my mind won't let me forget it. I don't want to lose you, though." I looked down at my shoes and swallowed the rising emotion. "You tore down my walls once, and I know you can do it again—my heart keeps reminding me of that. I know you're the only man in this world who can tear them down, but I just don't want to keep asking you to. You deserve someone who won't hold back. You deserve to be happy right now."

"Maggie," he said as he sighed. "I've never been as happy in my whole life as I have with you this week. We fit, and anyone else would just be settling. I want you, only you, and I always will. You don't have to figure this out on your own anymore. I'm here now, and I'm ready to help. I will tear down as many walls as I need to, as long as your heart is always the prize. I've always had a thing for demolition anyway." He smiled over at me, and I returned it. "We're too close and too connected for this to be the end of our story. And for the record, I don't think the woman on top of the mountain singing in the rain held back or the one I've been kissing all week..." He smiled and raised his eyebrows at me—it made me laugh again. "...or when you leaned back against me while we were panning, and I don't think you were holding back just now when you said you were in love with a piece of paper."

My mouth dropped open in surprise. "I am in *not* in love with a piece of paper."

"Then what are you in love with?" he dared.

My lips spread into a come-and-get-me smile. "The roguishly hot outlaw standing in front of me right now." Those words were all it took for John to cross the room in one second flat and wrap his arms around me. He pulled me in so close and kissed me so passionately. I wrapped my arms around his neck and pulled him closer. *This feels right. John feels right.* Just like that, my walls had turned to rubble at our feet. *I never knew I could be this happy and this in love.* John has always been my missing piece.

"Don't go," he whispered as he touched his forehead to mine.

I softly held his face in my hands and stroked his jaw with my thumbs. "I'm not going anywhere. You're my person too. I promise I'll never run again...unless it's to you." I held out my pinky finger to officially bind my words. He smiled as we interlocked pinkies, then I softly took his face in my hands again and looked right into his eyes. "I want to see where this goes too. I love you, John. Present tense *and* future tense."

"I love you back," he said. He kissed my forehead and let it linger before pulling me in close. "How do you feel about sticking around for a bit?" His voice was deep and raspy, and the sound made my toes go all tingly. "The leaves are just about to turn and a Utah autumn, like you, is worth the wait."

"I wouldn't miss it." I smiled. He leaned in again and pressed his lips to mine. I rested my hands on his chest and could feel his heart beating fast. I pulled back slightly and looked deep into John's blue eyes. "This is it. This is what people search their whole lives for—a love like this."

He smiled and touched his forehead to mine again, then whispered, "A love like ours."

Together, we found gold this week, but I also found something much more valuable than any amount of gold and something I would never be surrendering—*John's heart.*

EPILOGUE

I packed up my things—Alan the fish included—and moved out to Utah last fall to be closer to John. He and I have been inseparable ever since. It was February 12th and John said he was taking me back to Summit Springs for dinner tonight. He was up to something, but I just didn't know what yet. I looked over at him as he drove up the familiar road, and when he caught me staring, he smiled. I smiled back and said, "I love you" through my eyes. He caught it and said it back through his. We pulled right up to the check-in cabin in his black truck; nothing else would've made it very far in all the snow. He helped me down and held my hand as we walked to the cabin. There was a walkway through the snow that had already been shoveled, and the stairs had already been cleared.

"You're really getting involved here with this dinner tonight, John. Walkways through the snow?"

"I didn't want your feet to get cold," he said. He opened the door, and a warm wall of air greeted us. The fire was crackling, and the lanterns were all lit. There was a table set for two in the middle of the room.

"John! Look at this place! It's amazing." My eyes zeroed in on the big plate of cornbread on the table. "There's cornbread. You're buttering me up, aren't you?"

"Can't I just have a nice dinner with the woman I love without having an ulterior motive?" He teased and wrapped an arm around my waist to pull me close. Our footsteps sounded across the floorboards as we walked over to the table. He pulled out a chair for me, and I raised an eyebrow.

"This is about that Russian sage plant you ran over next to my driveway, isn't it? I told you it's fine. It was really pretty, but I can buy another one."

He laughed. "This definitely has nothing to do with a plant, but I am still sorry for running it over."

I took my seat and grabbed a piece of cornbread before he had sat down. I took a bite an eyed him suspiciously. He lifted the lids from our plates to reveal enchiladas for me and a steak with A.1. Sauce for him. "There's even extra salsa here. You really are up to something," I laughed. He smiled over at me but didn't say a word about it. After dinner and some really good cheesecake, we snuggled up on the couch next to the fire. John had his arm around me, and I leaned into him and rested my head back next to his. "I know what I want for my birthday." I said.

"What's that?"

"I want your wanted poster. I plan to cross off the "ed" to make it present tense, though."

I could feel and hear him laugh. "I think I can make that happen." He kissed my head through my hair.

"Thank you for tonight. It was perfect," I said.

"It's not over yet." He sat up a little. "I took the heart…"

My eyes went wide, and I sat up and faced him. "What kind of heart are we talking about?"

"Not that kind of heart, Maggie." He laughed. "The one we found together when we were panning for love…I mean gold." He purposely faltered, and we both smiled. He reached into his pocket. "Instead of plane tickets, because you're already here, I took the heart and had it melted down. I thought these rings might be a subtle way of letting you know just how much I love you." He pulled out two gold rings. My mouth dropped open, and I looked from his eyes down to the rings. I noticed an inscription on the inside. *J ♥ M.*

"You really did know what I wrote with that dip pen all those months ago, didn't you?" I asked. He smiled and nodded once. I started to reach for the smaller of the two rings to get a closer look, but he quickly closed his hand.

"I want to do this right," he said. My heart began to race. John slid off the couch and knelt close to me on one knee. Our knees touched, and he took my hands in his. I held my breath. "Maggie." He smiled. "You're my person, and I want you to be my wife too. Will you marry me?"

My stomach fluttered with an entire migration's worth of butterflies. I looked John right in the eyes. *I knew without a doubt that I want to marry this man.* "Yes. Of course, I will," I said as I gently held his face in my hands. "I love you."

"And I love you," he said. We leaned in until our lips touched, and as soon as they did, our kisses matched the heat of the flickering fire—hot.

When the flames had turned into glowing embers, I sighed, placed a hand on John's beating heart, then asked, "When should we get married?"

"Yesterday."

Summit Springs Cornbread

1 ½ c. cornmeal
1 ½ c. flour
½ c. granulated sugar
1 t. baking soda
1 t. baking powder
1 c. plain yogurt
½ c. cream corn
1/3 c. frozen corn
1 ½ c. buttermilk
3 eggs
½ c. butter
¼ t. salt

Heat oven to 375 degrees.

In a large mixing bowl, whisk all the wet ingredients together. Mix all the dry ingredients together, then add to the wet mixture to form the batter.

Spray a 9 x 13 stoneware pan with cooking spray before adding batter.

Bake for 25 minutes (or when a toothpick test in the center comes out clean).

*Cast iron skillets or Dutch ovens can also be used.

Hey! My name's Meg, and I'm so glad you're here! Thank you so much for reading my book!

Three things I like:
- The smell of the laundry detergent aisle.
- Old things (dresses, cheese, people, etc.).
- Driving under overpasses while it's raining.

Three things I don't like:
- Ants.
- Wrinkled food like sun-dried tomatoes and raisins.
- Cooking rice.

Three things you probably don't know about me:
- I could also write in the horror genre, but I won't, or I'd never sleep again.
- I slept in a round-a-bout once.
- I'm really good at catching worms.

Instagram - @authormegwenig
Facebook - Author Meg Wenig
Website - megwenig.com

Coming soon...

PINING

FOR

LOVE

BY
MEG CROSS WENIG